Fifth Avenue Devil

A Billionaire Enemies To Lovers Romance

Vivian Wood

Author's Copyright

ONE
NATE

"Four hundred thousand," the large Iranian man next to me declares. He grunts as he pushes a towering stack of poker chips into the middle of the table.

I lift the cards in my hand just high enough so that I can see them. A pair of jacks. With the other two jacks already laid on the table, I'm fairly certain that I've got the winning hand.

The dealer turns his attention to a tall, reedy man with a thinning crown of washed-out blond hair. "Mr. Gellar? It's to you. Four hundred thousand is the ante."

"Yes, yes," Archer parries. He eyes me, screwing his mouth up like the rat-faced weasel he is.

Archer Gellar is the CEO of Gellar Industries and my biggest business rival. I'd once thought we could work together. I am the CEO of the commodities giant ViaLife, and Gellar's dealings in oil and precious minerals meant we could have formed a partnership made in heaven.

But because Archer is such a repugnant piece of human waste, he fucked me over. On a deal that netted him a measly hundred thousand dollars, no less.

Here we are, several years later. And *rivals* isn't a strong enough word for what we are.

No, we are *enemies*.

I loathe him with every fiber of my being. You do not trick Nate fucking Fordham and think you're actually going to get away with it.

"You seem awfully sure of yourself, Fordham," Archer says. He narrows his eyes at me. "I think you've got a shit hand and you're just praying that I don't call your bluff."

I remain carefully impassive. Putting my cards face down on the table, I loosen my tie. We abandoned suit jackets over an hour ago, but my tie is chafing my neck.

Instead of answering Archer's question, I turn to the waitress working the bar next to our private poker table.

"Another whiskey. Make it on the rocks this time. And for fuck's sake, turn up the air conditioning. It's hot in here."

Archer's entire face lights up with malevolent glee. "Too hot in here for you, eh?" He chuckles dryly, which turns into a wracking cough.

"Mr. Gellar, are you in or out?" The dealer's frustration is evident in his tone. "We need to move this game along, sir."

Archer grins. "I'm all in." He stands up to push all of his chips to the center of the table. "Wait." He takes off his gold wristwatch and tosses it on the pile. "That's five hundred and fifty thousand. And..." He purses his lips. "How about I throw in my daughter? Hm? She's gotta be worth, what, a hundred k?"

The dealer clears his throat. "Sir, you have been warned repeatedly about trying to wager with illegal goods. Humans are not traded over a poker game, no matter how good you feel about your chances of winning."

I shift in my seat. I don't like Gellar's casual attitude

toward human trafficking any more than the next guy. But the idea of somehow owning Archer's daughter — pretty, blonde Annalise Gellar — makes a prickle of sensation gather at the nape of my neck.

Archer points at me, grinning. "Look at him. He's excited."

I frown at Archer, even though what he says is true. Owning and debasing Archer's little girl does have a certain appeal to me. But that's not what we are talking about right now.

"Gellar, get on with it," I growl.

Archer feigns a wounded look for a second. "I'm just trying to win back what you have taken from me, Nate. Have a heart."

I turn to the dealer. "Let's move this along. I don't know what funds Archer has left to play with at this point, as I've been picking his bones clean for the last three days of this poker tournament. But let's be done with it all. I haven't slept in a couple of days, and I have a date upstairs with my pillow."

Archer makes a disgusted sound. Before he can start whining again, the dealer turns to me. "Mr. Fordham? We have five hundred and fifty thousand on the table. Would you like--"

"Wait!" Archer grimaces. He wipes the flop sweat from his forehead onto his pants.

This is the expression of a hardened addict trying to get his fix. I've seen it many times before when I've attended these tournaments geared toward the ultra-rich. But none were so evident as Archer Gellar is now.

"Just wait," he says. He eyes me. "What if I put something you really wanted on the table?"

"Mr. Gellar-" The dealer does not sound amused.

I hold up a hand to stop his admonishment. "Let the

man speak." I know that nothing I could lose here would touch my billionaire status. But I have a feeling that Archer is about to dangle something I want in front of my nose.

"What if I put a merger on the table?"

I sit up a little straighter. "A merger?"

"You've wanted Gellar Industries for a long time. You can have a merger with my company and get all our ground-penetrating radar technologies. How would that be?"

I tilt my head and fold my hands, considering the possibilities. "It depends. Would you still be involved? Because I will not work with you, Archer. You're a snake."

He glares at me. "You're trying to drive me out of business!"

I look to the dealer. "Can we move this along?"

"Wait!" Archer grits his teeth. "Okay. I am willing to wager the company. And it would be under new ownership. I'd step aside. If you win this bet. Which I'm confident you won't."

I look at my watch. It's almost six in the morning, and I'm getting tired. I shouldn't be gambling anything big right now. But I want to squash Archer Gellar so badly that I can almost taste his whimpers of pain.

"And what do you want if you win?" I ask, sounding almost bored.

"Fifteen million dollars." Archer is too quick to come up with the exact figure.

I give him a long look. "Four."

"Twelve!"

I consider him for several moments, then sigh. "Six. And that's my final offer. Take it or leave it, and let us all go home."

"Fine, fine." He waves his hand. "I'm going to win. It's my turn. The universe owes me."

I exchange solemn glances with the Iranian. He tosses his cards in wordlessly.

"All right," the dealer says, taking control of the moment. "That's it. All bets are placed. Let's see what the river has to show us."

He deals an ace.

Archer shoots up from the table with the biggest grin on his face. "Woohoo!" Without waiting for the dealer, he flips his cards over. He has a flush, not even a particularly good hand. But he is leaning over the table to offer a high-five to the Iraqi gentleman.

The Iraqi waves his hand. "Why don't we see?" he says in heavily accented English.

"Yeah, why don't we?" I lay my cards out on the table. "Four of a kind."

"What??" Archer gapes at me. "That's... that's... cheating! You're a fucking dirty cheater!"

I push back my chair as Archer rubs the back of his neck, looking distraught. I point at him. "You lost, asshole. Fair and square. I have no idea how you thought it was a good idea to bet your fucking daughter on such a nothing hand."

Archer winces. "Ouch."

"You think that hurts? Wait till you realize that you're fucking fired."

Archer leans forward, clutching the back of his head, and begins to moan. "It... doesn't... feel... right..."

He lists to the side, and the Iraqi businessman scoots his chair out of the way just in time. Archer falls to the ground, a moan winding its way out of his lungs. "Ohhhhooooohh-hoh," he says.

Then he goes still.

The dealer is already on his feet, calling to the waitress. He tries to rouse Archer to no avail. "Mr. Gellar?" He kneels down and checks for a pulse. "He's got a pulse but I don't think he's breathing..."

I watch the dealer try to attempt a clumsy version of CPR. But it doesn't matter.

Archer Gellar just died after losing to me. Someone will be sad about it, I suppose.

But not me. No, I just gained a whole company. Not to mention Archer's lovely daughter Annalise. I don't know her well, but from what I remember, she's a little blonde vixen.

Gellar came into this room probably thinking that he would mop the floor with me. But I swept the decks clean of his rotten garbage.

And now all that's left is to claim my richly deserved reward.

Two
Annalise

I slip inside my father's office and close the door behind me with a long, silent sigh. While it's quiet and still in here, the hustle and bustle of the office outside doesn't stop until well after dark.

I look at my dad's stuffed padded leather chair and immense, polished-wood desk.

I've been CEO for two whole weeks, yet this is the first time I've allowed myself to break the seal of Daddy's office.

I guess a part of me is still hesitating. Wondering if my dad will wake up from his coma tomorrow and expect his office back.

But as the days pass, that becomes increasingly unlikely. And I can't keep up my initial tactic of having a roving hot desk anywhere I please. Lori says that it ruffles the employees' feathers.

Taking a deep breath, I walk over to the desk and sit down in the chair. Swiveling to face the window, I almost laugh at what I see. Though I'm wearing a knee-length pencil skirt, a white dress blouse, and dark stiletto-heels, I still look like a child sitting in her father's chair. My blonde curls are pinned into a loose knot at my nape.

My makeup is carefully done in shades of pink, purple, and brown. It's a more mature look, meant to age me a little. Gone are the bright pink polka dots and stylish white balloon-leg pants of two weeks ago.

Even though I've done everything I could to make it look like I have the authority to sit in this chair, I still look like I am a five-year-old in the middle of a game of pretend. I take a deep breath and try to psych myself up.

I think: *I am CEO Annalise now, not to be confused with the boss's daughter that hangs out in the office ordering expensive coffees. I'm in charge, damn it.*

"Are you in here?"

I spin, and find my mother poking her head into the office. She doesn't knock or announce herself. When she sees that I am, in fact, in here, she barges all the way in, slamming the door behind her.

God, she's upset again. What is it this time? I wonder.

I slide out of the chair as my mom approaches. She stops when she sees me and her eyes narrow.

"What are you wearing, Annalise?" she tuts in disapproval.

She is dressed, as always, in the mode of Audrey Hepburn à la Breakfast at Tiffany's. Today, it's a knee-length, black silk dress, bared arms, with diamonds on her wrists and at her earlobes. A sleek, black, quilted Chanel bag is hooked over her arm. I'm sure that if she didn't realize that people would look at her funny, she'd be wearing elbow-length gloves and carrying a long plastic cigarette holder, too.

She pats her hair, which is in the same elegant knot that I wear. I sigh. No matter what I wear, my mother never actually approves of my wardrobe. I've tried so hard for years to figure out what Mom is seeing when she criticizes me.

Is it really my haircut or my bland-bordering-on-dowdy dress that's bothering my mom? Or is it a need to criticize? Either way, I don't know what to say to her question, so I try to change the conversation.

"How's Daddy today?"

My question gives her pause.

"He was taken to the hospital for more scans. I talked to Dr. Stein about the likelihood of your father waking up and running this company. Dr. Stein keeps blathering on about waiting and having patience." Her lips twist with disgust as she looks down at me sitting behind Dad's desk. "I can't believe that you and your father made this little agreement behind my back."

I shake my head slowly. "I keep telling you, Mom. I had no idea that he named me as his successor. I'm as perplexed as you are."

Mom cocks her hip and looks testy. "You need to be out husband hunting. You were born and raised to find someone from a well-to-do family. The older the generational wealth, the better. This CEO business..." She wrinkles her nose. "It's ridiculous. You should let Donald Young step into the role. That's what vice presidents are for!"

My cheeks burn. "We agreed that I could try this for a bit, Mama."

She shakes her head and huffs. "When are you going to learn that you should listen to me?" She walks over to me, smooths my hair back and examines my face. "You need to get some Botox." She touches the tiny lines just outside my eyes. "I can see the beginning of crow's feet, darling."

Her touch is strangely hot. I'm not really used to either of my parents touching me and it makes me extremely antsy.

Breaking away from Mom, I walk to the office door. "I really have to work now, Mama."

My stomach flip-flops at the not-quite-lie I just told. I'm trying to fill my dad's shoes here; if I can't tell a fib to my mother, then I'll be up a creek without a paddle when it comes time to sit at the negotiating table.

One step at a time, I guess. My first step just happens to be lying to my mom.

My mother floats over to the door, her lips making a moue as she looks me up and down.

"You need a better wardrobe, darling." Mom reaches out and fidgets with my sleeve. "I'll send someone shopping for you."

"I don't need you to do that." My voice has an edge to it. Exasperation, my oldest friend. I'm usually much better at hiding it, though.

"Don't be silly. I'm your Mama." She clasps her hands before her. "I'll send someone to redecorate this office, too. You need new things, not your father's stuffy old junk."

"Hmm." My favorite sound. Totally noncommittal, to help fend off my mom and my dad. "I have to go. I need to freshen up my makeup now, so..." I open the door. "I'll see you tomorrow, Mama."

She gives me a staid smile. "I'm sure you will. And don't think I'm going to forget your husband hunt for too long, Annalise. As soon as I find some compatible matches for you, you are going to be introduced to them. That's final, darling."

She leans forward and says, "Kiss kiss!" Then my mom leaves my office.

Note that at no time during her little gesture of affection did she actually touch or kiss me. It's always been that way.

I peek out the door at the floor full of cubicles. The

company has about thirty-five employees up here, and another fifteen or so downstairs in the geology lab.

Hushed conversations stop when the employees realize that I am watching them. Then comes a sudden burst of activity. The copier starts going. There is a lot of typing and throat clearing, accompanied by several people noisily shuffling papers.

At this point, I have to wonder if the workers at my company are actually working or whether they are just slacking off ninety percent of the time. Or if it's the third option: that they are still so nervous when I'm around that they abandon their real work for this playacting.

In any event, it makes me wonder how things get done around here.

Lori Parker, Gellar Industries' general counsel, opens her office door and looks around. She spots me, arches a brow, and then waves me over.

I love Lori. She's been in her position since the company was founded and she's a red-haired firecracker.

I close my office door behind me and stride over to her. Lori steps back to let me in. Her office is decorated in bold pinks and delicate creams. It has a leather couch and a matching leather chair, with soft looking blankets tucked into both. I always feel at home in this room, as opposed to my father's sterile office space.

I give Lori a quick hug as I head over to the couch. Over my shoulder, I glimpse a wedge of city view just outside the window.

"How's tricks, kid?" Lori asks. She goes to a mini-fridge beside her desk and opens it, then offers me a Pellegrino. I shake my head.

"Do you think the staff is scared of me?" I ask.

She takes the chair and opens the Pellegrino. "Maybe. I

think a lot of the office staff are wondering if they'll get fired."

"I'm not exactly intimidating. I'm five foot two, and a hundred and fifteen pounds soaking wet."

She smiles, but her eyes stay cool.

"I think you are underestimating your father's hold on them. He liked to belittle and scream at them for the smallest infraction. So, I think they are just trying to figure out if you're like your dad or not."

I glance at the window. "Maybe I need to schedule one-on-one meetings with everyone.”

Lori shrugs. "You could do that. But I think you'll be more interested in the news I just received."

"Give it to me, then." I beckon her.

She takes a long sip of the bubble water, nodding her head all the while. "Do you know ViaLife?"

I purse my lips. "Yeah. They sell commodities. Oil, precious minerals, copper... coffee...."

"That's the one. Do you know who owns them?"

She's looking at me expectantly. Heat floods my cheeks. "No... Should I?"

"Nate Fordham is the CEO."

My eyebrows leap up. I've met Mr. Fordham a number of times. He attends the same charity galas, yachting regattas, and ballet patron dinners that my family does. He's never spoken directly to me, but I remember him well nonetheless.

Tall, black hair, silvery eyes, a perfect Tom Ford tux. And a tongue that would shame the devil with the wild things Mr. Fordham says. My father and Mr. Fordham always end up clashing any time that they're in the same room.

"Doesn't my dad hate Mr. Fordham?" I venture.

Lori snorts. "That's an understatement if I ever heard one. Mr. Fordham is your father's rival."

I try to frame my next question carefully.

"Isn't Daddy a bit old for rivals?"

A laugh bursts from Lori's mouth. "He didn't seem to think so." She schools her expression. "Mr. Fordham was in the room when your father had his aneurysm."

I scrunch my face up. "It sounds like they were spending more time together than rivals usually do."

Lori crosses her arms. "Maybe. Apparently, your dad was only there because of the poker game that Mr. Fordham puts on regularly."

"Oh. Dad does love a chance to gamble on literally anything." I huff a sigh. "Why do you bring Mr. Fordham up? Does Daddy owe him or something?"

She hesitates, then nods. "You could say that. Mr. Gellar ran out of funds at the poker table. So, he wagered something that he knew Mr. Fordham wouldn't turn his nose up at." Her expression darkens. "He proposed that Gellar Industries would undergo a merger with ViaLife if Mr. Fordham won."

The hair on my nape rises. "He did WHAT?"

Lori reaches out a hand and rubs my knee. "Relax. It's not the end of the world. Yes, a merger will be complicated. But it'll also give our company a fresh infusion of cash. And some resources that we really need. ViaLife is known to be flush."

I gape at the general counsel. "Are you insane? I'd rather give up the role of CEO than let someone else make decisions for the company on my behalf."

"Annalise, listen." Lori leans toward me. "We talked just last week about how you wanted to expand worker benefits. Weren't you saying something about more paid leave?"

I frown. "Well, yes. We don't currently offer any paid maternity leave benefits. Which, in my view, is criminal."

"And I said that we couldn't afford it. But with this merger, we could adopt ViaLife's leave policies. And we can use a cash infusion in the research and development department. You know that the department head has been begging me to get her more money for months now. With a merger, we could make strides with our ground-penetrating radar."

I make a sour expression. "My mother will have something to say about it, no doubt. Both of my parents think that mergers are a sign of weakness."

Lori smiles at me. "But neither one of them are in charge now. You are."

"That's true," I say, thinking about it. "But it might be the killing blow where my father is concerned."

"He should have thought about that before he bet the company in a poker game," Lori says, matter-of-factly.

THREE
NATE

I sit at the end of the table in my meeting room, staring at the CEO of HardDig, Davis White. Davis is wearing a rumpled suit, a tie stained with food, and even though it is cold in my office, he is sweating.

I look down at the file folder in front of me, frowning as I leaf through the stack of papers. It's just a bunch of blank sheets, but Davis doesn't know that.

I've insinuated that it is his file.

What file? I didn't say whether it is from the police, the FBI, or just a private eye. I don't need to, either.

Because as far as Davis knows, it contains all of his misdeeds, from HardDig, all the way back to cheating off some other kid when he was in kindergarten.

I pin Davis with a look and give him a grim little smile. "So... Davis. You've been a very bad boy, apparently."

"Mr. Fordham, I think there has been a misunderstanding." He mops his brow. "I don't even understand why I'm here."

I give him a frank look. "Really? You don't understand why the CEO of a well digging company would be asked to meet the CEO of a company that makes its money primarily from finding oil?"

He swallows. "Sure, but—"

I hold up a hand to stop him from further explaining.

"Davis, let's cut to the chase. I'm too busy for any more foreplay. You have been claiming losses for HardDig with the IRS for three straight years. But I have it on very good authority that you have a second set of books that hide the fact that your company earned north of thirty million dollars last year alone."

Davis looks like he's been hit in the face with a frying pan. His mouth opens and closes. "Mr. Fordham—"

"Here's what is going to happen. You're going to sell HardDig to ViaLife for a million dollars. I will take over the company. You'll get a golden parachute of... let's say, ten million. And we don't call the IRS and rat you out." I give him a smile as sharp as a razor blade. "How does that sound?"

He looks petrified. "I... I don't know..."

I stand up, checking my watch. "I think we're done here. Sign the papers or be prepared to see the IRS on your doorstep tomorrow. I'll be able to buy your company assets when they are auctioned off by the government. This is just a faster way for me to get them, and also the only way that you escape prison."

"P-prison?" he gasps. "I can't go to prison!"

I turn toward the glass door of the conference room and beckon for my assistant to enter the room.

Sal pushes the door open with a questioning expression. "All set?" he asks.

Davis is weeping and wiping his face. I jerk my thumb toward him. "He's agreed to sign. Get him the paperwork."

I stride out of the meeting room without another word, leaving the sobbing man behind. By the time I take a few steps into the hallway, my thoughts have already left this situation behind. I pass by a few glass-doored offices before I reach mine.

My office is the size of six smaller offices and it has the corner view of downtown Manhattan that any reasonable human being would kill for. Right now, I see a buttery leather wingback chair, a marble-topped chrome coffee table, and a sumptuous leather couch upon which a dark head is currently resting. It can only belong to one of my brothers; no one else has my permission to be in here when I'm not present.

I push open the office door and walk the ten paces to my huge slate desk. Perching on the edge with a sigh, I see that my visitor is indeed a Fordham. Cash is stretched out on my Maison Tallairdat couch, leaving scuff marks from his leather wingtips on the seat cushion. He greets me without looking up from his phone.

"Hey Nate." He continues swiping and typing on the small screen.

"Cash." I cock my head. "What brings you here?"

He keeps looking at his phone. "What happened to all the hot, available women in Manhattan?" he complains. "I'm in a real hot girl desert."

"Well, you've slept with most of the women in New York, married and unmarried. And since you profess to only have one-night stands..." I lift my shoulders in a shrug. "Honestly, if you hadn't gone to L.A. for a few years, you'd probably have encountered this issue before now."

Cash sighs and puts his phone on his chest. "Damn. I was afraid you'd say that."

I wait a few more seconds for him to get to the point. Then I pointedly check my wristwatch. "I assume that there is a point to you loafing on my couch?"

Cash sits up. "Do you feel like going downstairs for a drink?"

"It's three thirty, Cash."

"So?" He shoots me a dirty look. "You're worse than James and Grant. None of you are any fun."

I pin him with a look. Cash sticks out his lower lip and makes a begging gesture with his hands.

Shaking my head, I reach behind me to my massive slate desk and press the intercom button. When my personal secretary answers, I ask her to bring in two tumblers of superfine Japanese whiskey. She brings them in on a tray and then retreats, leaving us to sip our drinks in silence.

"Why are you really here?" I eventually prompt Cash. "Is it related to the Grecian papers?"

Cash shakes his head and stands up. Walking over to the window, he looks out at the crossing of Fifth Avenue and East 87th Street. Miniature people rush around below, cars zoom by haphazardly, and two buses nearly collide while he stands there.

"I looked into Gellar Industries."

That's not what I expected him to say. I did ask him to make inquiries. But honestly, I'd kind of forgotten, since it's been a few weeks since Archer Gellar literally died right in front of me. What can I say? My attention has been in demand every second since then.

I'm the CEO of ViaLife, one of the biggest multi-billion-dollar industries on the planet.

"And?" I prompt. "What'd you find out?"

"Gellar was expected to have entrusted his company to his VP, Don Young. You know Don, we were on that yachting team to raise money for..." Cash pauses, screwing up his face.

"Children's cancer," I supply.

"That's the ticket. Short guy, light hair, dresses like he just fell out of a 1970s Sears catalog?"

"Yeah, I remember. He was a stickler for the rules."

"That's him. Anyway, Gellar didn't appoint him as his successor. He appointed his daughter, Annalise."

I set down my whiskey, raising my eyebrows.

"Annalise? She doesn't have a business degree or anything, right?"

He grins and paces back toward me. "Nope."

Ugh. Of course Archer Gellar named his bratty daughter head of the company in his absence. It's what I expected, but still a disappointing move from a man I considered more or less a peer. I shake my head.

"I don't know why Archer would appoint his daughter. He doesn't really seem like the type to care about family."

"I don't know why. I asked, and nobody seems to have an answer," Cash goes on. "It's a bit of a mystery."

"It should make things easy for me. Annalise is a soft-spoken little thing. She's probably pretty stressed and over-whelmed, but she's doing it because her daddy said so."

"Could be." Cash drains the contents of his tumbler.

"I shouldn't have any problem buying the company outright, then. She's inexperienced and probably a pretty weak negotiator. It should be a piece of cake."

It should be a simple enough maneuver. And I like to think I'm a shrewd deal maker. As long as the girl doesn't put up a lot of resistance, I should be able to move on with my life and forget this ever happened.

Cash sighs. "I looked up her photo on the Gellar Indus-tries website. If you could do me a solid and not shatter her into a million pieces, that'd be great. I definitely want a crack at her after you're done, and I don't want a slobbering, whimpering mess. That's way too much emotion for me to handle."

I look at the ceiling briefly. "Cash, you are certainly welcome to the girl once I'm done. But if she puts up resistance to me buying her company, I'm going to crush her into fine dust."

"You sure about that?" He whips out his phone and shows me a photo. A sweet young blonde in a gray Chanel jacket, smiling at the camera. She looks almost exactly as I remember her.

Soft.

Sweet.

As tough as dandelion fluff.

Cash's phone starts ringing while he holds it up to my face. It's Drew Hastings, ViaLife's VP. He turns it around and curses.

"Shit, I should take this."

"Take it on the way out. I have to work a full day, unlike you, apparently."

He mouths goodbye as he heads toward the door. Propping his phone between his shoulder and his ear, Cash swans out of my office as he answers. "Is it done?" I hear his voice receding down the hallway.

Pushing out a long breath, I walk around my desk and sit in my leather chair. I set my tumbler aside and I turn toward the window. From this vantage point, I have a nice view of the azure Central Park Reservoir. This is my favorite spot to think.

I think about Annalise Gellar and how I'm going to dominate her the second we meet.

I think about how lonely I am, and how I could plan a date on the same apps my brother Cash frequents. But the last time I did, I felt much lonelier after the sex was over. My loneliness is at war with my personal quest for dominion over this whole damn city.

No one wants what I want. And no one *needs* to dominate like I do.

I decide to pull up my luxury realty app and peruse the multimillion-dollar listings until I hit a compound in Aspen that looks manicured and immaculate. I buy it without a moment's hesitation. I contact my property broker and tell her the property address before writing SOLD in solid block letters.

The satisfaction makes the threatening loneliness quiet down for a moment. Maybe only for tonight, or the next few days. Still, it's better than nothing.

Then I Google Annalise Gellar and scroll through her pictures, trying to formulate just what I'm going to say to her when I see her next.

Four
Annalise

My mother cuts her eyes at me as we climb the black marble stairs to the charity gala. "I wish you would have worn the outfit I laid out for you. It was classy."

"It was one of your old dresses, Mom. It has a high neck, long sleeves, and is ballroom length. It was clearly meant for a sixty-five-year-old."

She points her chin toward the top of the staircase. Her lips harden into a thin line. "Look at what you're wearing. It's disgraceful."

I glance down at the silver bodycon dress that I chose instead. It is a little short, as it ends midthigh. But it doesn't show too much cleavage. It has a pretty daringly low-cut back, but that's about it.

God, I have to get out from Mom's thumb. I can't stand the amount of control she has over me, even now.

Before I can say anything in my own defense, we hit the top of the stairs. As soon as we do, my mom sees a cluster of her friends gathered near the doorway leading into the ballroom. Their heads are bowed together, and they are all obviously gossiping about some poor girl's dress.

Mom grabs me by the arm and starts marching us toward the group of backstabbing snakes. But I yank myself free.

"Let me go!" I hiss. "People are going to talk if they don't see me mingling. I'm the CEO of Gellar Industries now. There are lots of business opportunities in this room."

My mom recoils as if I just splashed her with a bucket of ice water. "Just another reason why you shouldn't be CEO. You should be more concerned about finding the right husband than the day-to-day performance of our company's stock."

I summon my nerve and smile at her. "Dad named me his successor and you don't have a single word of say over any of it. I'm twenty-four years old, Mom. I'm my own person. Deal with it."

My mom glowers at me. But I turn on my heel and flounce into the ballroom, unaccompanied. As I walk through the crowd of men in their penguin suits and women in their glittering jewelry and slinky gowns, I suck in a breath. Grabbing a glass of champagne from a passing waiter, I drink it in three huge gulps.

Despite what I just told my mom, I'm little scared to be on my own out here. I feel like everyone is sizing me up, comparing me to my father as CEO, and then dismissing me.

"Miss Gellar?" a cultured, older man asks. I peg him as one of the people who were sizing me up.

"That's me!" I say, forcing myself to sound cheerful.

His brows rise, but he extends his hand. "Herbert Gimes."

I shake his hand a bit forcefully, feeling the need to overcompensate for my petite size. Herbert's thick, unkempt brows rise again, this time staying up near his hairline.

"Mr. Gimes. How do you do?"

He takes his hand back with a small smile. "Very well, Miss Gellar. It's good to see you out and about representing your company tonight."

"Yes, er." I rack my brain for a memory of Mr. Gimes. "Are you a friend of my father's?"

An off put expression flashes over his face.

"I should say so, Miss Gellar. I've been a member of Gellar Industries' Board of Trustees for fifteen years. I count your father amongst my closest friends." He rubs his jaw. "I made the initial motion during your swearing in before the board two weeks ago?"

He says the last as if I ought to remember him. And perhaps he is right. But honestly, I was so nervous that day that I spent it sweating and silently shaking, in shock over the fact that my father would put me up as his heir. As opposed to Don Young or even my mother.

Though I don't feel sorry, I smile apologetically, deciding to bluff my way through the conversation. "Oh, Gimes! I thought you said... Grimes! And I have a little bit of face blindness. It's a condition that comes and goes. I apologize."

He blinks. "Well... I guess... that's all right, then."

I put my hand on his tux sleeve. "Thanks, Mr. Gimes."

Herbert is quick to move back a step, giving me a distrustful look. "Miss Gellar, I hardly think that touching is appropriate here. One would think that you're coming on to me if one did not know that I am merely your father's best friend."

His accusation blows my hair back. I barely touched his arm! What the hell?

"I don't understand." I back away a step. "Why would you say that?"

"Because!" Herbert looks me up and down. "Look at yourself, Miss Gellar. You're a female, you're dressed provocatively, you're touching me—"

I shake my head, as confused as ever. "I'm just trying to imitate how I've seen my mother and father act. They are both so stiff and formal, surely they can't be acting in a way that you would find... unbecoming."

Mr. Gimes shoves his hands into his pants' pockets and gives me a long look. "They aren't a young, available woman, Miss Gellar."

I literally don't know what to say. I whisper sorry to Mr. Gimes, then whirl around and hunt for somewhere to cool down. I notice several doors leading to the outside. Turning my shoulder to cut through the crowd, I reach the exit and push on the glass door. The chilly air hits my whole body the second I step outside.

Brr. I pull my cashmere wrap closer around my shoulders as I look around the terrace that I've stepped onto. The night is too dark to make out much beyond the vague impression of bushes past the stone railing. As I walk out onto the flat flagstones, my steps sound like muffled gunshots.

I pause, startled at the sound. Of course, the noise dies when my footsteps cease.

I give a nervous laugh just as I hear the door opening behind me. Because I am already on edge, I jump and spin around, my heart pounding, ready to ward off any evildoers. Standing there, bathed in the single spotlight on the terrace, is a man unlike any other I've ever seen.

The man before me looks handsome as an angel, with a little smirk on his lips and his dark hair ruffling gently in the slight breeze. But this is no innocent man.

"Mr. Fordham!" The words are pulled from my lungs, a protest.

His dark eyes sparkle with mischief. "Annalise Gellar. I believe we've been introduced once or twice."

I feel my cheeks heat, though I don't know why.

"At some point," I say quietly. "Before you made a bet that gave my father a stroke, that is."

He frowns. "That's unfair."

He strolls toward me, his expression what I imagine a tiger's prey might see just before its gory death.

Nate Fordham is intimidatingly tall, dressed in a tuxedo that fits him like a glove. His collar is unbuttoned, tie askew. I glance at the patch of smooth, dark skin and a light dusting of hair. Something glints in the faint light.

"Are you all right?" he asks, tilting his head a few degrees.

Although I don't want them to, I can feel my cheeks heat again. "I'm fine." I wrap my arms across my chest and shoot him a glare. "Why are you out here? There's no one else to talk to on this terrace."

Nate takes another step toward me. Just what the hell is he doing?

"That's all right. I came out here to find you, Annalise."

"Me?" I try not to appear startled. The breeze starts up again and I catch a whiff of his cologne.

"Yes, you. You sound surprised."

"I'm just cautious with men I don't have any reason to know."

The smirk appears on his face again. "You have every reason to know me. Your father wagered a merger between our businesses. And I am here to collect it."

His assertion is so absurd that I can't help the laugh that slips out of my mouth. "You're crazy. No one in their right mind would think that winning a merger in a poker bet would stand up in court."

Nate puts his hands behind his back and studies me like I'm a curious insect that he's about to squash.

"My lawyers would be happy to sue your company. They are a vicious pack of thieves and liars and they're busily sharpening their knives, readying for their next victim."

I roll my eyes. "That's a horrible way to describe the people you employ."

He brushes that fact away with a sweep of his hand. His fingers are quite long. Pairs with being tall, I suppose.

I ball my face up. "So, you're actually here to claim that you have justification to force my company to merge with yours?"

He considers my words for several moments.

"Yes, I believe so. When your father said that he would step aside and name a successor, I imagined it would be someone... well... older. Someone who had run a company before, at least. But instead, I got Archer Gellar's daughter." His lips twist as if he's considering something humorous. "I'm trying to decide whether Archer was joking or high when he named you as his heir."

I bristle. "You really are a prick. Just so you know, my father named me as heir in secret six months ago. I found out about it when the rest of the world did."

"Come on. You have to be as confused as everyone else." He pauses, thoughtful. "Are you sure you're not in on it together somehow?"

My hands drop to my sides and ball into fists. "You know what, Mr. Fordham? You really are the worst. A no good, no account... scuzzball."

He smiles at me without a trace of warmth, showcasing a dazzling set of perfect teeth. "And you are Daddy's little girl, throwing a fit and messing up what would otherwise be business conducted between grown-ups! But you don't see me rubbing that in your face now, do you?"

What? Is this guy serious? No wonder my dad nursed a grudge against him for fifteen years. Nate Fordham is a complete tool!

My rage is near the boiling point. "That's it! I've had enough of this. I don't have to stand here and be insulted!" I stalk to the door.

Nate is lightning fast, whipping his hand out to catch my arm.

My mouth drops open. I stare at him, dumbfounded. Just who the hell does this guy think he is?

Nate pulls me close, his eyes flashing a warning. "Don't be a brat, Annalise," he hisses.

"Let me go!" I try to pull out of his grip, but he clasps me even more tightly. I can feel the delicate skin on my upper forearm throbbing in the shape of his big hand.

"If you don't agree to this merger, I will execute a hostile takeover of your board and then buy your little company. Do yourself a favor and just give in. It'll be quick and painless."

I clench my teeth. "Over my dead body."

"You have no idea who you're playing with, little girl."

Mustering all my energy, I break free and run for the terrace doors.

FIVE

NATE

When I enter the building where Gellar Industries maintains their offices and labs, I have a goal. I need to meet with little Annalise Gellar in the daylight, and make her see that the merger between her company and mine is inevitable. After meeting with Annalise, it is clear as glass that I can't actually expect her to sleep with me because Archer wagered it. But our companies are going to happen eventually... and it will go better for her if she just submits to my will now.

I stride through the lobby, not bothering to stop at the check-in desk. The employee behind it is clearly asleep anyway, and doesn't rouse as I hit the button to call for the elevator.

The elevator door opens with a creak. I raise my eyebrows and step in. The doors wheeze closed. I press the button for the top floor. The light flickers for a second as the elevator's gears grind. Then it carries me up to Gellar Industries without further issue until it arrives at the designated floor. When it stops, something in the machinery overhead bangs loudly.

I dart out of the elevator, reminding myself to take the stairs on the way down.

Gellar Industries, despite being on the top floor of the building and apparently doing ten million dollars a year of income, looks outdated by several decades. The bright, fluorescent lighting shines harshly down on a single, nonplussed-seeming secretary. She is sitting at a peeling laminate desk that was probably new in the late 1980s. The secretary clicks a mouse on an aged desktop, looking quite bored.

Shooting my suit cuffs, I step up to her desk.

"Can I help you?" She doesn't even bother to look away from her computer. Click. Click. Click. She jiggles the mouse.

I peer around the tan box of her screen and see that she is playing a poorly animated game.

"Nate Fordham. Here for Miss Gellar."

The secretary looks at me and takes a second before answering. "Do you have an appointment?"

"I don't need one." I spread my hands wide. "Our companies are merging. I'm the new boss."

The secretary sits up straighter. Her eyes widen. "One moment..." She picks up a telephone and mumbles something into it. She glances up at me and continues her muttered conversation for a few more seconds. Then she hangs up the phone. "Miss Gellar will be here shortly."

I smirk at the secretary, walk to the shabby, laminate oak door, and yank it open. Inside, I find quite a few cubicles filled with listless employees. They're either talking to their neighbor or playing computer games on outdated machines similar to the front-desk secretary's. They ignore me as I head down the side of the building toward where I predict the CEO's office to be.

As I pass office doors on my right side, I attract the

attention of one person. "Mr. Fordham!" A woman comes rushing out. She's probably in her late 50s, and is dressed as boringly as possible in ash gray slacks and a matching sweater. She thrusts her hand out to me, a first since I've entered this building. "Lori Parker. General counsel for Gellar Industries. It's nice to meet you."

I shake her hand, surprised at the strength of her grip. "Nate Fordham. I assume you know why I'm here."

Lori nods. "I assume that you've decided to take Archer up on his offer of a merger."

"That's right." I offer her a small smile and then look around the open room. "Is it usually like this?"

Her cheeks stain with color. "Just since Mr. Gellar fell ill. He used to rule this office with an iron fist."

I nod, digesting that bit of information. But before I can respond to it, Annalise comes storming over.

"What are you doing here, Mr. Fordham?" She doesn't look pleased to see me. Her hair is gathered in that same bun as she wore last night, and there are faint circles under each of her eyes. She wears a Chanel dress suit that makes her look twenty years older than her actual age.

"I'm here to check out exactly what I'm supposed to be merging with." I jerk my thumb over my shoulder. "Your employees seem to need something to do."

Annalise flushes and snaps at me. "They are doing fine. Why don't you come into my office? I thought I made my position on merging very clear last night. But I will explain it again if you need me to."

"Annalise!" Lori whispers. "You should hear him out at least."

Annalise gestures to the corner office. "This is just a chat between myself and Mr. Fordham. I'll let you know if I need any other points of view."

Lori nods her head and steps back to let us pass. It's too

bad that Lori isn't the person that I'm dealing with. At least she seems willing to accept the inevitable.

Annalise waves me in her office. I walk in and I'm struck by how masculine the energy is in here. Very little décor other than a big oak desk and navy curtains. There are a few photos on the wall, each of Archer with his arm around a president or dignitary of some kind.

Annalise Gellar is nowhere to be found in this room. It's still a shrine to Archer.

Walking over to her rather threadbare looking couch, I sit down, making myself comfortable. Annalise sits primly in the desk chair, looking like there are a million conversations she would rather be having than this one.

I cast a gaze over her. She's pretty, after a fashion. Her face is youthful, though she wears too much foundation and the muted colors she chose do nothing for her. If she wore a little color instead of the same damn pink nude color of her skirt and top, it would help.

"Are you going to explain what you're doing here, Mr. Fordham?"

The name brings a faint smile to my lips. "So formal, Annalise. Call me Nate."

Her green eyes study me for a second. "Fine. Nate, then. Why are you here? I told you last night that I am not interested in a merger."

"I'm here because I am interested. And I was promised a merger by your father. It's your right as CEO not to agree with it, but my team of lawyers will destroy you in court."

Her lips thin. "Yes, so you've said."

"Can I be candid with you?"

"I couldn't stop you even if I wanted to, apparently."

I smirk. "I am a man who is used to getting what I want. I would like you to agree. But I don't need you to." I stretch out on the couch, taking up space. "What I don't understand is why you wouldn't want to merge companies. I have seen your shabby little office and your unenthusiastic staff. Why would you not agree to a merger where you got much nicer offices, a person to do the heavy lifting for you and cut all of your dead weight, and a lot of money to boot?"

Annalise runs her tongue over her teeth, looking annoyed. "Because, Nate. First off, my father absolutely despises you. My job as his successor is to run things as he would see fit. He would never say yes to a merger. Secondly, I don't like you any more than my father does."

"And what about the undeniable benefits I'm offering?" I glance out her glass door toward the employees. I can see them standing and staring rather than working. "You need a hatchet man. Somebody unafraid to make bold cuts. Those people out there are not loyal to you, Annalise. They aren't driven to work hard for you. Let me be that person. Let me move you into much nicer offices in the ViaLife building. And for god's sake, think of your profits once I start making changes to the company structure."

She narrows her eyes at me. "I think you're missing something, Mr. Fordham."

"Nate," I correct her. "And what would that be?"

Annalise stands up and plucks a key card off her desk. "Let me show you."

Without another word, she leads me out of the office, to a stairwell, and down a floor. We're headed to the company's lab floor, I bet.

What could be interesting about that, though?

Annalise scans her keycard at the door, then steps back to do a biometric scan. Once the door unlocks, she ushers me into a hallway with a series of same-looking white doors. One is propped open and strange light flickers from the room into the hallway.

"Left! I said left!" a man shouts.

I look at Annalise, arching a brow. She ignores me and hurries into the room with the strange, flickering lights.

I blink a few times as I follow her in; my eyes have to adjust to the darkness.

In the center of the room, a large, three-dimensional map hovers midair. The map is being navigated by a young man working joystick. He presses a button and the map unfolds to reveal several sections of the ground, complete with layers of topsoil, sediment, and rock. The young man sticks out his tongue as he deftly works the joystick, descending through the strata on the map.

An older man lounges in a chair beside him. He stands up when Annalise enters, rubbing his hands together. "Bossy lady!" he says. His accent is reminiscent of the Eastern Bloc. "You come to see us, finally."

"Hi Mikhail." Annalise looks to me. "This is Nate Fordham. Mr. Fordham, meet Dr. Mikhail Popov and Dr. Lev Alexeyev."

"Please, call me Mikhail," the older man says. He elbows his co-worker in the ribs. "This is Lev. We are trying to perfect the mapping software. It has many glitches, still."

"Is this a model that you're working with?" I ask. "Is this a hypothetical project?"

In the next second, the software glitches and the projection vanishes. I hear Lev mutter a curse in what sounds like Croatian or Estonian. Then he walks over to flip on the light switch.

Annalise, in the meantime, answers my question. "It is a model of an actual site in Utah. We have done extensive work with ground-penetrating radar and sonar. Now we just need to debug the software so that we can actually use it."

Lev nods, talking to me slowly, as if I will surely have difficulty comprehending this information.

"If you can see all the ground at one time, you can see patterns. And from there, you can predict and explore where there might be large deposits of any kind."

He leaves it there, but there is an unspoken, "duh" at the end.

The back of my neck heats. I'm not used to being dressed down by anybody, let alone scientists. Annalise glances at me, fidgeting, and chimes in again.

"We are going to be able to find huge shale oil deposits. And any other kind of mineral or gas as well. Our project is mere months away from making us so much money that we don't even know what to do with it. That's why there are so many people upstairs playing solitaire. They are sales or support staff, waiting for the word to start making calls," Annalise adds.

My eyebrows shoot up. If what she says is true, I could be coming into this merger at the perfect time.

"We need to talk about the best way to roll this technology out." I can see how profitable her technology will be. I can also see how partnering with ViaLife can feed this little two-person department a stream of top-tier computer programmers. What she thinks will takes months could take weeks if it is given the right resources.

Annalise thanks the two scientists and steers me out of the room. She makes certain that we are in the stairwell again before she speaks.

"ViaLife is going to be one of many partners that pay for our services as soon as we are up and running." She starts climbing the stairs ahead of me, forcing me to follow her. I scowl as I look at her fantastic ass in that overly conservative skirt and her sleekly muscled calves in those black high heels.

For the first time since I've been in negotiations with Annalise Gellar, I start to lose focus on the merger itself. Instead, my brain fills with questions about Annalise herself and what she might look like in something other than those boring Chanel suits she seems to favor.

Actually, I wonder what she looks like in nothing at all. She would probably look utterly stunning naked, lying in the middle of my black silk sheets. All that creamy skin, ready to be explored...

"Mr. Fordham?" Annalise prompts.

I blink. She is holding the door open to the upstairs floor, looking at me with vague confusion.

Did I just sexualize Archer Gellar's little girl? Yes, I believe I did.

Smoothing down my tie, I bound up the last few stairs. My mind is already working overtime. I need to continue this conversation someplace much less formal.

"Do you like the ballet?" is what I come up with, grasping at straws.

Puzzlement settles over Annalise's delicate features. "I do..."

"The NYC Ballet is showing Sleeping Beauty tonight. Will you come as my guest?"

She lifts her chin, eyeing me. "Why should I do that?"

"So we can continue to talk."

She hesitates for a moment. "I don't think that's a very good idea, Mr. Fordham."

I smirk. "What if I pay you?"

She rolls her eyes and turns away. "I have everything that I could want already, Mr. Fordham."

I catch her arm, tugging her back into the stairwell. Annalise shoots me an annoyed look.

"Are you going to do this every time I try to leave?"

I slide my arm around her waist. She sucks in a deep breath, perhaps surprised at my boldness.

"Yes." I grab her hand and trail my fingers to her pulse.

Her heartbeat is like that of a jack-rabbit. "I think you like that I don't want to let you go, Annalise."

She blushes, two bright red spots high in her cheeks. "You barely know me, Mr. Fordham."

I cock my head, wrapping one of her blonde curls around my finger. "You really should call me Nate."

"No, I shouldn't." She looks up at me, her expression pinching. "I think you are a dangerous man, Mr. Fordham."

"You have no idea." My lips twitch with a sparse bit of humor. "Come out with me tonight. We can talk more business. If you still don't like what I have to say... I'll walk away."

I know it's a lie the second it comes out of my mouth. If Annalise keeps being stubborn, I'll eventually turn my legal team loose on her. But she doesn't need to know that.

"Really?" she says. "You'll back off?"

"Sure." I shrug. More lies. "Just let me try to woo you tonight."

Her hazel eyes study my face for a few seconds. She bites her lower lip, drawing my attention there.

I intend to be biting and sucking at her glossy lips soon. And if things go as I want, I plan to groan and clutch the back of her head while she swallows my cock soon too. The idea of messing up her perfect lipstick stirs my blood.

"Okay," Annalise relents softly. "I'll come."

"I'll send a car for you." My eyes skate down her bland dress. "Actually, I'll send a dress, too. I want you to fit in."

She rolls her eyes. "I've been to the fricking ballet before, Mr. Fordham."

I don't want to turn her loose. But I step back anyway, forcing my hands behind my back. "Be ready at six. I don't tolerate lateness."

Then, before I can be tempted further, I turn and

thunder down the stairs. Only one thought rings through my head.

I'm going to have Annalise Gellar. I'm going to take Archer's little daughter and pathetic his little company, too. I'm going to rub it in Archer's face.

Nobody gets revenge quite like I do.

Six

My lips twist sourly as I slide from the back seat of the chauffeured SUV that Nate Fordham sent for me. I wrap the expensive white cashmere and fur wrap that Nate had messengered to my apartment more closely around myself to ward off the chill evening air.

I look up at the broad stone steps before me that lead up to a slate-covered, modern-looking building. I let a puff of breath escape my mouth.

The New York Ballet could be the only ballet in the world, for all I care. Since it was taken over by Nate's cousin Calum Fordham, their dancers have put on nothing but incredible performances. Everyone who is anyone fights for tickets. Because of the size of the theater, I know that only the most vaunted patrons get box seats.

You can't buy your way onto the waitlist. You have to be *invited*. And I'm willing to bet that the Gellar family hasn't even gotten close to the top of that list.

Because the Fordham family is one of the founding families of New York City, here I am. Heading up to the door, knowing that a much-contested box seat will be waiting for me. I have to admit, my interest is piqued.

An usher holds open a massive oak door for me and I step inside. A soaring, three story space surrounds me. I can see that I follow a group of ballet-goers closely. But their sounds are muffled and distorted by this huge, slate-lined atrium. Nothing sounds like it should.

"Annalise."

When Nate touches my inner arm and says my name, I almost jump out of my skin. I turn to him, my heart thrumming. "Mr. Fordham!" His name from my mouth sounds like a curse. "Don't sneak up on me!"

He chuckles. "I said your name twice before I touched you, Annalise. You are a skittish little thing. I should call you Kitten."

I make a disgusted face. Even though I kind of like the way Kitten sounds, coming from him, it's hardly appropriate. This is a business relationship at best.

I try to remind myself of this as my eyes travel down his body. Once again, he's wearing a tuxedo like he was born in it, commanding my attention. "Mr. Fordham. I would appreciate if we kept things formal."

His eyes skate down my figure, but he doesn't comment on what I am wearing. Thank god for that. I don't need to know what he's thinking; the blaze of hunger in his eyes tells me all I need to know.

This guy is trouble.

Nate sticks out an elbow. "Let's find our seats, shall we?"

So he's going to pretend he didn't hear me. Great.

Sighing, I slip my hand onto his forearm and press my lips into a thin line.

His forearm radiates heat. It's everything I can do not to huddle closer to Nate's big body. They have the air conditioning jacked up in here, perhaps in deference to the ballerinas that will soon be dancing under the hot lights.

As we take the elevator up, and walk past other rich couples, I notice that Nate says hello to practically everyone. Mr. Fordham is a social butterfly? That's not something I had on my imaginary bingo card.

"Is there anybody here that you don't know?" I say wryly.

A smile tips Nate's lips up. A rumble from deep in his chest makes me shiver. "Did you really expect that there would be anyone here I wouldn't know? I'm from one of the oldest, and most well-connected families in New York City." He arches a brow. "But I don't expect you to know how that is. To my knowledge, Archer was penniless ten years ago."

I feel my cheeks heat. For a moment, I had almost forgotten that Nate and my dad operated as business rivals for quite a long time. Silly me. "You're not scoring yourself any points by bringing up the fact that my family hasn't been rich for long." I shake my head, my expression pinched.

He lets out a soft laugh and heads toward a row of doors with pink velvet hangings draped on either side of them. "Fair point."

I look at him skeptically. I can't tell if he is making fun of me or not. If he is, he's hiding his condescension well.

An usher spots Nate and hurries to open one of the doors. "Mr. Fordham, welcome. I wasn't told you would be here tonight," he squeaks.

"Hello, Jones." Nate pats the usher's shoulder as we pass. I am pretty sure I see him pass the man a large cash tip. "Make sure that we're not disturbed, will you?"

Then he slides his arm around my waist and hurries me on, not waiting for a response.

This must be what life is to Nate; he pays, and people rush to do his bidding.

The usher closes the door as soon as we are through it. Below us are padded benches that can accommodate a dozen or so patrons. Then the box drops off and the whole stage spreads out beneath us, misty and beckoning like a Siren.

I gasp and step down to peer over the balcony edge. There, I see the orchestra warming up and the audience that spills out behind them. From our vantage point near the stage, the floor seats seem quite far away.

And to think, I was going to be one of the people populating the tightly packed floor. Every seat is occupied. The noise that rises to my ears is muffled. Like everything in this building, it is distorted somehow.

"I take you like the seats?"

I blink, then look at Nate. Somehow, I managed to completely forget him for a full five seconds.

He wears not quite a sneer on his lips as he smirks at me.

Damn him. He's so handsome, it's irritating. He is just... infuriating.

"They're fine," I say.

His lips twitch with humor. "You know what I just realized?"

I tug my wrap around myself, eyeing him. "What's that, Mr. Fordham?"

A smile appears on Nate's lips. "You're very easy to read, Kitten. You really haven't lied very much in your life, have you?"

"I'm honest, if that's what you mean." I glare at him. I'm lying through my pearly white teeth when I add, "And don't call me Kitten."

Just because you like something doesn't mean you should make a habit of it.

Nate looks me up and down. "You need to be tutored,

Annalise. You'll never make it in this business if you can't lie." He flashes me a grin.

"I think I'm doing fine," I grit out. Again, it's not even close to the truth. But the idea of admitting something so personal to Nate makes me feel faintly sick to my stomach.

He waves a hand to the bench seat. "I don't think so. Take your coat off, Kitten. Stay a while."

My whole face must flush bright red. It has to, from the way it flames hot. I knew that he would make me take my wrap off at some point. I should've picked a much more conservative dress from my closet. I'm not entirely sure why I wore what Nate picked out. I guess I'm always doing what I'm told. That's been my whole personality for my entire life.

It's a hard habit to break. Plus, Nate's taste in clothes is, unsurprisingly, very chic.

My mouth twists with distaste as I walk over to the seat he's indicated and slowly peel my wrap off.

As I start revealing skin, I notice that his breathing hitches.

Coupled with my usual black pumps, I am wearing the beaded gold tube top and matching gold skirt he picked out for me. And honestly? The look on Nate's face right now is worth the embarrassment of wearing so little in public.

His eyes bounce to my tits, then to my belly button, then to my tightly-fitted, gold beaded skirt with a hem that is higher than any I have ever worn before.

For a moment, Nate doesn't even breathe.

For that moment, I feel like I have all the power in the world.

Then Nate seems to remember himself and forces his eyes back up to my face.

"You look good in the clothes that I picked out for you, Annalise," he purrs.

What do I say to that? If I were my dad, I would try to show no weakness. And I want Nate Fordham to view me as seriously as he views my father.

I lift my chin defiantly. "And you look like a cartoon dog with its tongue rolling out. Down, boy."

His expression of complete surprise delights me. "Are you saying that you wouldn't spend the night in my bed?" He sits down beside me just as the lights begin to dim.

"In your dreams, Nate Fordham."

As I say it, my heart thuds so hard against my ribs that I am sure it's about to break free and crawl out of the box we're sitting in.

His silver eyes narrow on my face. "No woman says no to me."

I shrug, trying to pretend that my heart isn't hammering in my chest as I speak. "I do."

The orchestra begins the overture and I slide forward, leaning my elbows on the box's ledge.

He stares at me for several seconds, then shakes his head. "We're going to talk about this later," he husks out.

"Not if I have anything to say about it," I fire back.

The first ballerina springs onto the stage. The orchestra is loud and wonderfully distracting. I try to focus my attention on the stage.

Nate slides closer on the bench. I glance at him and his eyes are on the stage, as they should be. I breathe a sigh of silent relief and turn back to the ballet.

But half a minute later, Nate's hand lands on my thigh. My heart starts hammering relentlessly. "Mr. Fordham!" I scold him.

"Shh." He nods at the stage. "Keep your eyes on the performance."

"But your hand—"

"Is comfortable where it's at," he finishes the sentence for me. "Now be quiet."

I feel like I've swallowed my tongue. Staring at Nate so hard that I should burn a hole in one of his perfectly chiseled cheeks does no good. He doesn't move his hand, which rests just above the hem of my skirt.

At last, I look away from him and stare angrily at the ballerinas that fly across the stage. My mind is working overtime.

Nate moves his hand ever so slightly. He plucks at the beaded hem of my skirt, his fingertips trailing down to skate across my bare thigh. I squirm, trying to move away.

What is he doing?

Most of the time, I want to throttle Nate Fordham. Not let him touch me so... intimately.

Just because he's handsome as sin doesn't mean that I want to throw myself at him. Maybe if he were a little less irritating, we would be having a very different conversation.

Am I just a prude? I wonder to myself. Sure, I'm still a virgin. And my parents kept me essentially locked up, controlling my social life until I escaped their home at twenty-two. But I don't think of myself as uptight or judgy. Especially compared to the illustrious Monique Gellar.

According to my mother, I have to be prim and proper until I marry... well, someone like the man I am sitting next to. Then I can be a freak and a slut once I have a Cartier ring on my finger. Sadly for Mom, that marriage is not on the table right now. If it were, my mother would be cheering Nate on, telling me to do whatever it takes.

The thought turns my stomach.

When Nate starts edging my skirt up, I bare my teeth at him. "If you don't stop, I'll scream."

He smiles at me, something devious flashing in his eyes.

"You can leave this booth if you want to," he says, looking at the door. "No one is stopping you."

I give him a prim little smile and try to brush away his hand. "I could, but I want to watch the ballet."

Nate's eyes turn toward the stage. "I want you to watch the ballet too, Kitten."

"Don't call—"

His fingers over my lips silence me. "So damn argumentative," he whispers. "I want to make you feel good, Annalise."

Does he mean... he wants to give me an orgasm? I stare at him, open-mouthed. "I'm not going to sleep with you!" I whisper.

"No one said you had to. Just focus on the ballet." He pauses. "Or we can leave. Your choice."

I clench my jaw. I'm not going to let him scare me. I'm not a little girl he can just order around. Nor am I anyone's Kitten.

Besides, I'm fully dressed and there are people watching us in this box. There is no way that Nate can actually embarrass me and make me weak. Not with those two impediments.

I lift my head, staring stubbornly at the stage. "I'm not leaving." The statement sounds an awful lot like a challenge. Inside, I'm frantically trying to figure out how I feel.

Angry? Frustrated? A little turned on?

Certainly scared. But...

I press my thighs together. I can't help but notice that Nate's touch has excited me, made my pussy grow damp. I can feel my *excitement* gathering in a small pool in my panties.

He leans close, tipping my head back. I look up into his eyes. I can smell his warm, slightly minty breath as it fans across my suddenly sensitive mouth. He smirks at me. "I can see that you want me, little girl."

I want to protest, but in the next second, his mouth captures mine.

His kiss is as shocking as if I've just touched an electric fence. I am frozen for a moment as he presses his lips to mine. A flood of pleasure swells in me and my lower body throbs.

"Kiss me back, Kitten. I know you want to," he murmurs.

And God help me, I want to.

I kiss him back somewhat timidly, not knowing exactly what I am doing. I feel like a clumsy fool. But then he slips his tongue in my mouth, eliciting a gasp from me. I moan and open my mouth, inviting him in.

I want this. I need his invasion, even if I'm not sure what it means. His fingers pluck at the hem of my skirt again and then skate up my thigh, under my skirt. I grip the collar of his tuxedo, pulling him closer.

His fingers brush the front of my panties, quickly finding the evidence of my excitement. He moans softly. "God. Is this all for me?"

My face heats, but I nod anyway. He kisses me again and his clever fingers brush my slit through my panties. My hips twitch, pressing closer. Nate's tongue slides against mine and I dig my nails into the material of his jacket.

I *need* something that only Nate can give me.

And that's the moment that there is a sharp knock at the door.

I freeze. Nate quickly disentangles himself from me, clearing his throat. I turn my head to stare at the door. Until this moment, I had forgotten that it even existed. Nate twists in his seat and leans over. "Who is it, goddamn it?!"

The voice on the other side is muffled by the thick door.

The person speaking sounds far away when he says, "It's Calum!"

"Shit." Nate stands up. He's got a huge erection and he adjusts himself for a second, then looks at me. "We will have to resume this later."

I stare at him, trapped like I'm a deer in headlights. Vaguely, I nod.

He turns and walks to the door, swinging it open. A handsome dark-haired man in a tux pokes his head in. He looks back and forth between us. "Should I come back?"

Nate clears his throat and hurries out to greet the man. "Calum! How are you?"

Nate doesn't tell me to follow him. I get up and straighten my skirt, wondering anxiously if anyone will be able to tell that I'd been turned on. My biggest concern is the wet spot on my panties. I can't feel it anymore, but I don't want to announce to everyone that I was getting felt up during the ballet.

I follow Nate's footsteps to the door, curious about our visitor. When I duck out my head out into the hall, Nate introduces me. "Annalise Gellar, this is my cousin Calum Fordham. He and his wife run the ballet."

My heart beats so hard that I'm sure I might die. "It's a pleasure, Mr. Fordham. I am a huge fan of your ballet company."

"Thank you, Ms. Gellar." Calum bows his head. "I hope you're enjoying *Sleeping Beauty*."

Nate smirks. "Calum, Annalise is Archer Gellar's daughter. She just took over his company.""

"Ah!" Calum says, then turns to Nate and adds, "I know you and Archer butted heads quite a bit. Hopefully you'll get along a little better with Annalise."

I bite my tongue against the urge to tell Calum that I did not give him permission to refer to me by my first name. I'm still hanging awkwardly in the doorway, clinging to the shadows.

"We'll see," I reply.

Calum smiles coolly. "I didn't mean to interrupt your enjoyment of the performance. I just wanted to reschedule our failed meeting, Nate."

Nate smiles. "Well, you had somewhere else to be, didn't you?" To me, he says, "Calum's wife went into labor a week early a day before we were supposed to grab a drink."

"It's true," Calum says. "I can't say that I'm especially regretful, though. I missed the meeting, but if I'd gone, I would have missed the birth."

Nate laughs. "You chose correctly."

"I think so." Calum smiles. "I should get back to my seat. But I wanted to say hi. Also to tell you that Christoph Meyer, the CEO of Pomegranate Tech, is holding court downstairs. I know you wanted to catch up with him."

"I'll have my PA call yours. We'll see if we can't find a few hours to play racquetball or something." Nate flashes a grateful look at his cousin.

"Or something." Calum smiles vaguely at me. "Nice to meet you, Ms. Gellar."

At least Calum doesn't call me by my first name, unlike Nate. With a parting smile, Calum heads out the door.

Nate turns back to me, raising an eyebrow. "Meyer owes me three-hundred thousand dollars for backing out of a deal at the last minute. I've been trying to catch him in person to pin him down to an agreement, so I'm going downstairs for a minute. Would you like to come?"

Licking my lips, I open my mouth to say yes. Then I pause, remembering my earlier concern. What if strangers can tell that Nate and I were fooling around? I would actually die of embarrassment.

I shake my head. "I think I'll stay and watch the ballet."

Nate shrugs. "Suit yourself." Without another word, he turns and vanishes down the hall.

I walk into the box and try to decide what to do. Should I stay?

Will that mean that I have to reckon with Nate again?

Feeling like a coward, I grab my wrap and drape it around myself as I flee, heading for a back door so I am not forced to see Nate as I leave.

SEVEN

ANNALISE

I walk into the ballroom of the Prestige hotel in downtown Manhattan. Several volunteers from the New York Endowment for Movement Arts are already setting up chairs to face a runway stage. I'm a little surprised. I thought I was here to volunteer. But I was told to be here at ten-thirty.

Am I late, somehow?

I look at my watch as a woman pops her head out from the curtains behind the stage. "You're here!"

I gulp and look over to find Ms. Vasquez hurrying down the discreetly built-in steps beside the stage. Ms. V, as she insists on being called, is my mother's best friend. She's waving me over with intense excitement.

I just came to help the charity put on their annual bachelorette auction. My mother being here was not a part of the plan.

Kicking myself for coming at all, I head over to the stage. Mrs. V looks me up and down. "Are you wearing a cute dress under that coat?"

I pull my white wool coat closer around me and frown.

Mrs. V always wears loud, bright colors and frankly scandalous outfits. She favors halter tops and miniskirts, as is evidenced today in her outfit of hot pink pleather pants and a bright yellow tube top.

"I didn't realize that I had to look a certain way," I mumble as she hustles me backstage. "I'm just here to volunteer."

"We will find you something good!" Mrs. V declares.

We walk over to the area where several women are being primped and made up for the auction. Poor things. They are being plucked and plumped as if they are cattle, being readied for sale. *Yuck. I'm glad that's not me.*

I sigh and check the time. After this, I am due to work a few weekend hours at the office. I'm determined to make it through my dad's mountain of personal papers by the end of the week.

My mother waits for me beside an empty chair, poised and smiling. "Hello, Annalise."

"Hey, Mom. Do you know where the person in charge is? I'd like to find out how I can help for the next—" I check the slim gold watch on my wrist. "Three hours. Maybe I can check names as people come in the door? Or organize the gift bags?"

"Actually, darling... one of the girls dropped out at the last moment." My mom shakes her head. "It was tragic, really. But I told the woman in charge not to worry, because you'd be happy to fill in."

"What?" I ask, alarmed. "I don't want to be auctioned off! How embarrassing!" One of the ladies having her hair done looks at me sourly. I'm quick to add on, "For me! Only for me, I mean,"

Mrs. V comes up behind me, pulling my coat off. "Don't be ridiculous. What reason do you have for not wanting to fill in as a bachelorette?"

"Stage fright, for one?" I supply. "I can think of half a dozen other reasons just off the top of my head."

My mother purses her lips and looks down at what I'm wearing. It's just a simple beige bodycon dress with three quarter length sleeves that ends just above my knee. Not exactly a demure dress, but it should meet her standards for modesty.

"Annalise Rebecca, you really need some help with choosing your clothing. What on Earth are you wearing?"

Smoothing my hands down the front of my dress, I smile despite the anger flooding my veins. I'm not taking advice from Jackie Kennedy Barbie, I remind myself. I lift my head and give her a little spin. "I'm enjoying myself, Mom. I've moved out, I've taken over as CEO, and now I'm even picking out my own outfits. If you don't like it, you can just deal with it."

"Christ, Annalise," my mom sniffs.

Mrs. V intervenes. "Girls, please don't bicker." She turns to me. "You need to head into the wardrobe room at the end of the hall."

"I'm not going onstage. Period." I try to glare at both of the women.

My mom sniffs. "Darling, don't be ridiculous. It's for charity. Quit being a petulant little girl about this. If you're as grown up as you claim, you'll do this without complaint."

My mom knows what buttons to push, because she herself installed them. I scowl at her. "Fine," I grit out.

"Annalise, don't frown!" She touches the skin just to the right of my mouth. "You'll give yourself wrinkles."

I move toward the wardrobe door that Mrs. V had indicated. My mouth is full of bitter words for my witch of a mother. But I don't let them out. I just strut past her, lifting my head up and putting my shoulders back.

"That's the walk you should use on stage," I hear Mrs. V hoot as I vanish through the wardrobe doorway.

An hour later, I'm transformed. I'm wearing a tight white minidress. My hair has been straightened and piled on my head so I appear to have gained a few inches of height. I'm wearing six-inch, see-through plastic heels. And I have so much makeup on that I feel like a circus clown.

"You!" the organizer barks at me. "Come here." I take very careful steps toward her. She puts out her hand. "Give me your information card."

I slip the index card crammed with my vital details and facts about myself against her palm. She peers at it for a second, then snaps her fingers and points to the two women already lined up for their turn to walk down the runway. I totter over to stand behind them.

The girl in front of me gives me a sympathetic expression. It would be comforting, if she weren't wearing the most distracting pink print midi-dress I'd ever seen. It looks like a print of scorpions about to sting. But I'm not sure if I should ask.

"You don't look comfortable in those shoes," she says.

"That's because they are two sizes too small and four inches taller than I'm used to."

She waves a hand. Her fingers are green and glittery. This girl seems otherworldly. "Two minutes," she says.

I feel like I'm in a stress dream. Like I'm going to walk out on that stage and the people sitting in the audience will slowly morph into my elementary school classmates and they'll laugh uproariously at me.

Gulp.

God, what if nobody bids on me? I'm not intrinsically valuable without being CEO of Gellar Industries, after all.

The girl in front of me goes out. I can hear the crowd now and it sounds bigger than I had imagined.

My heart races as she finishes, coming off the stage with a big grin. "Hon?" She touches my shoulder with her glittery fingers and I startle. She flashes me a sympathetic expression. "You're on. Go knock 'em dead." She practically pushes me out onto the stage.

My body goes into autopilot mode. I feel my lips lift in a smile as I scan the catwalk. It's a good thing my body decides that it still knows how to walk, because I am paralyzed inside.

I walk to the end of the catwalk as women in dresses and men in daytime suits look up at me from their seats. I pass my mother. She taps her shoulder, drawing it back, reminding me to have good posture.

Yeah, I got it, Mom.

I manage to make it to the end of the catwalk. I hear my name being said over the PA system. "Stop right there, if you don't mind, Miss Gellar."

I look around the room full of my peers, trying to locate the voice. A man waves to me and I focus my attention on him. "There you go. Miss Gellar is an exceptionally bright young woman who graduated from Yale two years ago. She loves fashion, watercolors, horseback riding, and traveling first class. She's fluent in French—"

None of the attributes that the emcee has ascribed to me are true. Did my mom make them up? Seems like a Monique Gellar move to me.

A man in a dark suit puts a paddle up. "Ten thousand." With the bright stage lights, it's hard to see his face. But I know his voice. I would recognize it anywhere.

It's Nate Fordham. Oh my god. Half of me is deeply embarrassed that he's here to witness my humiliation. And half of me is thrilled that he's here.

God, what the hell is wrong with me? My face flushes more and I press my lips into a thin line.

"Okay. I have more on the card—" the emcee says.

A middle-aged man cuts him off by raising his paddle. "Eleven thousand."

I squint to find that this man is Don Young, our company's VP. With his thinning, dishwater blond hair and his tall, stooped frame, he resembles a scarecrow. Don has never shown an interest in me before outside of talking enthusiastically about his oceanic exploration trips once. I feel in my heart that my mother has to be putting him up to this."

I clear my throat, feeling like a complete fool.

"I have eleven," says the emcee.

"Twenty," Nate says. "It's for a good cause."

A woman timidly raises her paddle. "Twenty-one."

"Twenty-two," Don volleys back.

I squint at Nate Fordham, expecting him to offer more. He locks eyes with me, smirking.

"Twenty-three," the woman says. "I'm bidding to win the weekend for my daughter, who is in high school. She could use a good SAT tutor."

Don stands up. "Twenty-five."

The woman also stands up, her jaw squaring. "Thirty."

They go back and forth for a minute. Thirty-five. Forty. Forty-five.

Nate finally raises his paddle. "Seventy-five thousand."

My jaw drops. Seventy-five thousand dollars just for a date? He must be joking.

"Wow! That is the most money ever bid here at the thirteenth annual New York Endowment for Movement Arts Bachelorette Auction!" the emcee gasps. "Do we have any challengers?"

Don glares at Nate. The woman sits down, a sour expression on her face. The emcee says, "Going once? Going twice?"

Don sits down and the emcee shouts, "Sold!"

The audience breaks into applause, but I barely hear it. I just stand there, looking directly at Nate. He looks pretty smug right now, even more so as the emcee shoos me off stage.

How could Nate Fordham think this is even a remotely good idea?

As I clomp offstage and straight to the wardrobe department to replace these painful high heels, all I can feel is dread.

When I step out of the changing area, Nate is waiting for me backstage. He's abandoned his suit jacket and rolled up the sleeves of his white work shirt. He straightens his dark tie as he looks me up and down.

"That was quick. You already changed out of that sexy outfit?"

I feel my cheeks glowing like two fire-red coals. He thinks I'm sexy?

"That was borrowed from wardrobe," I stammer. "It's not mine, obviously."

"No? That's too bad. I like you wearing gold. I think that's your color, Kitten."

I bristle. "Don't call me pet names, Mr. Fordham. I can't believe you spent seventy-five thousand dollars just to have lunch with me."

He raises a brow. "Is that what you think I paid for? Because I think I have my jet and my yacht all gassed up and ready to go. I think, for what I paid, I get to take you anywhere I want. For however long I want."

My jaw drops. "Are you serious? I'm supposed to be running Gellar Industries, not sunning myself on the deck of your boat while you ogle me."

Nate grins. "I think the lady doth protest too much. You like me more than you let on."

"No, I don't." My face flames again. "In fact, I'm very

close to hating you. I can't figure out why you are pursuing me so doggedly."

"Is it not obvious?" He spreads his hands wide. "I want you, Annalise. And I don't mean I just want your company. I want you in my bed, too. And I'm determined to have them both."

I shake my head in disbelief. "It will never happen, Nate. Never."

"So, I'm Nate now instead of Mr. Fordham? See? My charms are working on you."

"If by that you mean I can barely stand you, then sure. They're definitely working."

He reaches out, snags my waist, and hauls me against him. "A little fight in your blood, huh? That only makes me want to play with you more, Kitten."

His silver eyes are hard on my face. I tilt my head up, wetting my lips. My heart pounds.

"I will never want you, Mr. Fordham," I manage. Even to my ears it doesn't sound very convincing.

"Because you said that, I'm going to make you beg for me to make you cum the first time I fuck you." He says it so nonchalantly, as if I were throwing myself at him already. "When I slide my cock into that tight little pussy, you're going to scream my name and leave scratches on my back, Annalise."

As much as I hate what he's saying to me, my body responds to being pressed up against him. My breasts tighten and nipples pebble. I can feel dampness blossom between my thighs at the brush of his hips against mine.

My body is betraying me and I'm helpless to resist. All I can do is shake my head because even my words have left me high and dry.

Nate grips my hand, steps away from me, and starts

leading me out of the backstage area. And god help me, a small, secret part of me really wants to go.

But who will run Gellar Industries while I'm gone?

"Wait!" I protest. "We can't just leave. Some of my employees are at my office, waiting for me as we speak."

Nate gives me a moue. "Don't worry about that. Your Mom came up to me before the auction and offered to make excuses for you at the office."

"And you just went along with that?" I screw up my face. "God, you really don't know me at all."

"That's why we're going away for the weekend."

I arch a brow. "Oh, I thought it was because you wanted to fuck me."

Grabbing me by the waist, Nate starts pulling me inexorably toward the exit. "There'll be plenty of time for that, Annalise. Now come on."

That's exactly what I'm afraid of. I shiver, unable to resist any longer.

EIGHT
NATE

"Welcome aboard my yacht, Annalise." I sweep my hand behind her back, urging her forward as we step onto the boat. She cranes her neck upward, looking at the five stories that the yacht has to offer.

"It's bigger than I thought," Annalise murmurs. "Much larger than my father's yacht, that's for sure. Not that I'm impressed. I couldn't care less."

"Wait till you see the bedroom," I purr. She glares at me, making me grin.

I walk her into the boat's enticing lower deck. There is a large lounge here that is open to the sun and air because the large panel doors have been pulled wide. A butler waits at a small marble bartending station, a tray of drinks at the ready.

"Mr. Fordham, sir." He fires off a salute. "Welcome back. Your rooms have been readied. We are prepared to sail to Prince Edward Island at once."

"Thank you." I take one of the slender glasses that he offers, finding it to be full of carbonated water, mint, and ice. I offer one to Annalise, who is looking around nervously. "Here. It's just bubbly water."

She accepts it but doesn't sip it as I continue to guide her through the lounge and out onto the main deck. Her heart shaped face and windswept blonde hair make her expression unreadable.

I bring her up to the largest deck. It's dotted with a pool, sun chairs, and umbrellas to fend off the worst of the sun's harsh glare. Annalise surveys the deck with what I think might be an air of boredom.

"This is nice." She puts a hand to her forehead, trying to keep her wildly undulating hair out of her vision. It's obviously very windy out here and will only get more so when we start moving. So I jerk my head toward the elevator in the center of the boat.

"Why don't we head somewhere that's more sheltered?"

She offers me a small smile. "Is it that obvious that I'm miserable out here?"

That makes me chuckle. I wrap an arm around her waist and lead her back toward the elevator. Soon we step out of it onto the third deck. This has a swanky private observation room.

The deck is much smaller than the one we just left, almost cozy in comparison. A big bay window is framed by bookshelves, heavy polished cedar side tables, and several fine leather couches. While the window is bright, everything else in this room is brown, which increases the snug feeling. Annalise seems surprised when we walk in.

"Wow." She walks over to the big bay window as though drawn by a magnet. Outside, I see the Manhattan skyline slowly receding as the ship pulls away from the dock. Annalise sits down on the seat the bay window provides.

"Is that a wow of amazement?" I tease gently. I sit down beside her. Annalise has hiked her boring beige skirt to midthigh without even thinking about it, leaving a tantalizing strip of thigh for me to ogle.

"If you're looking for me to be impressed, you'll have to try harder," Annalise murmurs. Her eyes are still on the skyline. "You're not going to sway me to liking you by taking me on a boat, Mr. Fordham. I'm a little insulted that you should think that I would swoon at this."

The back of my neck heats. To myself, I can admit that I haven't tried to charm any woman of quite her caliber. But it can't be that hard. Can it?

"It's Nate." I grab her chin with gentle fingers and make her look at me. "That's one of the rules this weekend. No more last names, Kitten. It's much too formal for us."

Annalise pulls out of my grasp and puts an inch between us. "Look, Mr.—"

"Nate," I cut in.

She stares at me. "Very well. Nate. You said that you want my company. You also said that you wanted me in your bed. And I'm here to tell you, that isn't going to happen. I agreed to come along because you're so damn stubborn. I knew that if I didn't come, you'd make a scene. But now that we're here, I'm telling you that we can't sleep together."

"And why not?" I grin, smothering a bit of annoyance.

"Because! There are a ton of reasons. You might be handsome—"

"Can I quote you on that?"

She waves her hand away like she's swatting a fly.

"But I'm not interested in either proposal."

"Well, buckle up, buttercup. I won the merger from your dad already. That's basically done. My lawyers are drawing up the necessary paperwork as we speak. And as for having you in my bed..."

I look her up and down, all those curves in a tiny package. I'm going to find her trigger, make her let down her defenses. And I'm going to swarm over her gates until she is riding my dick like she was born to it.

"I get what I want. Always. You won't be any exception. Just watch."

She grits her teeth. "Are you always this pompous and arrogant?"

"Are you always such a whiny little girl?" I fire back, losing my cool. She's wearing me down and I'm fucking exasperated at this point.

She makes a little hmmmph noise and turns her head back to the window. I'm a little surprised by her tenaciousness; most women that I seduce aren't this fucking stubborn.

"We should get ready for dinner," I announce, standing up.

It's impossible to miss the side eye directed my way. "What getting ready do we have to do?" she asks.

"I'm so glad that you asked. First, I had my personal shopper pull a few outfits for you and I brought them here. So you can pick something different to wear, something that suits you more." And second, you could stand to be less cranky. Men don't really like cranky women."

She stands, folding her arms over her chest. "Good thing I'm not trying to attract you, you complete asshole."

I may have crossed a line there. Sensing that I'm not going to say anything that will make it better, I head to the door. "The butler will bring you clothes to change into presently. I'm going to talk to the steward and make sure everything is ready. I'll see you in half an hour in the dining room."

As I'm leaving, Annalise calls over my shoulder. "And where is that?"

"Just ask the butler. He'll take you."

I head to my suite, where I change into a fresh pair of

dark slacks and a white button-up I wear with the top three buttons undone. Then I go talk to the steward, who is frantically trying to oversee all the preparations that I have requested for tonight.

See, tonight is going to be perfect. I'm going to wine and dine Annalise, and really practice my seductive charms. By the end of the night, she will be putty in my hands.

And then I'll get exactly what I want: another notch to carve into my bedpost and eventually, Gellar Industries as a small part of ViaLife.

NINE
NATE

I head up to the dining room when it's time. There are two dining rooms on this boat actually, but this one is smaller and more intimate. The room is draped in dusky velvet, adorned with bright platinum candelabras. There is only enough seating at the big teak table for six. A few feet away from the table are double glass sliding doors. They've been thrown wide to let in the warm, salty sea air as the sun sets.

I step outside and look down onto the bottom deck. The pool glints where the sun catches it. Just beyond that, there is nothing but endless wild waves of the dark ocean waters.

"Nate?"

Annalise's voice is soft when she calls to me. I turn and find her standing just inside the doors, much closer than I thought. She tugs at the hem of her short white dress. The dress shows off quite a bit of leg and the neckline is low cut. My eyebrows rise and for a second, I'm speechless.

Annalise Gellar is gorgeous. The gentle swell of her tits. The sweetheart shape of her face. Those huge bright green eyes. The powerhouse of those long legs of hers in strappy sandals.

"You look incredible," I finally say.

Annalise blushes and brushes her hair behind her ear. "Thanks. I have to ask... how did you know my size? I'm a petite girl. No one ever gets my size right."

I shrug a shoulder, sauntering over to her. "Part of my charm."

She rolls her eyes, but I'm sure that I see a dimple flash in her cheek. I take her by the hand and lead her to the table, which is full set for two people. I pull out her chair. She eyes me as she sits down.

Is that distrust I see? Or curiosity?

I sit down and my butler pops his head in. Seeing that we are ready, he starts bringing in the first dish, caviar on a tiny portion of truffle custard. The steward fills our wine glasses with a fruity red. She purses her lips the whole time she's being served, seeming not to relax until we are alone again.

I raise my wine glass, offering her a toast. "Cheers to our embarkment."

She frowns but clinks her glass against mine and then takes the tiniest sip of the red wine. Her eyebrows knit and she looks at the glass as though it's surprised her. "This wine isn't horrible."

"I should hope not. It's eight thousand dollars per bottle."

She sighs and rolls her eyes for a second. "Got it."

I cock my head and take a sip of the wine. "Got what?"

"You're spending lots of money on me. You're making special note of how much things cost. I'll tell you now, you can't buy your way into bed with me."

I narrow my eyes at her. "Noted. I would've decanted this bottle tonight, whether you were here or not, though."

She pins me with an unamused look and then takes another sip of the wine.

For the next two courses, the conversation limps along. I ask about how her father is doing and receive a snippy, "he's fine". A follow-up question about the health of Gellar Industries stock merits a look of sheer distrust.

"Why do you ask?" she says, rather pointedly. "All these questions about my father. Are you missing him already?"

She earns a chuckle from me for that one. "Definitely not. If you don't mind me saying, your father is an absolute bastard."

She swirls her wine. "On that, we can agree."

"I bet there are more things that we both believe to be true. I think you'd be surprised just what we have in common."

"Us?" Annalise blinks. "We're fifteen years apart in age. What could we have in common?"

I wave my hand. "Support for the ballet, for one thing."

She cocks her head to the side and sticks out her lower lip as she considers my words. "That's true," she allows.

"And we're also interested in seeing Gellar Industries succeed." I list off. "I'm sure there are other things." Dabbing my lips with my napkin, I push out my chair and offer her my hand. Annalise looks at me for a long moment before hesitantly taking my hand. I lead her out onto the verandah.

This is the magic moment, I pep myself up. Now you turn on the charm and the dazzling smile and that's how you get her in bed. It's showtime.

The butler peeks in the room and I nod to him. Soft jazz starts playing through the cleverly hidden speakers.

Taking her by the hand, I whirl so that she is pressed against me, looking up at me with shocked eyes. I smirk and start to move in a slow waltz.

Annalise has no doubt been forced to learn to dance.

She follows the waltz without speaking, gazing up at me while she wordlessly follows my lead. Flattening my palm against her lower back, I press her close to me. She gives me a confused look.

But when my hand slides down to her ass and I press her body close to my hips and my semi-hard cock, her mouth falls open. "Nate!" she says, scandalized.

I notice that her breathing picks up and her breasts seem close to popping free of her low neckline.

"There's no one around to watch," I murmur in her ear. "No one will ever know what we do right now."

She wrinkles her nose. "Yes, but..."

She trails off. I dig my fingers into her ass again, flexing my hips against her.

"But what?"

Annalise's face turns red. "We can't take this too far. It's... it's unladylike."

"Fuck that." I laugh low in my chest. "I don't believe in that bullshit. It's not the 1940s anymore, Kitten. You want to be a real CEO? You've got to learn to take what you want, when you want it."

I kiss her then, because I don't want to hear what kind of nonsense she's about to spew next. She hesitates for the barest moment, then kisses me back. The kiss is a little clumsy at first. But I deepen the kiss, coaxing her tongue with mine, and soon her shyness has vanished. Any awkwardness is gone with it.

I pick her up, enjoying her tiny squeal of surprise. Then I walk back to the glass wall, pinning her against it while I kiss her neck and the tops of her tits. She goes crazy, provoked by my touch. She rocks her hips, moves her fingers through my hair, running her nails against my shirt.

Yes. This? This right here, Annalise going insane? It's what I have been building up to. The thought of her screaming my name while I bury my cock in her velvet pussy has me eager for more.

I'm a hungry man and she's a cupcake, ready to be devoured, bit by bit.

I run a hand down her stomach and between her thighs. The barest brush of my fingers against her sweet pussy leaves my touch damp.

"Your body is getting ready for me, Kitten," I husk out. She gasps and bites her lower lip. I slip my fingertips beneath the tiny scrap of material that stands in my way, seeking the source of her moisture. I brush her clit with my thumb by accident. Her reaction is the most satisfying moan I think I've ever heard from a woman. Instead of getting my fingers deep inside her pussy, I start to rub her clit.

Annalise braces herself against the glass wall and moans again, her head whipping back and forth. Like she's fighting it, for some reason.

After all the teasing between us, it's not really a surprise to me. She needs to be fucked. You can tell by how she walks, how she holds herself. So buttoned up and strait-laced. It pleases me to watch her defenses crumble.

I circle her clit in slow orbits, loving the earthy, slightly acidic smell of her pussy as it fills the air. I pause and then slip my index finger inside her pussy.

Anna's half-lidded eyes snap open wide. She stops moving and pushes against me, her eyes wide like I've just dumped a bucket of ice water on her head.

"Get off!" she howls.

I immediately withdraw, letting her body slide down the wall until she is caught by trembling legs.

"What?" I demand to know. I search her face, which is turning red as a beet. "Annalise, tell me what's wrong."

Her fists ball up. She looks like she might burst into tears. "I'm a virgin! At least, I was..."

"...what?!"

But Annalise is pushing past me, fighting back tears, hurrying out of the room. I had no idea that she hadn't had sex... though honestly, if I did, I don't know that I would've done anything differently. Maybe I would wait until we were in bed...

Annalise vanishes out the door, fleeing toward the elevator. I stick my head out the door as she goes, a little aghast.

Annalise Gellar is a virgin?

Suddenly, her reactions to my come-ons make more sense... but how do I come back from this?

TEN

ANNALISE

The next morning, I'm leaning on the balcony of the boat, lost in thought. We're no longer just in the middle of the ocean. I see the dark outline of land ahead of us. But my thoughts are anywhere but here.

Shame fills me, coursing through my body. I hear my mother's voice so clearly.

You let a man put his fingers inside you? Only sluts do that.

I don't have to actually talk to my mom to know exactly what she would say. But is what she'd say correct? Did Nate do something naughty and forbidden?

It felt good. When he was touching me, it felt like I was on fire, being eaten alive by flames. And yet I wanted more.

But is that feeling... wrong?

My mom would definitely say yes. But my heart wants to feel that taboo heat again.

Okay, maybe that is coming from somewhere lower in my body, not my heart.

"We're going to dock in twenty minutes."

My whole body tenses. I turn around and there Nate is,

looking tempting in his khakis and white button up. His dark hair is unstyled and shoved back. A golden vee of skin and dusky chest hair peek at me from where his shirt is unbuttoned. He's casual here. But not exactly relaxed.

He has that same hungry look in his eyes that he had last night before he... touched me. I gulp.

Is it bad that I'm turned on just by the desire burning in his eyes?

"I wasn't informed of any stops," I say, just to have something to say to him. The words sound foolish.

His eyebrows rise. "This is me, informing you."

"Oh." I can feel blood rushing to my cheeks. The damn things always give any kind of embarrassment away.

Nate walks to the balcony, looking out. "About last night—"

Oh my god. Of course he would bring up how I ran out of the room. He's so irritating that I can't even let him finish.

"Can we not talk about that?" I grit out.

He hesitates, then shakes his head. "I think we'd better clear the air, Annalise. First off, I didn't know you are a virgin."

I sniff, unable to even look at him. "Was. I was a virgin."

Nate does a double take. Then he reaches out to me, turning my body so I have to face him.

"You're still a virgin," he says, searching my face. "Anybody that tells you otherwise is crazy. Also, in case you haven't heard, virginity is a really outmoded concept. If it's really important to you, fine. But your value doesn't increase or decrease just because you've had sex."

I drop my gaze. My entire body burns with shame. How can he be so casual about sex?

Before I can even think it over, the words are already coming out of my mouth. "If that's how much you care about sex, I'm glad that I haven't fallen under your spell. I only want to share a bed with someone that thinks sex is a big deal."

Nate grips my upper arms and looks at me intently. "Some sex is a big deal. Some sex is casual. I think you will come to see that when you're more—" He pauses, searching for the right words.

"Old and wise, like you?" I spit out.

He looks amused. "Emotionally mature. Listen to me, Annalise. I don't want to fight about this. I don't want you to run away from me. Can you just take me at my word?"

His face holds no hint of deception. If I had to pin his plea down, I would call it earnest. My defenses don't know how to handle that approach. No sarcasm, no hint of dark humor?

Gulp.

I slowly nod and Nate eases his grip on my arms. "Good. Come downstairs. Let's get ready to disembark."

Half an hour later, I am walking on to the sandy beach of an immense coastal estate. His mansion has a weathered Cape Cod cottage quality to it, but it is immense. Only a short walk up the decidedly private beach and we're at the front door. I turn and cast my gaze back to the rolling sea, the miles of sandy beach, and the untouched greenery. This? This is actually the first display of wealth that Nate has shown me that is somewhat impressive.

Okay, *very* impressive.

We are greeted at the doorway by the starched and polished staff. As we head inside the beachside mansion, several younger staff members hurry outside. Going to the yacht, if I had to guess.

I'm taken off to my room by a maid, who tells me that my clothing will be transferred here shortly. In the meantime, I might avail myself of a swimsuit and a cover up. In the large walk-in closet are racks upon racks of swimsuits and a ton of white coverups. The maid says that Nate usually likes to go to the beach right away, so I should get ready.

After sifting through the bathing suits, I find one that suits me. It's a shiny gold one-piece, low cut and nearly backless. I grab a long, loose tunic and a pair of gold sandals. Everything is my size, which is amazing. With my very short torso and extremely petite waist, I am hard pressed to find bathing suits that fit me properly.

By the time I'm changed and head downstairs, I am told that I can find Nate on the beach. So I head out, appreciating the sunny weather. It's the height of summer right now, so it's almost ninety degrees. I'll soon need sunscreen, I remind myself.

Nate stands by two surfboards, stripped bare to his waist. His ass and legs are perfectly defined in a tight Lycra wetsuit. He picks up a paddle as he glances back, catching sight of me.

He grins, although I can't see what's in his eyes because he wears sunglasses. "Finally," he says. "I thought I was going to grow roots waiting for you."

I sidle up beside him, surveying the surf boards. "No one told me to hurry. What are these?"

Nate's grin widens. "Paddle boards."

I scrunch my face up. "I hope they're not for us. Because I don't know how to do that."

"Relax. This first time, we'll just paddle out and sit on the boards. You're a paddle board virgin, so I'll take things slow. A little further each time you ride."

I can't help but feel that he's talking about more than the paddle boards. But he hands me a wetsuit, quickly moving on.

"Come on," he urges me. "I'll carry your board to the

water for you. Then you can hold onto the board for balance."

Nate heads to the water, leaving me to follow behind. I feel ridiculous, like a fish that has ended up on dry land, gasping for air and quickly dying. But I don't want Nate to see my insecurity, so I hustle after him.

Even in my wetsuit, the water is cold when I wade in. I stop just a few steps in, waiting for my body to acclimate. Nate doesn't stop, yelling over his shoulder. "Come on! Get your whole body wet at once."

He sets my board down, letting it drift with the waves. While I hurry deeper, trying to catch it, Nate puts his arms in his wetsuit and zips it up.

"This water is freezing!" I complain.

"Let's go a few feet further and then we can sit on our boards."

He strides out, assuming I will follow. I take a deep breath and steel myself. Then I plunge forward, heading into waist-deep water. Nate turns around and grabs the nose of my board.

"Go ahead and climb on. I'll hold it." He smirks. "I am a gentleman, after all."

Rolling my eyes, I scramble onto the board. Nate hands me a paddle he unstraps from his board, then lets me go. To my surprise, I am not immediately swept out to sea. Instead, I float next to him as he masterfully climbs on his board, producing his paddle with a flourish.

"See? That was painless."

"It would have been harder if you hadn't held the board for me," I admit.

He dips his paddle in the water. "Let's paddle a bit. I don't want you to freeze to death."

I dip my paddle in the water, testing it out. "My mother

would absolutely have a stroke if she found out that I was here right now."

Nate looks back at me. "Your mother knows where you are. Who do you think tipped me off to your presence at the bachelorette auction?"

"Wait, she called you and told you? You probably only had about twenty minutes to rush right over. That sounds pretty desperate on your part."

I should feel a sense of betrayal over my mom's actions. But I'm too flattered by Nate's interest to feel my mom's claws. I have no idea why Nate is so interested in me. I haven't done anything important or interesting in my life. Yet Nate seems to find bickering with me *fascinating*.

He pauses, then raises his sunglasses a few inches. "Your mom is next-level crazy. I can tell why you are the way you are, coming from a house where she was in charge. She invited me to the auction days ago, all sweet talk to butter me up."

I gape at him. "Wait... you knew that far in advance? Mom told me that a girl dropped out at the last minute!"

"Your name was in the pamphlet that the auctioneers handed out. Seems like your mom planned for you to be there as a bachelorette."

"That... absolute... cow!" My jaw hardens. I paddle the board furiously for a few minutes, steaming about my mom's deception.

All this time I thought I was defying my mother and sneaking around with Nate Fordham. But it turns out that my mother knows everything. She orchestrated it! The fact fills me with a blinding fury.

"Anna! Slow down!" Nate calls.

I stop paddling and look back. I blink a couple of times, searching the shore for the house. In just a few minutes, I have paddled far enough that the mansion is a tiny gray dot at the edge of my vision.

My chest is also heaving from the exertion. Whoops.

I paddle back to Nate more calmly.

"Sorry. I just... I didn't know that my mom set me up. She knows I don't like crowds or being on stage in front of people."

" I would have told you sooner, but I didn't know you were going to be ambushed. I thought you were a willing participant."

I shake my head. " There's nothing that you could have done. It's a totally Monique Gellar thing to do to trick me to go on a date with someone she considers an appropriate match." The last two words drip with sarcasm. "My mom is obsessed with me marrying someone from old money and giving up the CEO position to be a happy little wifey. It's gross."

Nate is quiet for a long second. Tension blooms in the space between us, nearly palpable.

"I'm not interested in a wife, Annalise. I'm not even looking for love. In fact, I would say I'm pretty anti-love."

I hope Nate can't see my face turning red. "I don't expect anything like that from you. Just so we're clear, I'm not interested in love, marriage, or even dating. I have enough to worry about with Gellar Industries right now. My company is the only relationship I'm interested in right now."

He sits there, his expression impassive. "So we are on the same page."

"About dating? Yes. About everything else..."

"Annalise." His voice sounds tight. "I keep telling you. I already won the merger. This little weekend getaway is just supposed to help you open up to me. Things are going to change for your company as soon as we touch down in New

York City. I'm—" He sucks a breath in. "When it comes to running a company, I'm a fucking genius. If you only agree to let me help you, tutor you, you could learn the basics of being a CEO from me."

His words are only a little surprising. I had been expecting him to make a gambit to seal the deal between our companies.

But the tutoring stuff... I didn't see that coming. Is it terrible that I desperately want someone to tell me how to play the CEO game? Maybe...

I tilt my head. "What if I say no?"

"Then I'll spend the next month leveraging the board to fire you and elect me as CEO. I'm not interested in the role, but I'll take it if I'm forced to. The question is, will you make me?"

I swipe my lips, tasting salt water. This is not a position I want to be in. But when Nate puts the question to me like that... I'm going to lean toward having him as a tutor.

Setting my paddle down, I cross my arms and pin him with a look.

"One month. You tutor me. I make the merger easier for you."

And I can stick it to my mom in the process.

"Oh, this is a negotiation?" He barks a laugh. "Six months. You make the merger easy. You warm my bed. And we move the company to my office. Yours are... not nearly as nice as ours."

"Six months! No way. And we definitely don't move. One month, final offer."

He gives me a tiny smile. "Two months of tutoring, in the office and in bed. Someone needs to teach you the ropes. And moving is a deal breaker."

Show me the ropes? What could that mean?

"Nate—"

"Kitten." He takes off his sunglasses. "Don't deny your-self. You want what I have to offer. So just say yes."

My heart is trying to beat its way out of my chest. He's right. I do want his tutoring... both kinds. What's holding me back?

When I speak, my voice sounds faint. "*Yes.*"

I don't know if I'll regret this, but there is only one way to find out.

ELEVEN
NATE

The whirring beat of the helicopter blades unsettles me, puts me on edge. Or maybe that is the presence of the sassy little blonde sitting next to me.

Usually, I ride in the co-pilot's seat any time I take the helicopter. The only way I can relax is to have a bird's eye view of the sky. It's the same with chauffeured SUVs and my private jet. For some reason, I don't feel that way on my yacht. Which is probably part of the reason that I brought her to the boat in the first place.

But I don't want Annalise to see how badly I need to control my surroundings. I'm not interested in her knowing that much about me.

"Is this line private? Like... can the pilot hear me?" Annalise asks. She points at the oversized pair of headphones that she wears. I have a matching set, but mine aren't cartoonishly large.

I glance over at her and nod. "Just the two of us."

She twists her mouth to the side. "Can I ask you a question?"

I tilt my head. "You mean another question? Be my guest."

She looks down at her hands, which are clasped and twisted in her lap. "Right. Um. Why didn't we... do... other things? You've been on me to agree to let you tutor me or to agree to the merger, at least. All in the name of getting to sleep with me. So... why didn't you... try to fuck me? You had all weekend."

"What, having a private chef cook haute cuisine for you wasn't enough? A private sommelier to pick out your wine wasn't impressive? Sleeping in a huge bed with thousand-count sheets didn't feel special?"

She furrows her brow. "To be honest, not really."

I chuckle. " I only do hostile takeovers in the board-room; I don't need them in the bedroom. I told you that I would have you begging me, and I'm going to wait until you do."

Her eyebrows fly up in surprise.

"You don't want to have sex until the paperwork is complete?" She laughs. "Wow. Of all the things I thought you would say, that is not one of them."

I give her a frank look and a slight shrug of my shoulders.

"I'm worth billions, sweetheart. It's lesson one from me on being a CEO. Document everything. Look at every document. Read it, understand it before you sign it. If you don't understand it, pay somebody impartial to translate it for you." I pause, thinking of a way to sum up the point. "Basically, you have the golden signature. Be sure to use it wisely and often."

Annalise frowns. "I don't think I've signed a single paper since becoming CEO. I guess other people do it for me."

"Not anymore. As part of the merger, I'm going to let

most of your non-essential staff go. The rest will get with the program, I guarantee it."

She blinks, looking as though I have struck her in the face. "You're going to fire people?"

Just then, the chopper touches down on the top floor of the ViaLife building in downtown Manhattan. I give her knee a reassuring pat. "We'll talk about it later."

I climb out of the helicopter, helping Annalise out behind me, and hopefully I leave the dull conversation about firing behind. We rush downstairs, past the corporate offices of nosy C-level staff. There is no point in hiding Annalise anymore. Word is bound to get out about the merger and spread across the offices of Manhattan like wildfire.

I try not to grin as I escort her into my office. I'm about to get just what I want. A company that makes a unique service that is useful to my empire. And soon, the sweet Annalise in my bed.

I'll have the last say over my rival Archer Gellar. And teach sweet Annalise all the dirty things I can think of in the bargain. What could be better?

Ushering her into my corner office, I try to keep my delight hidden. "Would you like something to drink?"

I wander over to my desk, ready to call my personal secretary in. But Annalise tugs at the neckline of her frothy white button up shirt, which is tucked into a form-fitting bronze pencil skirt. Paired with simple black stilettos, she looks like a billion bucks. But the neckline is lower than she wanted; I know because she has already complained about it.

"No thank you," she sighs, looking around my office. "I will say that you have an excellent view out your office window, though."

I grin. "There is a reason they call me the Fifth Avenue Devil."

"They call you a lot more colorful things when you're not around. I'm just guessing." Her quip is off the cuff and not really meant to wound. But it's sharp as a honed blade.

I'm impressed with how intelligent and quick-witted Annalise is proving herself to be. "If this is you when you're back in the office, I like it."

Her cheeks color but she turns to the window, saying nothing. She's got some serious walls up. And that's more than okay in this setting.

But I'm going to break down every barrier she puts between us on a personal level. Raze her and rebuild her, model her after a woman I've only imagined.

Searching my desk for the legal papers I had my team draft for the purpose, I call her over.

"It's time to use your golden signature. Here are the merger documents. And you'll find a non-disclosure agreement, and a consent to rough sex as well."

She whips her head around. "A what now?"

I spread my hands, trying not to grin. "Just a precaution. We don't have to get into it now."

She marches over and picks up the papers, then turns and walks back to the window, studying them intently. I check my email and answer a few requests. My VP of finance has sent me a pretty intriguing email.

N, I have an idea about the merger that I think could make us a lot of money. Come talk to me when you get a chance. —D

Hmm. I wonder what that could be about. Drew is generally a genius when it comes to making money in inventive ways, so I have no doubt that it will make for an interesting conversation at the very least.

Annalise walks back to my desk, laying the contracts

down. I sit down in my desk chair, leaning back. She leans on the desk as she reads, her silky hair slipping into her face. She brushes it away, biting her lip.

"I consent to spanking, slapping, binding, gagging, bodily fluids, amaurophilia—" She glances up at me nervously. "What the hell is that?"

"Being blindfolded."

"O...kay. Role play, voyeurism, public sex, anal sex..." Annalise swallows, the fine muscles of her throat working. "God, do I even want to have sex with you? It sounds terrifying."

I tilt my head. "I only fuck women that are begging for my touch."

"*Oh.*" She licks her lips and shivers, admitting, "You're extremely handsome. I'm sure you have women lining up around the block just for a chance to hop in your bed. Why do you want *me?*"

"Because of your last name, primarily. I want to fuck Archer Gellar's little girl."

Annalise opens her mouth, her brows knitting. But I hold up a hand to stop her protests.

"I also think you're fucking sexy, Annalise."

Her cheeks turn a vivid pink. "You do?"

"I'd be crazy not to. Plus, I think our chemistry will prove combustible."

She looks down at the contract for several seconds, pushing her cheek out with the tip of her tongue.

"You would take care of the company. Right? This contract says that everyone that works for me is going to get a little bonus when the merger is complete."

I school my expression. "Everyone that I don't fire. It would be better to build your sales team from scratch under your management only. That way there aren't any resentments among the staff for you doing things differently than Archer."

She narrows her eyes. "Can we wait and see if that's actually a problem first?"

I purse my lips, studying her face. "All right. I'll give you a few extra weeks to sort through the staff. We'll keep everyone at the current offices until then. But I'm going to be standing over your shoulder, helping you make the tough decisions. I think this will be a good learning experience for you."

Her jaw tightens and I see stubbornness in her expression. But in the next second, she manages to tame it, forcing it down. "Fine," she agrees, her tone clipped. "It's a deal. You have a pen?"

I open the desk drawer and pull out a gold pen. Her lips twitch with humor when she takes it. "You weren't kidding around when you said that your signatures are golden."

"I rarely joke about business."

She leans down, giving me an ample shot of her cleavage as she signs the contract. She was right; the neckline of her top is cut too low for the workplace. If I saw anyone else baring that much skin, I would almost certainly fire them.

But I look at the soft swell of her breasts and my cock stirs. Annalise isn't just signing the merger contract.

She's also agreeing to have sex with me. And I can't wait to take advantage of that.

As she initials each page, I press a discreet button under my desk to make the glass walls facing the inside of the office fill with a gray, smoke-like substance. The effect is cloudy and nearly opaque without being too indiscreet to the C-level offices around me. The walls aren't soundproof here, but I can make sure Annalise is quiet when I touch her.

She finishes with a flourish, pushing the thick stack of

papers across the desk at me. She tosses the pen on top and then cocks her eyebrow at me. "Is that it?"

"Not a chance," I say. I crook a finger at her. "Come here, Kitten."

She looks surprised. "Here? In your office? You've got to be kidding me."

I rock back in my chair. "I'm not, though. Do what I say."

Analise's eyes widen but she comes around the desk. She's as skittish as a colt right now. I take her hand, bring her closer and part my thighs to make space for her. As soon as she is close enough for me to slip my hands around her petite waist, I drag her against my body. My cock stirs as I look at her perfect hourglass figure framed well by the pencil skirt. My hands are at her waist, skimming down the flare of her hips and then wandering to her ass. When I knead her ass, I hear her sharp intake of breath.

I won't take her virginity here in the office. But I'm desperate to touch, taste, and see more of her bare skin.

Pushing her against my desk, I reach behind her body for the zipper attached to her skirt. She sucks in a breath.

"Nate!" she protests. "Control yourself. We're in your office, for god's sake."

I pin her in place with my eyes. "Not a fucking chance, Kitten. I've held back too many times now. I have to see your pussy splayed out over this desk. I don't want it. I need it."

Her cheeks flush and she opens her mouth but can't come up with the words to deny me. I slowly unzip her skirt and then push it down. It falls to the floor, unnoticed.

I stare at her pale legs, her naturally small waist, and the tiny pair of panties that hug her hips. The panties are absurd, light pink with dark pink hearts. They're almost see-through. I touch the spot where they dent her hip, trying to get my urges under control.

I want to fuck her until she begs me to stop. I want to bury my face in her pussy and eat it until I die from starvation. I want to turn her over this desk, spread her thighs, and fuck her ass like there is no fucking tomorrow.

But I won't do any of that. Annalise has asked me to tutor her. I'm going to do it right if my life depends on it.

I look at her as I drag her panties down her legs. The fabric sticks and stretches where her thighs touch.

"Spread your knees, Kitten." I bite my lip and look her in the eye. My cock is throbbing, the tip leaking in my pants. But I ignore my need for the moment.

She swallows and moves her thighs. The panties fall down her legs as I push her ass back against the desk again. Her button-up covers her pussy for a moment. I make quick work of the buttons, laying it open. She moves to cover her breasts, hidden in a light pink lace bra. But I grab her hands.

"Don't you dare hide anything from me," I husk out. "I want you to show me how you touch yourself when you're in bed all by yourself."

Annalise tosses her blonde hair, her face flame-red. "Nate, that's... private."

"Show me," I command. "I want to see it, baby. I'm dying for you."

She blinks. "For me?"

Her question makes my chest tighten. I need to brush past it before I start thinking about it too much. So I push her back onto the desk, gently nudging her knees wider. "You wanted me to show you the ropes. Now do as I say."

She gulps and runs her hands over her tits. Then she touches her knees, raking her fingers inward.

. . .

I kneel in front of Annalise. Her blonde curls fall down her back as she leans back slightly on my desk. Her panties lay forgotten on the floor. My cock strains against my pants, desperate to lay claim her.

But I want to take my time with her. Now isn't the time or place to take her virginity. At this moment, the most I can do is tease her and make her come.

"Touch yourself for me, Kitten," I rasp. My voice is thick with desire. "Rub your pretty pussy. Show me how you like it."

Annalise, the embodiment of the good girl, shyly complies. Her fingers slowly tease her wet folds. My cock twitches in anticipation. "That's it, Kitten. Close your eyes. Lean your head back. Rub your clit and think of whatever turns you on the most."

I trail my tongue up her exposed belly, tasting her delicate scent of wildflowers and arousal.

"Oh, Nate," she moans. Her eyes sink closed and she throws her head back, making her breasts jut out.

I need more of her. With a growl, I start unbuttoning her blouse. Her tiny, perfect tits are showcased in her see-through lacy bra. My mouth finds her hardened nipples, sucking and biting them through the fabric.

"Oh, God, Nate, I'm going to—"

I slide a hand between her legs, feeling her hot wetness against my palm. "That's it, Kitten , I want to hear it all," I growl. I slip two fingers inside her tight channel, flexing them. "You're so wet, Annalise. Is this all for me?"

She bites her lip and nods, her eyes still shut tightly. I thrust my fingers in and out of her hot pussy a few times, moaning quietly. She's so fucking hot. I can hardly keep myself in check.

Annalise cries out as her hips buck against my hand. I pull her hand away from her clit and bring it to my mouth, savoring the taste of her arousal on my tongue. She tastes so decadent.

"You taste like sin, Kitten. I'm about to show you just how much of a sinner you can be."

With one swift motion, I push her back onto the desk, spreading her legs wide. Kneeling between her thighs, I bury my face in her heat, inhaling her intoxicating scent.

"Oh, fuck," she groans. My tongue explores every inch of her swollen clit, swirling around it. Her fingers tangle in my hair, her nails scraping against my scalp, but I don't mind. I love it.

I love seeing Annalise let go and surrender to me. She's taking the pleasure that only I can give her. I slip my fingers back inside her tight pussy and feel her walls clench around my fingers. I add another one, curling them in a way that drives her wild.

She whips her head back and forth, fighting the oncoming sensation. "Nate! Nate, I'm so close..."

I intensify my movements, sucking her clit between my lips and flicking my tongue over her most sensitive spot. Her moans grow louder and more urgent. Her inner muscles spasm around my fingers. She reaches her climax, shattering with a wordless shout. I feel her juices cover my fingers and drip down onto my hand. I taste every drop of her like she's the most delicious thing in the world.

Slowly and gently, I withdraw my fingers, leaving one last lingering kiss on her folds. I'm as shaken as she is, and I haven't even taken my clothes off. I can already predict the nuclear fission of our first time fucking.

One thing has become clear: I need to hear many more of Annalise Gellar's breathy moans.

TWELVE
ANNALISE

I sit, gazing at a Matisse still life, in the upstairs hallway of my parents' mansion. The painting is mostly dull red and shadowy gray, with the exception of an apple and a bunch of red-purple grapes.

I lean my head to the side as I consider the fruit.

Namely, I wonder if the fruit in the studio was fresh.

Oil paintings take quite some time to paint. So, were there several apples before this one? Or are they rotting and Matisse just left that detail out?

You can never tell how things really are just by glimpsing an image. This is the only 20th century artist in my parents' otherwise stodgy collection of dour portraits. I love the modern, fresh take, the way he forces us to see things as he wants us to see them, not as they might appear to our own eyes. It didn't matter that the fruit might really be rotting.

My phone buzzes in my hand. A text from Nate.

I'll be there in 15.

Of course he picked today to get stuck in traffic. He's only supposed to be meeting my mother after I tell her the news of the merger.

I let out an exaggerated sigh just as the door to my father's bedroom swings open. My mom looks me up and down.

"Annalise Rebecca Gellar, what on earth are you wearing?"

The high-pitched sound of her voice grates on me as I stand up. "Hi, Mother."

She puts her hands on her hips, looking with horror at the gold velveteen dress that hugs my body. "Did you get robbed on the way over here? Or are you making some kind of horrid joke?"

My mouth pinches. "It's a Givenchy dress, Mother. I know it's not what you would pick out for yourself, but it's very much en vogue."

"It looks terrible. And your makeup! God, it's like a clown slapped it on."

The urge to touch my face is strong. But I ball my hands into fists and force a smile on to my face. "You made a huge deal about me flying out all the way out here to Newport this morning. How about we just go in to see Dad?"

Mom sniffs. "I'm glad that your father won't be awake to see you dressed like that."

I throw my hands up. "Maybe I should come back when you're feeling up to hosting people."

My mom shoots me a glare and then starts to walk back into the bedroom. "Come on. Look alive, then."

Rolling my eyes at her retreating figure, I hurry to follow her.

When I enter the room, the drapes are drawn tight. The only light comes from a small lamp on the bedside table. My father lies in the bed, hooked up to several monitors. I approach and see his salt and pepper hair and papery, pasty skin. He appears asleep, his blue-and-white striped pajamas sticking out of a dark blue comforter.

"Hi Dad," I say. I sit down beside him and take his hand. It's clammy to the touch. "It's Annalise. Just coming to check on you. See how you're doing. It seems like your color is a little better than the last time I saw you."

That might be a lie. I can barely make out his features because it's so dark in here.

"Can we open the drapes and let the light in for a little while?" I ask no one in particular. "It's a bit stale-smelling in here."

I smooth the back of my dad's wrinkly hand with my fingers. Someone opens one set of drapes, casting enough light on Dad's face to make him seem alive, at least.

Our relationship was contentious, at best, before he fell into this coma. But he's still my dad. I might want the company, but I don't want him to die.

A man clears his throat, which makes me jump. I turn to find Don Young standing near the opened drapes. He waves a hand at me uncertainly.

"Hi, Annalise."

My mouth thins. "Don. I didn't realize that you were here." I pause, thinking. "What are you doing here, exactly?"

"Just checking on your father," he says. He looks at my mother, who smiles enigmatically.

Something is rotten in the state of Denmark. I can feel it in my bones.

"That's nice of you. Would you give me a minute alone with Dad?" I ask, keeping my tone light.

"Actually, Annalise," my mom cuts in. "I thought that you and I could sit down and talk about Gellar Industries. Your dad will still be here when we're through."

I shrug. "We can talk about it right here."

I stroke Dad's hand, looking between Mom and Don. What are they up to now? Hard to say, but it's not exactly unexpected that my mother might be up to something.

She has a history of betraying me whenever she can.

"Anna, darling," Mom coos. She comes to stand close to me. "Look at you. You're a basketcase. Stressed about Dad. Lonely because you go home to an empty house—"

"I'm not a basket case," I reply, tartly. Looking over at Don, I jerk my head toward my mother. "Have you decided to team up with her?"

Don spreads his hands. "We're just thinking of the company, Annalise."

Mom smiles sweetly in his direction. Which is strange, on its face. My mom doesn't do saccharine. She only does bitter poison.

Are Mom and Don somehow involved?

"I think you need to focus on your marriage prospects, sweetheart." My mom pats my shoulder. "You should sign the CEO position over to Don temporarily. You would still be on the board, of course. But this would—"

"Not interested," I cut her off. "And I think Don should leave now."

My phone chimes with an incoming text notification, ringing in the tense silence. I check it, finding a text from Lori. As I'm reading it, my mom tsks.

"Don't be rude. We are having a conversation," she rebukes me.

"Annalise, I really think you need to listen to your mom," Don says. "She has your future in mind."

I grit my teeth and glare at them both. "What's the game here? Huh? Mom, what do you gain by pushing Don to take the CEO spot from me?"

Mom flushes. "Nothing!"

My gaze slides between them. They're acting awfully shady for two people who haven't agreed to some under-handed deal.

My phone chimes again. I hurriedly silence it as a knock

sounds on the door. Nate's face appears in the doorway. "Ah. There you are."

If my mom were a cat, her ears would flatten. She is instantly on edge.

"Mr. Fordham," she says. "What are you doing in my house?"

"I invited him here," I announce, waving Nate through the door. "I didn't realize that you would try to corner me and make me give up the CEO position to Don. But your intentions are irrelevant, really. Nate is here to discuss the merger."

Don's face gets red. "What?? What merger?"

"I signed the contract yesterday. Dad would have signed the contract himself, but he had a stroke before he could execute anything."

My mom is speechless. "Archer would never agree to a merger with Mr. Fordham."

Nate eases across the bedchamber, looking at my dad as he does. "He lost a poker game. He was running out of funds, so he put the merger on the line. It's as simple as that."

My mom looks at my dad, then begins to usher everyone out of the room. "Let's talk about this somewhere else. Archer needs quiet and rest."

Nate catches my eye as we walk out into the hall. Mom shuts the door firmly behind her and puts her hands on her hips.

She seems like she's about to lay into me, but Don cuts her off before she can get a word out. "I can't believe that you were so foolish to believe anything that this snake in the grass whispered in your ear," Don hisses at me. He stabs his finger in my face. "That was incredibly stupid of you, Annalise. We will be lucky if we're able to take the contract to court and get it invalidated."

Nate smoothly steps between me and Don, his expression hard. "The fuck you will. You're not in charge, Donny boy."

Don's eyes widen. Then he steps forward and pushes his finger into the center of Nate's chest. "Now you listen here—"

Nate catches Don's hand and twists it hard, spinning him around and pinning his hand at a painful angle behind his back. Don yelps, making me wince.

"Don't touch me," Nate says coldly. "And if you ever think about touching Annalise again, I'll fucking end your life." Don makes a grunting sound. Nate grits his teeth. "Do something about it, you bastard. I'd love a reason to break your fucking arm."

"Mr. Fordham, let him go!" my mother cries.

Nate eases his grip and steps back. Don yanks his arm in front of his body and cradles it. "You fucker!"

My mom rushes to Don's side. "Are you all right?"

Don glares balefully at Nate and then at me. "You know," he seethes at me, "I would watch my step if I were you. You're just a little kid playing in a grown man's world. It would be a real shame if you got hurt."

"Don!" my mom says, her voice rising. "Don't threaten my daughter."

"It doesn't matter what this little crybaby says," Nate announces. "His days are numbered at Gellar Industries."

"I'm going to kick your ass!" Don flings back.

I grab Nate's arm to keep him from responding to Don's threat with more violence. "Nate, we need to leave."

"I think that would be best," my mom says sourly. "Don't come back here until you're ready to give up the CEO position. I can't imagine why your father willed it to you, but I'm absolutely certain that you don't deserve it.'

I back away, leveling a glare at my mom while digging

my nails into Nate's forearm. "Thanks for your support as usual, Mom."

Mom flaps her hand at me dismissively. I drag Nate away, quickly walking toward the mansion's front door.

"I think I changed my mind about letting you fire people," I say out of the corner of my mouth. "Don has to go."

Nate seems unruffled, as if he didn't just do some kind of jujitsu move on my VP. He shrugs. "Think of it as streamlining," he jokes. Then he puts his arm around my back as we step out the front door.

THIRTEEN

ANNALISE

When I take three steps into the office, I am immediately ambushed by Lori.

"Where have you been??" she demands. She grabs me by the arm and starts hauling me toward her office. "I texted you five times!"

Knowing that Lori is loyal to my dad, I grimace. "Yeah, about that..."

"Never mind." Lori pushes me past the cubicles and drags me into her private room. She closes the door behind us and whirls to put her back to the door. "We have a huge problem."

Looking at Lori's wild eyes and her unusually messy desk, I surmise that is true. But what kind of problem could have arisen over the long weekend? Will it still be an issue once I explain about the merger to Lori?

"Slow down." I take a seat on her couch and pat the seat next to me. "Tell me what's happened."

Lori perches on the couch next to me. "There are serious accounting irregularities."

I furrow my brow. "That's not what I expected you to say. How did you find out? What's the probable source?"

Lori looks down at her hands. "Lance came to me with his suspicions Friday afternoon. I begged him not to tell anyone while I get to the bottom of things." She takes a deep breath. "The irregularities started six years ago. And they stopped the day your father fell ill."

"Whoa. Slow down." I shake my head slowly, trying to absorb the information. "You think my dad had something to do with the accounting irregularities?"

"Yes." Lori bites her lip, her eyes filling with tears. "I spent the last few days piecing a document trail together. Your father used his office computer to log into the company's accounts and move funds out of the employee pensions and insurance accounts. I added it all up and it is something like twenty-two million dollars that was taken in regular withdrawals."

I put my hand over my heart, feeling its frantic pace. Nothing could have prepared me for this news.

Dad is a lot of things. A prick? Sure. A narcissist who only cares about himself? Definitely.

But a thief? And a poor one at that? After all, Lori was able to find a paper trail in a matter of days.

"Annalise?"

"Sorry." I shake my head, at a complete loss. "I'm just trying to wrap my head around it. Twenty-two million dollars?"

"It's shocking, I agree," Lori shoves her hand through her hair. "But I have multiple records of logins from your father's password-protected account, so..."

"I can't believe it. I mean, I know Dad likes to gamble. But taking money from the company's coffers?"

As soon as I say it, I realize that it isn't much different

from my dad wagering the merger on a fucking poker game. I don't know why I'm so damned surprised.

My dad has a real problem.

"What do we do?" I look to Lori for help. "Can we just return the money?"

Lori purses her lips. "I don't know. Do you have a spare twenty-two million lying around?"

I scrunch up my face. "No."

"Me neither. We can cover with the company profits, but that's only a few hundred thousand." She hesitates. "I respect your father. But I think we have to come clean with the board about this. We should formulate a plan. Maybe we could take Nate Fordham up on his offer to buy the company?"

I wince. I hadn't even thought about telling Nate. If I told him about it, that would be the end of my dad's run as owner. If my dad wakes up, Nate will probably force him to go to jail. If my dad never regains consciousness, his legacy will be the laughingstock of Wall Street for years to come.

I put my hand to my brow. "Can we keep this between ourselves for a little while? I need to make a plan."

"Of course." Lori frowns. "That's why we're talking about it right now."

Just as I am winding up to tell Lori about the merger, a knock comes at her door. "Go away!" she responds.

"Nate Fordham is here to see Ms. Gellar!" a voice calls through the door.

Lori looks surprised. She stands up, glancing at me. I grab her hands and yell, "We'll be out in just a second!"

Pulling Lori closer, I whisper to her. "I trust you to keep this between us. Okay?"

She nods. "Of course. I can only keep it under my hat for so long, though."

"I swear. It's just until I make a plan. I'm not looking to

excuse my father or hide his misdeeds. You know I wouldn't do that."

She offers me a hug, which I take. But while we're hugging, I tell her, "Nate Fordham is here because I signed the papers to begin the process of a merger between our companies."

Lori pulls back, her eyes searching my face. "Wait, really?"

I give her a half-smile and nod. "Yeah."

She squeezes my upper arm. "That's great, Annie."

Her use of my childhood nickname makes me smile. "Should we go see Mr. Fordham, Lor-Lor?"

Lori chuckles. "Yes. We'll talk more about the other situation later."

I open her office door and Nate is right there, scowling at me.

"Mr. Fordham!" I say. My cheeks are probably the color of a ripe summer tomato about now. "Were we expecting you? It's almost six thirty."

He smirks. "You should always expect me, Annalise."

His eyes burn into my face. I swear, I could actually die from embarrassment. Mercifully, Lori cuts in.

"It's nice to see you, Mr. Fordham."

"Ms. Parker." Nate shakes her hand, looking her up and down. "You know, you actually went up against my brother Cash's start-up a number of years ago. They were making a new block chain currency and you sued them for some reason?"

Lori lights up. "I remember. Block chain currencies are a scam. That's still a hill I will die on."

Nate grins. "They're mostly used to trick the unwise into parting with their money. There are some exceptions, of course."

Lori gives him a knowing smile. "Of course." She turns

to me. "Well, I won't keep you. I imagine you two have quite a bit to hash out before you get to the contracts, right?"

Nate and I exchange a look. "Actually, I'm going to take Annalise out to dinner."

"Oh!" Lori smiles. "That's nice. Well, you two have a great time. Annalise, don't do anything I wouldn't do."

Does that include moaning Nate's name? Because I have a feeling that I'm going to be doing plenty of that tonight.

"I'll be careful," I say with a wink. "See you around, Lori."

Nate puts his elbow out and I take it. He escorts me from my office, not saying a word until the elevator doors close. He presses the button for the lobby, then turns to me.

"You look good in that dress, Kitten."

I look down at my dress, a Givenchy design. I paired it with something from my own wardrobe, an oversized black sport coat with gold accents on the pockets.

"Of course you like it. You chose it." I bite my lip. "You look good. But you always look good."

Nate leans down and gives me a single, searing kiss. I kiss him back, feeling my engine begin to rev up.

He quickly moves away, flashing me a grin.

"Later. I promise. First, I want to take you somewhere special. Are you ready, Kitten?"

I want to roll my eyes at his use of my ridiculous pet name. But I don't.

If I am being one hundred percent truthful with myself, I think I am starting to like the sound of the word rolling off my lips.

Kitten.

"I'm just waiting for you," I say with a secretive smile. "Lead the way."

He kisses me again and I forget everything else.

FOURTEEN
NATE

When my driver pulls to stop at the Metropolitan Museum of Art's distinctive Greek revival-style entrance, I smile. I have set up the perfect date. A private showing during the hours that the famous museum is normally closed to visitors. A self-guided tour through the most famous gallery. Dinner for two set up in the grand rotunda while a string quartet plays Bach and Handel.

Annalise only mentioned loving modern art in passing, so I'm pretty sure this will be a complete surprise to her. I'm about to woo her so hard that I'll sweep her off her feet... and into my bed.

Getting out of the SUV, I dash around to the other side to wait for her. When the driver opens Annalise's door, she is fidgeting with the strip of black silk that I tied around her head to keep her from seeing where we were going.

I step in, scolding her in a joking tone. "Are you trying to spoil the surprise?"

I can't see her eyes, obviously, but I like to imagine that she rolls them.

"No. I'm being patient." She sighs heavily, touching the delicate strap of her gold and silver evening gown. She looks so innocent and lovely in the dress. It stirs my darker impulses. "Have we arrived?"

"Yes. But don't open your eyes yet," I tell Annalise. I unbuckle her and help her from the car. "I'm going to guide you inside. There are some stairs that we'll have to ascend to get to our destination."

Annalise clings to my arm as we head up the sidewalk and down the red carpet. We hit a short flight of stairs, heading between the khaki-colored columns that tower on each side of us.

Whisking Annalise through the entryway, I pause when we are just about to step through into the grand foyer. "Hold on."

"As if I could do anything else," she quips. "You've literally blindfolded me."

I smirk, untying the silky piece of fabric and letting it fall from her eyes. She gasps when she sees where she is, her hands flying to cover her mouth.

"The Met??" She looks at me, eyes wide and excited. "How did you know that I love art?"

I give her a sly smile. "You mentioned it once."

She walks into the rotunda, gazing straight up at the frosted glass ceiling. "How on earth did you convince the museum to let you in after hours?"

I follow her, enjoying her innocence. "You can do almost anything you want if you write a big enough check."

"Good evening, Mr. Fordham," a staff member greets us as he approaches. "Welcome to the Met, Ms. Gellar. Please, follow me."

The peculiar scent of aged wood and centuries-old canvases fills my nostrils as we move inside.

"Did you know that the Met houses over two million

works of art from around the world?" I casually mention to Annalise as we stroll past the darkened galleries that are not open tonight. Their masterpieces are protected from prying eyes by velvet ropes.

"I did actually know that. I have been to the Met before."

"And I might or might not have read that fact on the museum's website." My mouth curls in a smile.

"That counts." Annalise takes my arm and looks at me with sparkling eyes. "Keep telling me museum facts. It makes me forget what an ass you've been to me for the last couple of weeks."

"Will do." I smirk, but something like pride blooms in my chest at her approval.

As we meander through the hushed halls, we're guided by the soft footsteps of the staff member who has introduced himself as Mickey. I point out several artworks that catch my attention.

We venture deeper into the museum and our conversation flows effortlessly. With Annalise, nothing is ever stilted or a lot of work. It's just... natural. Like it should be between a man and a woman.

The hushed silence of the museum hangs in the air around us as we continue our exploration. We walk through a gallery with entire assemblages of knights in medieval armor, beautiful faux-outdoor Japanese pagodas, and several rooms devoted to 18th-century paintings. My gaze lingers on Annalise's slight expression of awe as she studies the artwork hanging on the walls. Her wide hazel-green eyes take in everything.

One thing about Annalise, is that she is always learning, calculating, digesting information.

It's a good trait to have in the business world. Doubly so for a CEO.

Annalise pauses at one particular painting and I stop to admire it too. It depicts a sunny day in a lush garden, filled with vibrant flowers and delicate butterflies. The style of painting is stunningly realistic. It's hard to believe that it was painted over a hundred and fifty years ago.

Annalise studies the painting for a moment. I can see something stirring within her, underneath the surface. There's a hint of wistfulness in her gaze.

"My grandmother had a garden just like this," she shares softly. Her voice is soft and faraway. "I used to spend hours there when I was a child, exploring every nook and cranny, discovering all sorts of hidden treasures."

"Really?" I ask, genuinely intrigued by this unexpected glimpse into her past.

She nods, her eyes still fixed on the painting. "It was my secret garden. Just like the book. You know?"

"Interesting," I say. It sounds a little forced coming out. I damn sure haven't read whatever book she's talking about.

Her lips twitch with humor. She gives me a little side eye as she moves on. I follow, feeling like I said the exact wrong thing. Curious, as I'm normally so well-spoken and quick with my quips.

We walk on, slowly passing through several rooms before she speaks again.

"This is gorgeous," Annalise says, nodding to a large painting. It's from the 1600s and it depicts a woman in a transparent dressing gown, draped across her bed. "It's so... raw. Powerful. She's obviously beautiful but also sort of sickly and apathetic. But there's also something deeply troubling about the way she looks off at something we can't see."

My eyebrows rise. Again, I can't help but appreciate her keen dissection of the feelings that the painting evokes. She's so fucking smart.

A completely novel thing for me to notice about a girl I

am only interested in sleeping with. And I am still firmly in the no-relationship camp. But damn, this little girl is really fucking with my head.

I stare at the painting, trying to grasp for some comment, something to say. "It's... unusual to see a painting of a naked woman in the 1600s. Right? Most art was like... biblical scenes?"

"Most nineteeth century art was commissioned portraits, I think." Annalise's eyes light up. "But your point still stands."

I narrow my eyes on Annalise. "This isn't fair. You're just out of college. You've probably taken an art history class in the last few years."

"Correct." She smiles winningly. "I took Women Depicted in Art two years ago."

Rolling my eyes, I glance at my watch. To my complete surprise, almost two hours have slipped by. "Annalise, I have another surprise for you."

I start guiding her down a secluded corridor adorned with delicate frescoes.

"Another surprise?" She raises an eyebrow, a playful smirk gracing her lips. "You really know how to keep a girl on her toes, don't you?"

"Only the best for you," I reply, a hint of mischief in my tone.

As we round the corner, a beautifully set table comes into view, nestled in a quiet alcove surrounded by master-pieces from centuries past.

"Wow, Nate, this is...." She pauses, searching for the right words. "Incredible. It's really thoughtful. I didn't think you were capable of thinking about anyone other than yourself."

"I'm trying to get you in bed, not proposing marriage." I toss off the words like they don't mean anything. But inside, the strange feeling of pride expands because she gave me a compliment.

Take it easy, I tell my swelling ego. *She's just a girl. No need to react like the queen of England just offered to make you a knight.*

We approach the table. Apparently, I want to be considered gentlemanly, because I pull out her chair, gesturing for her to take a seat. As she does, I can't help but marvel at how effortless she looks in this elegant and refined space. Like Annalise herself might be a piece of art.

"Thank you, Nate," she says.

As the dinner unfolds, a string quartet begins to play. Their quiet melodies provide the perfect backdrop for our conversation. Between sips of wine and bites of exquisite cuisine, I find myself talking about my childhood.

"Growing up, I always felt like I had to prove myself," I admit. "We were rich, but my parents were distant. My grandfather was the only one who seemed to believe in me. But his expectations were so high that it felt suffocating at times."

Annalise listens intently, her gaze never leaving mine. "It made you into the man you are." She pats her mouth with her cloth napkin, then reaches out to trace the veins in the back of my hand. "A powerful CEO with a secret heart of gold. Or maybe bronze. We'll see."

Her tinkling laugh spreads and fills the air between us. My whole setup is working like a charm. We're sitting close. She's touching me. I'm telling her stories that make me seem sympathetic.

But damn if this moment isn't also working on me. I shouldn't be feeling the intense connection that I'm feeling between us right now.

I raise a glass to her. "We will see. Tonight, I think."

She blushes and drops her gaze, pulling her hand away.

Damn. I tripped on my own words again. But she starts speaking, taking me by surprise.

"You know, Nate, I've also felt this immense pressure to prove myself," she admits, her voice wavering slightly. "I have always felt that I was not good enough or strong enough or..." She waves her hand. "But I'm determined to make things right. I plan to earn the respect of those around me and show them that I am capable."

"Annalise, you're incredible," I blurt out. "You couldn't let anyone down if you tried."

"Hah!" She laughs dryly. "That tells me that you don't know my mother."

I spread my hands. "I get the picture, though."

I try to keep my tone light. But I mean every word. Our eyes meet, holding.

The air between us seems to crackle with electric energy. I reach across the table, taking her hand in mine. Her hand is warm, and I revel in it for a moment.

"Annalise," I say softly. "In another life, I can picture myself with you, laughing and vacationing on my yacht somewhere off the coast of Santorini."

Her breath catches in her throat and she shivers slightly. Her eyes seem endless at this moment.

"Nate," she replies, her voice equally soft. "You still don't want a relationship. Neither do I."

"Who said anything about a relationship?" I quip, attempting to lighten the mood. "I just meant that if we ever found ourselves stranded on a deserted island, I think we'd have a hell of a time."

A smile tugs at the corner of her lips.

"Oh. Well, when you put it that way," she teases. "Maybe I could see myself there with you too."

"Well, in that case." I feel a wave of relief wash over me.

"I'd like to take you back to my penthouse now, so we can discuss this in more depth."

Arousal flashes in her eyes as she nods, her breath hitching in her chest. "I'd like that too," she agrees.

"Then let's not waste another second," I say. I stand up and offer her my hand.

FIFTEEN

ANNALISE

The elevator to Nate's penthouse seems to creep along its track. Nate looks at me with a smirk. He's not touching me as the elevator lifts us skyward, but the sensitive skin on my bare arm breaks out in gooseflesh.

I'm desperate for him. I'm desperate to touch his silken skin, to feel his lips on my neck, to wrap myself around him and swallow him whole.

Once we reach the penthouse, the view is breathtaking. The glittering lights of Manhattan unfold below me like a sea of stars, twinkling faintly from the floor-to-ceiling glass windows.

His strong arms encircle me from behind as I gaze out at the city below us. His lips trail kisses along my neck, sending shivers down my spine.

"Kitten," he murmurs into my ear. The pet name flushes me with desire. "Are you ready for this?"

"More than anything," I reply, my voice barely above a whisper. I've been craving this moment for far too long.

Now it's finally here but somehow, I can't seem to grasp it with both hands.

This moment seems surreal.

"Good girl," Nate says. He spins me around to face him and slides me a predatory grin. He raises his hand to my face and runs a thumb across my lips. "Come with me."

He leads me toward the large window overlooking Central Park. The cityscape provides an alluring backdrop. As we reach the glass, he turns to me with a commanding gaze.

"Strip."

My heart races as I obey. I remove each article of clothing until I stand before Nate completely naked. His eyes drink me in, bright and hungry. He undresses as well. As he drops each article of clothing on the floor unhurriedly, I can't help but admire his sculpted body. Every inch of him seems to be exuding power and raw sexuality.

"Back up against the window, Kitten," he commands.

My breath leaves me in a rush. I comply, shivering. Nate sinks to his knees and grips my hips, nuzzling a spot just below my belly button. I let out a half giggle, half moan as he lifts one of my knees and trails kisses down to the cleft of my pussy.

I moan, closing my eyes for a brief second. His mouth is hot and wet. Anticipation pounds in my veins because I know what is about to happen.

Nate moves closer and lifts my other leg, sliding his arm underneath it to support my weight. The move opens my pussy to his gaze. He growls as he leans down to run the tip of his nose against my slick flesh. His lips find my pulsing clit, sucking on it. I buck against him, crying out.

"Nate!" My fingers tangle in his hair. My hips instinctively rock as the pleasure builds within me. I'm already drenched and quivering at every touch.

He licks and sucks my clit, focusing on it with an intensity that is almost too much. My orgasm sneaks up on me, springing forth as he brings me to an earth-shattering climax. I cry out. Nate moans against me, the vibrations from his mouth giving me pleasure mixed with pain.

"Did you enjoy that, Kitten?" he asks as he disentangles himself from me and rises. He smirks at my disheveled state.

"Yes," I pant, still trying to catch my breath. "But I need more."

"More, you say?" he teases. "You'll have to beg for it."

My pride bristles at the thought of pleading with him. But I know the desire coursing through me is too strong to resist.

"Please," I whisper, raw and vulnerable. "I need you. I need... more."

He sweeps me off my feet and carries me to the opulent bed. His strength leaves me feeling both cherished and utterly dominated. As he lays me down on the plush sheets, I reach out to his naked form. My curious fingers touch his hip before wrapping around the throbbing length of his cock.

"Teach me," I beg. I dare to meet his smoldering gaze. "I want to know how to please you."

"Good girl," he praises, his voice laced with approval. He places two fingers against my lips. I part them willingly, taking his fingers into my mouth and swirling my tongue around their length.

"Suck, Kitten, and bite gently."

I do as he instructs. He closes his eyes, then opens them and stares at his fingers as I suck them. He lets out a stifled groan.

"Enough," he growls. He pulls his fingers from my mouth before pressing a searing kiss to my lips. "You're doing so well, Kitten. But there's much more for me to teach you."

As Nate reclaims his position above me, I find myself again at the mercy of his skilled hands and unyielding presence.

"Please, Nate," I beg. My voice is barely a whisper as I arch my back, hungry for more. "I need you."

"Patience, Kitten," he murmurs. His gaze is intense, his tone dark and commanding. "I want your first time to be unforgettable."

I know for a fact that it already is, but I'm willing to listen if he has more.

He leans in to capture my lips in a devastatingly sensual kiss that leaves me breathless and wanting.

My body trembles with anticipation. Nate slides his hand between my thighs, his fingers deftly finding my clit again. He begins a slow, deliberate dance, exploring my slick folds. I moan, the thought that his stiff cock will soon be filling my pussy exciting me.

"God, you're so wet for me, Kitten," he whispers. The possessive gleam in his silver eyes stoking my desire even further. "Tell me you're ready for me."

I blush, stammering, "M- more than ready. I... I want you, Nate."

"God damn," he curses. He presses his fingers deeper inside me. I throw my head back and a guttural cry escapes from my throat. "I am going to destroy you, Annalise."

I gasp. I don't want Nate to stop moving his fingers inside my pussy, but I can't wait for him to actually fuck me.

"Take me, Nate," I whisper hoarsely. "Make me yours."

Nate expertly positions himself above me. I look up at him, my breath hitching. His chiseled face is a study in determination and control.

With slow, deliberate movements, Nate fists his cock

and aligns himself with my entrance, steadily pushing forward. Each inch of him fills me, stretching me.

I wince, experiencing a twinge of pain. Nate is watching me closely and he slows down. My hands touch his back. As much as I feel the pain, I also feel the urgency of my libido telling me to fuck his brains out.

At my urging, he groans low in his throat, his eyes never leaving mine.

"You're so incredibly hot and tight, Annalise. So fucking perfect."

His praise sends shivers down my spine. I arch my back, desperate for more contact between our sweat-slicked bodies. The pain ends and now the sensation of his cock inside me, filling me, overwhelms my senses.

I don't mean to come, but I can't wait any longer. As Nate begins to move, my climax crashes through me like a tidal wave. The tidal wave of pleasure sweeps away all my rational thoughts.

"Fuck, Nate," I gasp. "Fuck!!"

My fingers clutch at the silk sheets beneath me. The pleasure is almost too much to bear. But Nate's eyes lock on mine, keeping me tethered to earth.

"Annalise," he breathes. His thrusts ease into a slow, steady rhythm, stoking the embers of my passion until they begin to glow once more. Our bodies move together in perfect sync. We come together, our cries of ecstasy echoing through the luxurious penthouse.

He stills for a moment, panting, before withdrawing from my body. He kisses my lips and then falls onto his side, a great beast sated for only a moment.

SIXTEEN

NATE

Will Annalise be at the gala I'm heading to? A part of me hopes so.

The sleek black car slides to a halt at the curb, its polished surface reflecting the bright city lights of Manhattan. I step out, the cool night air starkly contrasting with the warmth of the car that I just left behind. My gaze lifts to the grand hotel that dominates the skyline. Its facade is a testament to elegance, power, and most of all, money.

The revolving doors sweep me into another world. A world of glittering chandeliers casting prisms across the sea of high society. The hum of conversation fills the ballroom and blends with the subtle strains of a string quartet nestled in the corner.

I scan the crowd, noting the elegantly dressed attendees as they mingle, holding crystal flutes of champagne and nibbling delicate hors d'oeuvres.

There's a certain electricity in the air.

"Fordham!"

Heads turn when my name slices through the air. With a confident smirk, I stride forward.

"Nate." I pivot toward the familiar voice. Cash stands there, his eyes gleaming with mischief. Alongside him is Drew, ViaLife's VP, who looms with that stern frown that seems etched into his features.

They're an odd pair. One dripping cocky charisma, the other as personable as a stone slab.

"Thought you'd never make it." Cash's voice is pissed, and it draws me away from the crowd. We move to the corner, our backs to a towering sculpture of abstract metalwork.

"I can't remember a time when you two have ever willingly hung out together." I cross my arms and look suspiciously from Cash to Drew. "What have you two been cooking up?"

"Archer Gellar," Drew says. His voice is low enough to be lost in the hum of the string quartet and clinking glasses. "The CEO of Gellar Industries? Well, he was the CEO until recently."

I make a face. "Yeah, I certainly know all of that already."

"Well, we have a plan to wring the last dollar from that old goat." Cash looks pleased with himself. Which in turn makes me doubly suspicious.

Cash always comes up with outrageous plans to short the stock market that only work out part of the time. It's made him rich, but the amount of money he's lost in the process is nauseating.

I raise an eyebrow and push out a breath. "Go on, then."

"His affairs are more than just rumors," Cash says. A crooked grin unfurls across his face.

Surprisingly, Drew nods along, complicit. "The affairs aren't hard to uncover," he adds. "And we can prove it."

"So what?" I ask.

"So we leak them all to the press. We could get a bunch

of the women together and pay them to sue him. You know the press will fall all over that kind of information. They're always looking for a reason to shred a well-known man to ribbons."

"So you would 'Me Too' Archer," I muse, rolling the concept around like a fine wine on my tongue. "Archer would be publicly shamed. Share prices would plummet. Then Gellar Industries becomes ripe for the picking."

Annalise already signed the merger docs, but I'm not ready to share that with Cash just yet.

"Exactly," they chorus, their eagerness palpable.

"Low-hanging fruit," I say. I keep my voice noncommittal, but I'm considering the prospect. "How deliciously underhanded."

Cash and Drew think I'm enticed by the thought of taking down my rival. Little do they know, my ties to Gellar's empire are deeper, more... personal. But that's a card I'll play close to my chest.

"Interesting proposition," I say. "But before we proceed with such a Machiavellian maneuver, tell me how you found out about this. Surely Archer has wall-papered the whole Upper East Side with non-disclosure agreements."

Cash chuckles, a sound as slick as his carefully styled hair. "A former Gellar nanny has come forward with her story. She gives a colorful account of working for the family for over five years."

I allow myself an inward sigh of relief. Nothing in Cash's cavalier tone suggests he knows about Annalise and me. Drew doesn't give away anything, either.

My secret is safe for now.

"Drew, what are your thoughts?" I probe further, feigning interest in the details of their plan. I need to keep them talking while also not giving myself away.

The VP's eyes are sharp as flint. "We've been compiling

evidence quietly. It's solid. Once exposed, it'll spread like wildfire through the media. Archer's reputation will be ash. Gellar Industries' stock will be practically worthless."

"Scandalous," I murmur. "Give me some time to think it over."

"Of course, take all the time you need," Drew says. He gives me a conspiratorial look, which means he thinks I'm on board.

Cash cuts in. "And by that, he means a couple of weeks at the outside. We must move on this soon before someone else gets wind of it."

"Of course." I give them a little bow. "Gentlemen, enjoy the rest of the gala. I must circulate."

Cash and Drew both make their way to the bar. I turn in the other direction, wondering how their plan will affect my relationship with Annalise. After all, she is Archer's daughter. If the company suffers a reversal of fortunes, she'll likely feel it too.

As though I'd summoned her just by thinking her name, the glint of Annalise's golden curls catches my eye, a Siren's song in a sea of monochrome suits and dresses. I watch Annalise navigate the room with an elegance that belies her inexperience at the helm of a corporate empire.

She's a vision in crimson, the dress clinging tightly to her petite curves, provoking more than a few appreciative glances.

"Annalise," I call out. My voice cuts through the din of the gala as I intercept her.

Her head turns. Her nostrils flare and her eyes widen as she takes me in. "Mr. Fordham." Her tone is cautious, yet she is unable to mask the excitement in her eyes.

An electric current sparks between us. But before I can say anything more, Cash materializes beside Annalise, his trademark charm dialed to eleven.

He looks between us, and I can see him slowly putting the puzzle pieces in place.

If I'm not careful, he will know every wicked thing I've done to Annalise before I can interject. I want to go on the offensive. But I steel myself. It's not exactly good business to growl and snap at my own brother over a girl.

Even if the girl is Annalise Gellar.

Cash extends his hand to Annalise. "Miss Gellar, isn't it? I'm Cash, Nate's brother. And you are far too beautiful to be standing here alone."

Cash's smile is slick. His intent is clear as daylight. She's a pretty girl. And Cash? Cash is a ladies' man.

It makes me wish I had never invited Cash to woo Annalise when I'm finished with her.

"Mr. Fordham," she replies, her voice steady even as her body language screams discomfort. "You say that as if I mind being alone. But I don't."

"Ah, but that doesn't mean I can't make your night a little better by joining you," he purrs, leaning closer.

I watch, torn between intervening and compromising what little distance remains between Annalise and me.

"I don't think your presence would make anything better," she says tartly.

Cash raises a brow. He's obviously not used to getting this much pushback from women.

"Hard to get, I like that," Cash says. He appears unfazed, but I've reached my breaking point.

I've watched Cash charm women for most of my life. I'm not about to stand here like a cuckold and let him seduce Annalise.

"Enough, Cash." My voice slices through their exchange like a blade. "She said she's not interested. Take the hint."

"Touchy, aren't we?" Cash smirks. There's a question in

his eyes now as he gazes at me, a puzzle with pieces still missing.

"I'm not interested in standing here and watching you bully your way into Ms. Gellar's bed," I growl. Possessiveness suddenly rears its head and demands to be heard. "Or maybe she'll surprise you by punching you and breaking your nose. Archer Gellar is known to have a mean sucker punch."

Cash rolls his eyes. But he does take a step away from Annalise. He smiles at her. "I could introduce you to the right people, you know."

She stiffens like a cornered doe. "I just spotted a friend that I haven't seen in a while. If you will both excuse me–"

Cash grabs her arm. "Wait a second."

Annalise rears back. Dark intent sparks in her eyes. Immediately I step between them, physically separating her from my brother to keep her from attacking him.

"Go," I order her. "Cash and I are going to take a walk outside."

Annalise stares at me for a second. I swear I can see her deciding whether or not to attack Cash anyway. Then she gives a tiny shake of her head. She turns and walks away.

"Jesus, Cash," I say, once the crowd has swallowed her. "I thought you were supposed to be a smooth operator. What in the fuck was that?"

"Easy, big brother," Cash replies, his eyes wide with mock innocence. "Just having a bit of fun. Sometimes you meet girls that say they aren't interested, but it's just them playing coy."

"Annalise didn't look very coy from where I'm standing." The words are out before I can stop them.

Cash's eyebrows arch. "And since when do you care about Archer Gellar's daughter?"

"I should tell you that Gellar Industries is already

merging with ViaLife," I concede through clenched teeth. I hate the need to justify my protectiveness over Annalise. Like it's a tactical diversion, nothing more.

"A merger?" A laugh bubbles up from Cash's throat, rich and knowing. "Is that all it is?"

"Back off," I hiss, my jaw setting like concrete. "Annalise is young, Cash. She's certainly not old enough for you to be messing with her head."

"I see." Cash smirks, the corner of his mouth lifting. "Now about the merger. Did she sign anything?"

"Yes." I pause. "I haven't filed the papers with the courts, though."

"So you're hesitating. That's good for me. What's it to you if I kill the merger and make it easy for you to buy Gellar Industries for pennies on the dollar? Are you Annalise's boyfriend now, Nate?"

His question hangs heavy between us. I clench my jaw and my blood boils beneath my skin.

"Watch your mouth," I growl, and with a swift motion, I grab him by the arm. No one lays claim to Annalise—least of all my brother. "Now let's go."

I frog march Cash toward the ballroom door, seething.

SEVENTEEN

ANNALISE

I sit in my father's sleek corner office at Gellar Industries. The large windows in the cavernous room frame the breathtaking Manhattan skyline. My fingers twitch rhythmically on the desk as I anticipate Nate's arrival.

My stomach flutters with a mixture of anxiety, excitement, and some other unnamed feeling. I'm still not sure how I should perceive him.

I stretch my legs out, still feeling the remnants of a lingering ache. The feeling is bittersweet for me. Nate finally took my virginity. Spectacularly, I might add. I feel like I can finally understand why women in romantic movies lift their feet during a particularly romantic kiss with their partners.

If they feel anything like the fireworks Nate made me feel, they have every reason to let it show.

And last night's display of Nate's possessiveness in front of his brother Cash? I almost *swooned*.

I check my phone again for messages.

Meet you at your office at 10. – N

That's the enigmatic, early hour message I received from

Nate. Nothing about his sleazy brother. Or about missing me.

Of course not.

Nate remains a mystery to me.

The door swings open, cutting off my thoughts. And there is Nate Fordham in all his infuriating glory. His silver eyes meet mine. And of course, I can't help but notice how the sunlight streaming through the window makes them glint like silver.

"Ms. Gellar," he greets me curtly, striding into the room with an air of authority.

"Mr. Fordham," I reply. I am attempting to maintain a professional façade, to act as if my heart isn't beating faster just at the sight of him in his crisp Armani suit.

"Are you ready to get down to business?" he asks. His eye contact is blunt, his tone sharp and unyielding.

"Of course," I respond. "Once you tell me what you're here about."

"I have a printout of all the employees on the company payroll." Nate drops a file folder on my desk. "We need to go through each person's job. Then I'll assign them a rating."

I eye him. "And what will that accomplish?"

"It'll let me know who is essential, and who is potentially redundant, when it comes time to make personnel cuts."

I rear back. "Are you sure that is the best use of our time?"

"This is what CEOs do." Nate looks at me sternly. "We function to help the company prosper and deliver profits to the shareholders."

I can feel my cheeks tinge with heat. "...right..." As if that much should be obvious to me.

Nate pulls up a seat beside me and starts looking at the long list of names, starting with A. I force myself to focus on the matter at hand. After all, it's not just my own future at stake here. I'm making big decisions that will affect my employees.

As we dive into the discussions, I find myself admiring Nate's quick-witted intelligence and ruthless drive. Sure, his cold demeanor can be off-putting at times. But there is no denying that he knows how to command attention.

Nate taps his pen impatiently against my desk as we pore over the employee lists. "We need to be strategic about this. Not every single person is critical to the company's operations."

I grit my teeth. "I disagree. Each employee contributes something valuable. We can't just slash our workforce without considering the impact on the company."

His steely gray eyes bore into mine. Tension crackles between us, sudden and electric.

"Do you really think the mailroom clerk is indispensable? What about the fifteen administrative assistants?" Nate challenges. He leans forward and his crisp white shirt stretches taut to show the lines of his muscular chest. "Be rational here."

Anger flares inside me. How dare he question my judgment like I'm some wide-eyed ingénue straight out of college? I've worked my ass off to prove myself capable of leading Gellar Industries.

"I am being rational. Cutting jobs left and right is short-sighted. It destroys morale."

My pen moves deliberately down the list, marking almost every name as vital. Nate's brows rise in disbelief. I won't be cowed by his magnetic presence or ruthless business tactics.

"This company needs me to make tough calls. If you're too softhearted to do it, I will."

I scoff. "Softhearted? These are people with families, Nate. I'm sorry that I'm not ready to give them all the axe."

Nate smirks, confident and aggravating. "Keep telling yourself that, Kitten. We'll see who's right in the end."

God, I hate how much he affects me. I shake my head.

"I'm making a list of employees that are not superstars. Don't get too excited, because it will be short."

He rolls his eyes. "If you don't make a substantial list, I will fire employees based solely on their metrics."

"Do what you think is best." I square my chin and start making a slightly longer list than I'd originally intended.

As I'm making a few final notes on the employee list, I notice that Nate's hunched over a separate sheet of paper out of the corner of my eye. His pen moves quickly, decisively, in stark contrast to my own hesitance.

Curiosity gets the better of me. I lean forward slightly, trying to catch a glimpse of what he's working on so intently. Is it a counter to my own list?

Nate's head snaps up and he catches me looking, eyebrow arched in amusement. With a soft smirk, he casually flips the paper over, hiding the contents from view.

"Can I help you, Annalise?" he drawls.

I feel a flush creep up my neck at being caught snooping. "Just wondering what you're scheming over there."

Nate chuckles, low and sinful, as he stands over me. "So suspicious. If you must know, it's a list of employees I think will thrive in the new Gellar-Vialife offices."

"Let me guess. It's a fraction of the size of my list?"

"It's called trimming the fat. Something you'll need to learn if you want to succeed in this business."

His condescending tone makes me bristle. I stand abruptly, palms flat on the mahogany table as I glare at him. "Don't patronize me, Fordham. I'm not some wide-eyed girl you can manipulate."

Nate towers over my petite frame. "Believe me, I'm well aware of that."

The way he looks at me, hungry and heated, sends a shiver down my spine. I inhale sharply, willing myself to focus.

"This company, these employees? They are my top priority. I won't let your ruthless tactics destroy what my family built."

"Like it or not, Annalise, we're in this together now. So you better get used to me and my methods."

He plucks the list I made from the desk, frowning.

"Interesting choices. But you know as well as I do that not everyone here is going to keep their job."

"Then maybe you should teach me," I shoot back. "Show me how to be the ruthless, callous CEO I apparently need to be. That's part of the deal I agreed to, if you'll remember."

Nate studies me for a moment, as if weighing his options. Then a sly smirk appears on his face.

"All right, Miss Gellar," he whispers. His breath is warm on my cheek. "I wonder if you even know what you're asking?"

I jerk my chin up defiantly. "I think I do. My father named me CEO for a reason."

"Your father named you CEO because he knew you wouldn't rock the boat. And he was right. But that's okay. I will rock the boat for you."

He leans over the paper and writes a list of eleven names in his elegant, slanted cursive. Eleven names, a reduction from the sixty-eight on the printed list.

My jaw drops. "You can't think that I'll let you fire fifty-seven people!" I gasp.

Nate narrows his eyes at me. But after a long moment,

he nods. "You can keep three corporate-level managers when we move to the new offices."

I stare at him, my heart pounding with frustration. I scan over the names on the list. How can I possibly choose just three?

"But–"

He stills my protests with a hand on my arm. "This is a difficult task. There's no doubting that. But you have to do it. If you don't, there will be a CEO turnover. I've seen it happen time and time again. A company merges or is bought out, the new CEO doesn't make drastic changes. The next thing you know, the board announces a new CEO. And then, whoever is in your place will make these cuts without knowing anything about your employees."

He slides me his revised list. I suck in a breath as I see that Nate has been severe and heavy-handed. But his words ring through my head.

Nate could be right. There's no one on the board that will stand up in my defense. I won't get another swing at this fastball.

"All right, all right," I say. My finger hovers above the list, hesitating momentarily before scratching out several names. I can only hope that firing so many people is enough to salvage what remains of my father's legacy.

"Are you satisfied?" I ask, looking up at Nate.

He nods, but there's something different about him now. He exudes a calmness that wasn't there before.

"Let's move on to business strategies," he suggests. He opens a thick binder full of charts and graphs. I can't help but be a little intrigued by his change in demeanor.

"You're so relaxed," I tease him, trying to lighten the mood. He smirks at me and the familiar edge returns to his expression.

"I'm very comfortable doing my job, Annalise." His tone

is firm as he guides me through the intricacies of mergers and acquisitions. He talks about cost-effective marketing strategies and the advantages of vertical integration.

As we dive into corporate strategy, I find myself growing more and more fascinated. Not just by the subject matter, but by Nate himself. The intensity with which he discusses these topics reveals a passion I hadn't seen in him before.

Discussing synergy with him should be boring. But it's actually a little bit hot? I can't help feeling drawn in by his smooth talking.

"Okay, so what do you think is the best approach for Gellar Industries regarding market penetration?" I ask. I slyly move my chair a little closer to his. I want to soak up whatever charm and charisma bomb has just gone off all over Nate Fordham.

"First and foremost, you need to identify your target market and define your value proposition," Nate explains, his voice oozing confidence. "Once you have that down, it's all about staying ahead of the curve. You must anticipate trends and pivot when necessary."

His words ring through me, and I nod in agreement. The more time I spend with Nate, the more I realize that beneath his prickly exterior lies a wealth of knowledge. Perhaps behind that gruff demeanor lies a genuine desire to see Gellar Industries succeed.

"You know," I say, my voice laced with genuine admiration. "You're a fantastic teacher when you let your guard down."

Nate looks at me, his gray eyes locking onto mine with a hint of surprise. "Well, you're a quick study, Annalise."

A smirk plays at the corner of his lips. I feel a flutter in my chest.

There's so much more I want to learn from him.

Eighteen
Annalise

My workday goes long. At half past seven, I look at my watch with a blustery sigh. My head pounds faintly and there is a crick on my neck from sitting at my desk for so long. I get up and call for a car to take me home.

The Manhattan street glows like a string of diamonds as I head to my small, but luxurious, apartment overlooking a small park on the west side. My body aches for the comfort of home. I need a glass of wine and the sweet relief of kicking off these damn high heels. They make my ass look great, but they are torturous after a long day.

As I unlock the door, it swings open with unexpected ease. I'm alarmed to see a woman in my house.

And not just any woman. My mother.

She stands in the middle of my living room, her hands on her hips, surveying the chaos around her feet. The furniture is in disarray, with couches and chairs rammed into an odd configuration. The wall art lies in a messy stack leaning against a window, broken and ruined. One corner of a painting sticking through the delicate stretched canvas of another.

My chest tightens. This is what my mother does to her surroundings. She hates anything outside her chosen color palette of bland beige, drab gray, and muted pink. She is also outspoken about finding most places too cluttered and messy. I call her aesthetic 'bleak brutalism.' Mom prefers to refer to it as refined minimalism.

"Mom," I say coldly. "What are you doing here? How did you get in? And what the hell did you do to my stuff??"

She turns to me, gesturing to her destruction as if she has done me a favor. As always, she is entirely unbothered by my irritation.

"Darling!" she greets me. "I just thought your apartment could use a little sprucing up. It was so *disorganized.*"

"You're not even supposed to be in here. This is my house. I don't have to abide by your silly rules about house-wares here."

Mom smiles at me, waving away my concerns with a hand. "Don't be ridiculous. I came to see you, but you weren't in. Your doorman was kind enough to let me in. I'm just sprucing up a little since I had time to kill."

I sigh, rubbing my temples. Of course, Mom would find a way to worm herself into my sanctuary, even going so far as to charm the doorman. That doorman is getting *fired* later.

"I am not relitigating the issue of my chosen color palette, for my living room," I growl, putting emphasis on the word 'my'. I could wring Mom's neck. "Just leave every-thing as it is right now. I'll have the maid try to reassemble the living room tomorrow."

"Oh, Annalise. Don't be so melodramatic," she chastises. "I'm your mother. I know what you like."

If I weren't so angry, I would burst into laughter. My

mom wouldn't know what I liked if it was smack in front of her face.

I grit my teeth. This woman has controlled every aspect of my life since I was old enough to walk: what I wore, who I socialized with, and even what I studied at Princeton. Moving into this apartment was meant to escape her iron grip. Yet here she is, invading my space and uprooting the sanctuary I've worked so hard to cultivate, nosing in like a pig hunting for truffles.

"Mom," I say, forcing a smile onto my face. "Come on. I'm going to have a glass of wine and unwind. Why don't you join me in the kitchen?"

"All right," she says airily. She carefully steps around my expensive pink pouf and my white leather armchair and follows me as I lead her to the kitchen.

As I pour each of us a glass of Grunër Vetliner, I can't shake the nagging feeling that there's more to my mother's visit than rearranging furniture. I wait for my mother to tell me the real reason for her visit. There's a tension in the air.

As a kid, I became an expert at reading the mood in any room. Between my father's bouts of rage and my mother's need to control every single element of our lives, it was essential to my survival to know when to fade into the wallpaper.

I take the first sip of my wine and brace myself for the storm I know is coming.

"So." My mother looks at me, toying with her glass. "What came of the bachelorette auction?"

There it is.

I sigh. "Nothing, Mom. Nothing came of it. I don't know what you expected."

Mom takes a small sip of wine. She narrows her eyes at me as she swallows. I'm not sure how she manages to imbue her expression with so much disappointment and anger, but she does.

"Annalise, you need to take this process of finding a husband seriously. I can't tell you how many pretty girls that are full of potential I've seen go down the tubes because they aged out of the marriage market."

"This is my life, not yours," I spit out, staring her down. "If I want to pursue being a CEO, I will. If I want my art on the walls and my furniture arranged a certain way, that should be my decision."

My mom straightens, visibly irritated by my defiance. "Fine," she snaps. "Have it your way. But don't come crying to me when you realize how lonely and unfulfilling your chosen life is."

"Lonely?" I scoff, rolling my eyes. "I have friends, Mother. I have Dana. I have other casual friends. They aren't all just socialite puppets."

"Friends won't keep you warm at night. Friends won't secure your future," she retorts. "You need a partner who can match your status and ambition. Someone who can help solidify the Gellar legacy."

"Legacy? What legacy? We'll be lucky if I can right the ship."

"Oh? With Nate Fordham on your side?" She smiles victoriously, as if she's somehow gotten dirt on my misdeeds.

"What do you know about it?" I ask calmly. It's important that my mom doesn't know that her poking and prodding rattles me. "What do you even know about the merger?"

"Enough to know that you decided on it without my consent," she snarls. "How dare you make such a monumental decision for our family without even consulting me?"

Gritting my teeth, I fight the urge to lash out at her. Why does she continually try to butt into company business? She believes she has the right to control every aspect of my life, from my wardrobe to my career.

"Mom, you have no say in the company's operations," I remind her, straining to keep my voice level. "I'm the one running things now, remember?"

"Only because your father is too ill to do so himself," she snaps, her words slicing through the air like a whip. "And don't think I don't know what you're trying to do, Annalise. By proving yourself as CEO, you're hoping you'll finally earn your father's love. But you're only setting yourself up for failure."

My anger finally boils over, getting the better of me. "Is that what you think? That everything I do is just some pathetic attempt to win Daddy's approval? News flash, Mom. Not everything revolves around you and your pathetic little mind games. I'll call the board meeting," I tell her sharply, "But understand this, Mother. There's nothing anyone can do about the merger now. It's done."

"Is it?" she asks. "You're certain of that?"

I cross my arms over my chest, refusing to back down. "I'm certain. Dad wagered the merger in a poker game against Nate Fordham and lost. I may have signed the paperwork for the merger to happen. But all that I did was save the company millions in legal fees. Nate won fair and square."

"Annalise." She looks at me pityingly. "Do you even know the state Gellar Industries is in? Your father's reckless gambling has left us on far less stable financial ground than you might think."

Her words give me pause. "What do you mean?"

"Your father dipped into the company coffers to finance

his lavish living expenses." She smooths back a strand of her hair.

My heart skips a beat at her words. How could she possibly know about Dad's embezzlement? And why is she bringing it up now?

"Don't you mean *our* expenses?" I pin her with a stare. "I don't recall Dad spending hundreds of thousands of dollars at Bergdorf Goodman or redoing our house every couple of years. That can't have been cheap."

My mother simply smiles. It's a cold, calculating expression that sends shivers down my spine. "Annalise, honestly, I don't see why you're getting so worked up," my mom replies. "This is probably why no one at the company felt comfortable coming to you with this information."

I narrow my eyes, studying her carefully. It's clear she doesn't want to divulge whatever knowledge she has. How much does she really know about my father's actions and Gellar Industries' precarious situation?

"Mom–" I start. But she looks at her watch, tsking.

"Darling, I must jet. I can't be late for my charity luncheon."

"Mom, we're talking here. Either you want to be part of Gellar Industries, or you don't. Which is it?"

She lifts her chin. "Sweetheart, I don't think this merger is in the company's best interests. We need a board meeting to discuss it."

I throw up my hands. This whole conversation has been infuriating. "Fine! But it won't change anything. The merger was Dad's choice. I'm just cleaning up the mess he left me to contend with."

"Well, I'm glad you agree. I'll see you tomorrow at the board meeting I have convened," Mom announces.

My jaw drops. I realize that her entire visit led to this statement.

She smiles coldly and adds, "That dress is much too fitted for you. I'll send some more appropriate dresses over for you to wear."

She pats my hand, passes me, and walks out into the hall. I am left with my mouth open, unsure which thing I should even respond to. I turn around and shout, "Don't send me any dresses!"

But I know that Mom isn't listening to me. She never does.

Nineteen

Nate

If Annalise hadn't texted me *911* last night, I wouldn't be here right now. After all, I still have a whole business empire to run. But now I lean against the oak desk in Annalise's office, lips pursed. My gaze drifts over the Manhattan skyline outside. The sharp lines of skyscrapers slice through the morning haze and cast long shadows over the rest of the city.

Annalise still hasn't put her personal stamp on her father's office. It's still polished and masculine in here. Someone, a secretary probably, cleared away any files that Archer left open. But his chair remains, his large desk dominates the space, and even his 1980s books on making money are still on the shelves. Large dark blue curtains hang at the windows. There's nothing of Annalise in here.

I told Annalise that I planned to move Gellar Industries into new offices in my building. Could she just be waiting for me to make the move?

The door swings open, and Annalise stands there. Her beautiful curls spill from her face like a burst of honeyed sunshine. I look down at the rest of her and frown as I take in her conservative pantsuit. This is a far cry from the elegant ensembles I had picked out just for her.

She's still pretty, but her dowdy pantsuit hides the svelte curves that her new wardrobe emphasizes so well. Not to mention that I'm pretty sure Annalise's color is gold, not this awful beige shade that she's currently wearing.

"Annalise. Is there a reason you're dressed like that?"

She looks down and rolls her eyes, a hint of defiance sparkling in their depths. "My mother visited me last night. After she left, I realized that she ransacked my wardrobe. This is the best of what she left intact."

I can't help but snort. Monique Gellar, always the meddling presence.

"That's an unpleasant surprise," I say, pulling out my phone. My fingers fly over the screen, texting my personal assistant for help. As I slip the phone back into my pocket, I can't help but think how infuriatingly attractive she looks in that outdated outfit.

"It's not the only thing my mom dropped in my lap. She called a fucking emergency board meeting behind my back." She shakes her head, a strand of golden hair falling into her eyes.

"An emergency meeting?" I raise an eyebrow. "Why did she call it?"

"My mother thinks that I should not be running this business. If she had things her way, I would be meeting her friends' eligible sons, not trying to turn this company around."

I let out a low growl. My temper erupts at the thought of Monique trying to control Annalise. Annalise is more than capable of making her own decisions.

Annalise puts up a hand to stop my protests. "I know! I know. Honestly? My mom doesn't have a great grasp on reality in general. But especially not about her role in my life and my career. It's kind of sad."

"So... what? Are we just going along with it?"

"Unless you know how to stop the board meeting that we are about to be late for, there's nothing *to* do about it. I just hope that she'll confine her obsession with my dating status to one-on-one meetings and leave the board out of it."

Annalise walks to the door, shaking her head. She's too preoccupied with her thoughts for me to do anything but follow her as she heads out into the hall.

I haven't been in the Gellar Industries boardroom yet, but I see that it is cut from the same cloth as the rest of the office once we're inside. A polished but worn wood conference table. Faded carpet underfoot. Paper water cups that make me feel like an invalid. The art is dated, and the frames could use a good dusting.

Monique, the queen bee, sits at the head of the table in her designer suit while a balding man with a big suit and definite vice-presidential energy sits to her right. As I follow Annalise into the room, I can feel the piercing gazes of the other board members on us.

Annalise exudes confidence as she greets everyone, introduces me, and takes her place at the opposite end of the table from her mother. I sit next to her, studying the faces of the board members as I smooth down my tie.

To everyone's complete surprise, Annalise stands, signaling her intent to begin the meeting.

"Thank you all for attending this emergency meeting," she starts. She smiles at the board, seeming completely at ease. "As you may have heard, Gellar Industries has begun the process of merging with Mr. Fordham's company, ViaLife. It was my father's decision to offer the merger before he fell ill. But even without that judgment made, I think Mr.

Fordham offers many benefits that we, as a small company, could never hope to have."

Annalise picks up steam, pacing now, talking with her hands.

"ViaLife and Gellar Industries have an opportunity to revolutionize our industry. We, at this company, have some technologies that could really thrive if given the proper resources. Mr. Fordham has those resources. I believe that by working together, we will achieve something remarkable."

As I watch Annalise talk passionately about our companies joining together, I can't help the fact that my cock stirs. But it soon becomes apparent that Monique is glaring at me.

As though I'm responsible for anything that Annalise says. In this case, I wish I were, but I know better than that.

Monique pushes herself up, her jaw tensed. She cuts in, "Annalise, while your passion is admirable, I question the practicality of some of your ideas. After all, you're still new as CEO. Maybe it's best to stick with what has always worked for Gellar Industries."

I clench my jaw. Snapping at Monique in front of the board won't help my cause. Instead, I smile coolly. "I understand your concerns, Monique."

She looks at me as if I just splashed her with a bucket full of dirty water. "*Mrs. Gellar.*"

"Fine then. Mrs. Gellar, you have no choice. As I explained to Annalise weeks ago, I could either sue you into oblivion or you could let the merger proceed. Now that Annalise has signed the paperwork, we can get on with the business of making Gellar Industries profitable."

"Uh, Don Young here," says the suited man beside Monique. "VP of Sales. I'm just wondering about your personal reputation for buying companies and stripping them for parts. You are known for that, are you not?"

I frown and touch my tie. It took me a minute to place

him, but I realize now that he was one of the fiercest bidders at Annalise's bachelorette auction. One I crushed, I might add.

"If a company has reached the end of its lifespan, I'm not afraid to keep any good bits and trash the rest. But that's not the case here. If it were, we'd be having a different conversation," I specify.

Monique flaps her hand at me. "Annalise lacks critical skills that are required to be the face of our company. She says that you are helping her adjust, but... how can we trust you to guide our new CEO?"

"Well said, Monique," Don chimes in.

"This conversation is getting off track," Annalise interjects.

I put up a hand to silence her. "Mrs. Gellar and Mr. Young, while I acknowledge your concerns, it's important to recognize the potential benefits of taking calculated risks. Successful businesses have thrived precisely because they were willing to embrace change and think outside the box. I've been in the trenches with your CEO. I can assure you that Annalise has a very good grasp of the day-to-day goings-on of Gellar Industries. I think your anxieties about the company's direction are unfounded."

Tension fills the room. I glance at Annalise beside me. She's stone-faced and it's clear she is unhappy, but she's weathering the storm of Hurricane Monique pretty damn well.

Monique and Don glance at each other. I can see them growing more frustrated. Their arguments crumble in the face of my bloodless logic. They're not used to being challenged in this way. But they don't usually work with me, either. I won't tolerate their petty rebellion.

I try to engage Monique. "Do you truly believe that stifling innovation and clinging to outdated practices will benefit Gellar Industries? Or are you simply afraid of losing your grip on your daughter?"

Her eyes widen with outrage. I can see the fury simmering beneath her carefully maintained facade. But before she can respond, I turn my attention to Don, my gaze as cold and unyielding as steel.

"And you, Don. Are you here to serve the best interests of this company? Or merely to advance your own agenda? I bet that if Annalise steps down, you're the next logical successor."

Donald's face contorts with indignation. "I won't dignify that with an answer."

I smirk, relishing the knowledge that I've struck a nerve.

"I'm determined to turn this company around. Hell or high water," Annalise adds. "With Mr. Fordham's help, we've already made plans to streamline the employee rosters and to start moving to our new headquarters in the ViaLife building."

A murmur ripples through the board members, who until this point have remained silent. One of them raises two manicured fingers.

"Does that mean the boardroom will be moving to the ViaLife building as well?" she asks.

Annalise nods. "Yes. Everything will be upgraded when we move. Right, Mr. Fordham?"

I clear my throat. "Yes. We have the company move date scheduled for three months from now."

Throughout this exchange, I can feel Annalise's presence beside me. She's not cowering, but she is tacitly permitting me to sweep the street clean of trash. Our eyes meet briefly. At that moment, an unspoken understanding passes between us.

We make a formidable team, united in purpose and resolve.

"Annalise," Monique begins, her voice dripping with condescension. "You may have your... 'supporter' here. But do not forget that you are not the only one with a stake in this company."

"Indeed," Donald chimes in. His eyes flicker with annoyance. "We all want what's best for Gellar Industries. If we feel your vision doesn't align with that, it's our duty to challenge you."

I scoff at their thinly veiled attempts to undermine Annalise. "Don't be ridiculous."

But as I prepare to rip into them again, I notice a subtle shift in Annalise. Her posture straightens, her chin lifts, and a new kind of confidence shines in her eyes.

"Fine," she calls out. "Challenge me. Question my decisions. But get your damn ducks in a row first. Don't come at me with these pathetic personal attacks. I will prove to you all that I can lead this company."

I can't help but smile. Without a doubt, Annalise is a force to be reckoned with.

The tension in the room is palpable. I can feel the energy shift as board members exchange nervous glances, uncertain which side to choose.

"Is that all?" I ask Monique. "If so, I have places I need to be."

Not anywhere in particular, but she doesn't need to know that.

Monique flushes with anger. "Enough!" she exclaims. "We will resume this discussion at a later date. This meeting is adjourned."

As the board members file out of the room, I can tell that we've made an impact. Monique and Don are on notice and they know it.

"Come on, Annalise," I say. I grab her by the arm and

guide her out of the conference room. "Let's get out of here."

When we get into the elevator, Annalise turns to me with those perfect hazel-green eyes. Her eyes are endless and seem to suck me in, making me move closer.

"Where are we going?" she asks, her voice soft.

I slide my hands around her waist and give her a smirk. "Anywhere you want, Kitten."

Her laugh is melodic. "Anywhere? Like the Champs-Élysee? Or Saint Basil's Cathedral?"

My lips twitch with humor. "Paris and Moscow are pretty far. If you want me to, though, I will call my flight crew. I could probably have them get my plane gassed up and ready to go in an hour."

"Nah." Annalise scrunches her nose. "I know where I really want to go."

"Oh really?" I ask casually.

She steps close to my, kisses my ear, and then whispers, "Take me to your bed."

My heart speeds up as the elevator doors open. I put a hand on her waist, propelling her forward. "Your wish is my command, Kitten."

TWENTY
NATE

Not yet. Just let me spend a few more minutes of this delicious space between the dimness of sleep and the harshness of being awake.

Sunlight streams through the floor-to-ceiling windows, casting a warm glow over the penthouse. I don't want to wake up yet. As I drowse in my king-sized bed, I think about how incredible last night with Annalise was.

God, I barely recognize myself. Who am I? I used to be so cool and detached. Now it seems that despite my usual one-night stand policy, I can't help but crave more of Annalise.

I'm honestly not sure how to feel about my current predicament. Mostly I'm confused, but there is a strange undercurrent of energy. A thrum of excitement over breaking my own sacred rule.

Rolling over to feel Annalise's warm, sleeping form beside me, I'm startled to realize that the covers on the other side of the bed are thrown back. Her pillow is cool to the touch. Where the fuck is the woman who just bewitched me so?

I sit up, stretching my muscles and feeling the soreness from how hard I fucked her last night. Or was that this morning? I can't remember. The night and morning blend into a lust-filled haze. The sheets tangle around my legs. As I sweep them aside, they still hold the scent of her intoxicating perfume.

With a groan, I roll out of bed. I'm usually not this groggy. I pad across the hardwood floor to the kitchen and fire up my state-of-the-art espresso machine.

As the rich aroma of freshly ground beans fills the air, I hear soft footsteps approaching. My chest tightens just before I see Annalise entering the room. She's wearing nothing but my rumpled button-up shirt from the day before.

God damn. Looking that sinfully sweet should be illegal. I'll admit to a bit of relief that Annalise actually stayed here last night.

I thought she had slipped away with first rays of dawn.

My cock stirs at the sight of her. A possessive feeling I can't quite shake fills my chest. But I have no right to be possessive.

It's not as if we are an item or anything.

"Morning." She greets me with a coy smile. Her hazel eyes sparkle with knowledge.

"Morning. I thought you'd left. How did you sleep?"

"Best sleep I've had in ages," she says. She's too pert as she takes a sip of her coffee and lets out a satisfied sigh. "Oh, this is magic in a cup right here."

"Would you expect anything less?" I ask with a smirk. We stand for several long beats, sipping our coffee and enjoying each other's company in the sunlit kitchen.

Annalise shakes her head. She toys with a strand of her hair, curling it around her finger. "About last night..." she starts.

My heart sinks. Is Annalise about to tell me that we're making a mistake? Or maybe that it should never happen again? I brace myself.

"Yeah?" I prompt.

"Thank you," she says softly. She moves closer, her eyes meeting mine. "Last time that we had sex, I was wrapped up in the fact that it was my first time. But last night was different. I really... got to feel cherished, I guess."

Her admission makes the back of my neck flush with heat. "It was perfect. You were..." I pause, searching for the right word. "Amazing, actually."

Annalise smiles, fully dazzling me. Only a fool wouldn't smile back.

"You think I could have another lesson sometime?" I can tell that she's teasing me. Her gaze drops to my pajamas. My half-hard cock stirs underneath the pesky layer of clothing I'm wearing.

"You have so much more to learn, Kitten." My voice is thick with desire as I pull her closer. We might not be an item. Hell, we both have our reasons for not wanting a relationship. But there's no denying the electric connection between us.

And I'm not ready to let go of Annalise just yet.

I kiss her. She deepens the kiss, her tongue sliding against mine. She makes this soft, hungry sound just at the base of her throat. Almost a growl, louder than a purr.

I will fucking kill to hear that sound pulled from her chest again. But soon, she eases back, kissing the corner of my mouth. "It would be a sin to let this coffee go cold."

I grip my mug, nodding. But inside my chest is a ravenous tiger clawing and gnawing its way out. Being civilized for the sake of Annalise takes all the strength I have left.

Annalise adds some cream from the fridge to her coffee.

I didn't even know I had cream in there. Cream must be something that the housekeeper stocks.

We lounge in my living room. Annalise gawks at the view for a minute and then settles into my deep, sumptuous couch. Our legs entwine on the plush sofa. We make small talk, bantering while we sip our coffee. The conversation flows so easily with Annalise.

Why is that? What makes her different from the countless women that came before her? I honestly can't name a single thing, but I know the answer is *almost everything.*

"I wanted to mention something," I announce nonchalantly. "I'm going to participate in a poker tournament next weekend."

I balance my cup of coffee on the back of the couch as I look at her.

Annalise whips her head around to look at me. "I would think after causing my father to have a stroke, you'd be less enthusiastic about going to another poker event."

"Well..." I wince. "It's a longstanding commitment. My brothers and I always go every year. My parents will likely be there, too."

"Ah." She puts her elbow on the back of the couch and leans her head on her hand. "Why are you telling me?"

"Just making conversation." I school my face. "And I was wondering if your father getting sick at a poker tournament means that it would be crass for me to invite you to watch. If you need a business reason to come, it would be a master-level lesson in detecting deceit."

She balls up her mouth and releases a sigh.

"My dad always talked a big game about how the best CEOs are poker players at heart."

"Your dad was right. Learning to bluff, looking for other people's tells, wagering just what you have to and not a penny more... There is a lot to be learned from watching people play cards."

Annalise looks off into the distance for a few moments before waving a hand. "If you think I should be there, I will be."

Not the enthusiastic yes I was looking for, but I'll take it.

"I'll make sure you're on the list," I say smoothly. But deep down, unease begins to coil in my chest. My brothers will all be at the poker tournament. "Be forewarned, though. My family will be at the tournament."

The idea of introducing Annalise to James and Grant makes me tense. But she already met Cash. And he did try to make a play for her. If she's still interested in the event knowing that Cash will be there, she might be tougher than she looks.

"It's a deal." Annalise puts her hand out for me to shake. I take it, just because touching her is always preferable to not touching her.

"Just try not to swoon when I win everyone's money," I tease.

"You're so full of yourself," she rolls her eyes playfully. "I don't see how your massive ego doesn't get in the way of your poker game."

"And yet..." I wave a hand to indicate myself.

"You're the worst." She laughs as she takes a sip.

"I think you're confusing me with the best." I settle a casual hand on her knee and enjoy how she blushes.

A surge of possessiveness rushes through me as I study the curve of her knees and the delicate arch of her neck. She's a vision. Truly stunning.

"Your parents... do they know about your penchant for poker?" she asks, her voice soft and teasing. She turns to face me, sunlight glinting off her curls. It makes her look like a fucking angel.

"Hardly," I scoff, taking a sip of my coffee. "They disapprove of almost everything I do. As far as I'm concerned, the less they know, the better."

"Should you invite the girl you're sleeping with to your very important poker tournament?" Her eyes hold genuine curiosity, underpinned by concern.

"Who said you were just the girl I'm sleeping with? Maybe you're the girl I'm *interested* in. Besides, I don't care what anyone thinks. I want you there with me."

"Even though we're not... an item?" she asks. She drops her gaze and looks away. I can't miss the hint of vulnerability in her voice.

I want to soothe that ache. I pull her against my chest and inhale her intoxicating scent. "Especially because we're not an item," I reply.

To my surprise, she doesn't push me on that front. Instead, she sips her coffee. Silence grows between us, but it doesn't feel awkward.

Annalise pushes back slightly, tilting her head as if considering something. "Nate, you play the stock market and win millions, right?"

"Yes." I narrow my eyes, trying to understand where she's going with this. "Why do you ask?"

Annalise's tone is casual.

"I'm just curious. I did some research on you. There are quite a few articles mentioning your prowess at the stock market." Her gaze is direct and unapologetic.

"So you've been stalking me online?" I joke. Really, I'm trying to mask my surprise.

"I spent a whole day researching you online," she fires back. "Right after we met. I decided I needed to know everything that there is to know about you. Now, are you going to answer my question?"

I think over my answer for a few beats. "Playing the market is all about strategy and timing. You need to know when to buy, when to sell, and be ready to take risks. I am as excellent at the stock market as I am at poker."

"Interesting," she muses, pursing her lips. "Give me a tip so that I know that you walk the walk instead of just talking the talk."

"Psh. You just want to make a little money."

Annalise licks her lips and then smiles wanly. "Okay. Say you're right. Tell me the next stock you're going to make millions off of."

"All right," I say. "I'm about to short a stock on the brink of collapse. It trades under IVZE. It's risky, but the potential rewards are immense."

Annalise's eyes widen. "Tell me more," she demands, her voice low and sultry.

I find her boldness nothing short of charming. "It's a tech company. Inflated valuations have propped them up, but their product is little more than vaporware. When the truth comes out, their shares will plummet. Those who bet against them will make a fortune."

"Sounds exhilarating," she says. Her luscious lips curve into a wicked grin. "I'm in."

"Great." I draw her closer and kiss her. She tastes like coffee and cream and luxury. "We can discuss the details later...."

Annalise interrupts me by capturing my lips in a searing kiss. Her hands tangle in my hair. I suck in a breath. God, I can't get enough of her. She's driving me out of my mind.

She pulls me closer as she straddles my lap. The feel of her body pressed against mine sends a shiver down my spine, erasing any lingering doubts about giving her advice.

TWENTY-ONE
ANNALISE

Beautiful people in tuxes and ballgowns press in on me from all sides. I smile and examine their faces, hoping Nate will be among them. But my gaze slides off the laughing women and jovial men.

He isn't anywhere to be seen.

The Take Back the Night Gala glitters around me as I circulate through the well-dressed crowd. I make sure to nod and smile at the right people. Inside, though, my mind races.

It's been three days since I laid eyes on Nate Fordham and I'm dying to know just where he is.

I snag a flute of champagne from a passing server and sip the bubbly beverage. What to do now?

I should turn my attention to my flagging company. It's no secret that Gellar Industries has been slipping these past few years. Our stock price is slowly sinking. But I refuse to let it continue. I'll do whatever it takes to right this ship and steer us back to success.

I desperately need to pay back the money my father stole before Nate finds out about it. He could take the merger over even the allegation of financial infidelities.

I work my way into social circles with venture capitalists, talking about how bright the future of our company is. "We're confident that we will perfect the ground-penetrating sonar. We plan to use it to find the next big shale oil deposit within a matter of months," I say.

Is that true? That remains to be seen. But the venture capitalists and CEOs that I schmooze seem impressed.

A familiar red-headed firecracker catches my eye as I talk to a new clique of silver-haired, Hugo Boss-wearing CEO types. To my shock, Lori Parker marches toward me. Even more bizarrely, she has Gellar Industries Chief Financial Officer Lance White in tow. Lance looks awkward in his tuxedo, running a finger under his bowtie. He's tall and storklike and his quiet demeanor makes him a dead fish at events like this.

It's strange to see them here. I thought I only authorized a single company ticket for appearances. But they each take one of my arms, tugging me firmly toward the deserted balcony.

"My apologies!" I call to the CEO I was just talking to.

"We need to talk. Now," Lori hisses under her breath. Lance's face is grim.

As they steer me outside, foreboding prickles down my spine. I paste on an imperious look and fold my arms to hide the goosebumps from the chill night air.

"What's this about? I'm busy securing our financial future in there."

Lance and Lori exchange loaded glances. My heart pounds traitorously.

What could Lance possibly know? About the missing funds, my secret stock market scheming?

"Well?" I lift my chin, my pulse beginning to race. "Out with it. I don't have all night."

Lori takes a deep breath. "Annalise, Lance came to me about some improprieties in the company ledgers."

I arch my eyebrows, feigning faint surprise. "What are you alleging?"

Lance clears his throat, straightening his bowtie with twitchy fingers.

"Well, Ms. Gellar, I was conducting a standard audit of the ledgers when I noticed some discrepancies. Small ones at first. Payments out misaligning with funds received."

"And?" I fold my arms across my chest.

"Right." Lance swallows hard. Perspiration dots his thinning hairline. "I printed duplicate copies to cross-reference. The figures were inconsistent across versions. They gave me completely different numbers. It's my opinion that someone deliberately cooked the books."

Lori interrupts, placing a manicured hand on my arm. Her expression is carefully blank. "Annalise, there's a significant sum unaccounted for. Millions. Upward of twenty, I think."

"Twenty-two million, four hundred twenty-seven thousand." Lance looks between us, pushing his glasses up the bridge of his nose. "To be exact."

Blood roars in my ears as I process the implications. Fuck. I wasn't ready for anybody else to find out about the missing money.

How much does Lance know?

I level Lance with a cutting glare, channeling all the authority of my pedigree. "Are you insinuating that I had something to do with this so-called missing money?" I let out a derisive snort. "I don't believe it. Millions disappearing without a trace under my watch? I find that quite difficult to believe."

"No one is saying that you had anything to do with it.

The money started disappearing twenty years ago," Lori says soothingly.

"That's right. You couldn't possibly be responsible." Lance wrings his hands. His eyes dart between Lori and me like a frantic rabbit. "When I made my discovery, I thought I was going crazy. That's why I consulted Ms. Parker for a second opinion."

"I'm afraid he's right." Lori gives me a sympathetic glance. "The evidence is all there, plain as day. We wanted to come to you quietly before jumping to conclusions or making accusations."

I survey them both with impassive eyes. My mind races behind the mask of stony composure. How should I play this? Would it be better to feign ignorance and righteous outrage? Will Lance fold under threats?

"You say we don't have proof yet that my father is involved in this, and I won't throw him under the bus just because it's convenient. What's our plan?"

Lance hesitates for a moment, weighing his words carefully. "If you're willing to take this seriously, we could bring forensic accountants to investigate the discrepancies. They'll scour the books and determine any merit to these claims."

"Forensic accountants? That could take months. If Gellar Industries is indeed hemorrhaging money as you claim, we don't have that kind of time."

"Annalise, I understand your concerns," Lori says. Her eyes are steady on my face. "Let's not act rashly. It's better to take time to figure out what exactly we are dealing with."

"Ms. Gellar." Lance's tone is impatient. "If there's money missing, I'm committing a crime by not notifying the FEC immediately. I put my career in jeopardy. Not to mention the company's reputation."

"I hear you." I put my hands behind my back and start to pace. "I agree that we have to proceed with the investigation. But we have to keep this discreet. No red flags. Lance can contact an outside team of forensic accountants and the team can scrutinize the trail of the missing money."

Lance looks relieved. "Thank you, Ms. Gellar."

"No, I should thank you. Not every finance man is as ethical as you are, Mr. White."

He blushes. "Of course, ma'am."

Lance's footsteps echo across the polished marble floor as he strides back into the lavish gala. Lori and I are left alone in the cool night air.

"Annalise," Lori begins. "I'm sorry that we pounced on you. Lance sandbagged me. I didn't even have the time to send you a text."

"It's okay," I assure her. I exhale a long breath. "God, I was hoping to replace all the missing funds before anyone noticed."

Lori sends me a distressed expression. "There's something you need to know. I've done some digging of my own. I checked the IT logs, trying to see if the person who did this was stupid enough to leave their digital fingerprints all over their logins. The login used to make those money transfers *was* your father's login. But it probably wasn't him."

"What?" My heart skips a beat. "What are you saying?"

"I looked into the dates more deeply. I just checked your father's business calendar before, to line up the dates of the withdrawals with his availability. But it turns out that your father was actually out of town during two of the transactions. His personal secretary had the dates and times of every flight he took, including two flights that would have taken him out of the country just before two of the transactions." Lori takes a beats. "The level of sophistication needed to fake the login records is beyond anything your father could have done himself. It's *possible* that he hired help, but I know you father very well. It's doubtful that he committed this fraud."

"Then who could've done it?" I demand, incredulous.

I already know the players in this game, though. My father, Don Young, even Lori or Lance. There's also the distinct possibility that it was someone else. But who? Who else would have the company knowledge and access to the bank accounts?

Without further evidence, there are just too many suspects.

"Thank you, Lori," I murmur. "I'll find the damn truth, no matter what it takes."

"We'll find out who is responsible. Lance and I have that covered. Your job is figuring out how you'll handle this when it becomes public."

I look at her with surprise. "You think it will?"

"Lance just assured us that the information will be public knowledge sooner or later. Your task will be disciplining the perpetrator. It's easy to fire the guy if he's a VP like Don. But what if Lance starts making noise?"

I raise a trembling hand to my heart. Lori is right, of course. The public will need a strong response from the acting CEO to ensure the survival of Gellar Industries.

When I don't respond, Lori squeezes my arm comfortingly. Then she leaves me alone on the balcony with my thoughts. All I can think is that someone is playing a dangerous game.

And I won't let them sacrifice me or Gellar Industries as part of their endgame.

Twenty-Two
Nate

The sun casts long shadows across Central Park. I'm dressed in loose, gray sweatpants and a black t-shirt. As I lean against a bench, I stretch my quads, mindful of the run I will go on soon.

If my damn private investigator ever shows up.

I search the park patrons for his face. A nanny pushing a stroller. Two young guys at a hot dog stand, and an older vendor. Several older women with austere expressions speed-walking past.

I walk impatiently to the nearby Alice in Wonderland statue and check my watch. The cool breeze of early autumn brushes against my face, but it does little to soothe the burning that I feel.

Annalise Gellar has been on my mind for far too long. I have questions about her that only Rahim can answer.

"Mr. Fordham." A gruff voice pulls me from my thoughts. I turn to find Rahim Abbas standing behind me. He's dressed in a ratty gray sportscoat and worn jeans.

There is nothing noteworthy about Rahim whatsoever. He blends in perfectly on a New York City street.

"Let's keep moving," he suggests, jerking his thumb over his shoulder. Without waiting, he starts walking. Rahim's natural walking pace is quick and I have to jog a few steps to keep up.

"Have you found anything?" I demand. "You've been following Ms. Gellar for a few weeks but you haven't reported anything."

"Nothing out of the ordinary," Rahim answers, shrugging slightly. "Ms. Gellar is just going about her business. Other than her frequent overnight visits to your penthouse, she doesn't go anywhere other than work and home."

That's not terribly surprising. I didn't expect Rahim to find any skeletons hidden in Annalise's closet. She's too young to have much to hide.

"I'd like you to switch your focus. I want you to dig up dirt on the board members of Gellar Industries. I want to know anything that I can use as leverage against them."

He raises an eyebrow, clearly not expecting this change of direction. But he is the very definition of discretion. "You got it, Mr. Fordham." He doesn't ask questions about what I need the information for. He is the consummate professional private investigator.

I slip my hand into my pocket and pull out an envelope stuffed with cash. He looks at me coolly as I hand it over. He gives me a nod as he slips the envelope into his jacket.

"Anything else?" Rahim asks.

I shake my head. "No. Contact me as soon as you have something."

"Will do." He shoves his hands into the pockets of his jeans, then begins to jog quickly in the other direction.

My fingers tap restlessly against my thigh as I watch him dash away. My mind runs over the information that Rahim just gave me.

Annalise is living a quiet life. No surprise there. But it

does warm me to know that she's not some party animal in the hours that I don't see her.

What am I doing? Annalise Gellar has wormed her way into my thoughts in a way no other woman has before. I can't seem to help it. And it infuriates me.

But her determination, stubbornness, and intelligence make me infatuated with her. The fact that it's all wrapped up in that petite, blonde package drives me wild.

It's causing me to lose focus on what matters. When was the last time I went to my office to do some work alone? It's been weeks.

"Get a grip, Nate," I mutter. "Annalise Gellar is just a girl."

I wind my way over to the Central Park Boathouse, where my brothers Cash and James wait. Their laughter rings out like a familiar song, forcing me from my angsty thoughts. They approach me with wide grins.

"Look who finally decided to show his ugly mug." Cash jabs an elbow into my side.

I can't help but smirk at his playful banter. "I wouldn't miss it for the world," I retort, matching his tone. "You two always know how to treat me well."

"You bet we do," James chimes in. "Come on, slowpoke. We'll get you in shape one of these days."

"I am in shape!" I protest.

James looks at Cash. At once, they exclaim, "Nahhhh."

I roll my eyes. Just because I don't run in the park often doesn't mean that I've ever skipped a day at my gym with my trainer.

We set off slowly, allowing ourselves to settle into a comfortable rhythm.

"Hey, did you hear about Cash's latest conquests?" James chuckles. He glances at me with a conspiratorial grin.

"Conquests?" I raise an eyebrow. "As in multiple? No, do tell."

Cash smirks, reveling in the attention. He's such a fucking ham. "I'm simultaneously juggling a supermodel, a lawyer, and a diner waitress. My life's hectic right now, just how I like it."

"Sounds like a disaster waiting to happen," I say. A hint of admiration lurks beneath my words. Cash has always been the Casanova of our brothers. He unapologetically embraces his hedonistic tendencies.

"Don't be such a nag, Nate." Cash dismisses my concerns with a wave of his hand. "That's what we have James for."

"Why am I catching stray bullets?" James gripes. "I'm always looking out for you guys, and this is the thanks I get."

I flash James a grin. "Don't forget that I'm technically the oldest son by twenty-seven minutes."

"Oh, don't worry. I'm pretty certain that your tombstone will read, *Nate Fordham: a decent poker player, a lousy skeet shooter. Oldest brother by twenty-seven minutes.*"

His words make me laugh hard enough that I fall behind my brothers for a few paces. By the time I catch back up, Cash is saying, "I've got everything under control. The three girls don't know anything about each other, and I plan to keep it that way. What's life without a little risk?"

"Speaking of risks," James grumbles. His tone is as prickly as his personality. "I've got enough on my plate without worrying about Cash's escapades. Have I told you about Charlie?"

"Charlie?" I ask, getting winded.

"My best friend Derek's eighteen-year-old whirlwind," he explains, shaking his head in exasperation. "Derek has been sick, as you know. He's got stomach cancer. Well, Charlie has been staying at my place because Derek has been in and out of the hospital a lot lately. And she's been ruining my life. She has temper tantrums like a fucking child."

"She sounds like a handful," Cash smirks. He seems amused by the idea of our grumpy brother dealing with a rebellious teenager.

"More than a handful," James confirms, his frustration evident.

"She's driving me crazy. I've caught her sneaking out to clubs and coming home at ungodly hours. This week, she's suspended from her high school..."

I give James a sympathetic look. "And how is Addison taking it?"

At the mention of his long-term girlfriend, James pales. "Not well. I keep telling her that it's just temporary. When Derek is back on his feet, I will gleefully kick Charlie out."

"Good for you," Cash chuckles. "It's good to have a plan so your girlfriend doesn't murder you in your sleep."

I scoff, rolling my eyes. "I'm sure James will be fine."

"Yes, well." A mischievous glint appears in Cash's eye. "Nate, it's your turn in the hot seat. Isn't it time that you came clean about your latest obsession?"

"Obsession?" I feign ignorance. My heart rate spikes despite my best efforts to play it cool.

"Annalise Gellar," Cash grins, practically salivating at the opportunity to tease me. "I heard you two have been spending a lot of time together lately. Tell me the truth. Have you got a thing for her?"

"That's just a stupid rumor." I dismiss his words with a snort, even as images of Annalise flood my mind.

Her blonde curls, her fiery defiance, the way she challenges me at every turn. The way she looked wearing nothing but my button-up last week...

I grit my teeth. "You know I don't mix business with pleasure."

"Sure, sure," James chimes in, clearly not buying my denial. "Stone cold Nate Fordham. A man never distracted by anything but the bottom line."

"Exactly," I retort. My jaw clenches as I push myself harder. My muscles scream in protest.

But no amount of physical stress can hide the truth. I have definitely mixed business and pleasure. And in Annalise, I've found a wealth of desire, a deep well of confusion, and a hint of vulnerability that I refuse to acknowledge.

"Whatever you say, brother," Cash smirks. "She's just a girl that you know. Right?"

I don't answer, pushing myself ahead. "I'll race you to those benches!"

Sweat trickles down my temple just as we reach a row of benches beneath the dappled shade of a cluster of oak trees. We sprawl out, chests heaving and limbs aching from our punishing run through Central Park. Once we start to cool down, Cash resumes needling me.

"All right, Nate," Cash says. "Unless you plan to marry Archer Gellar's daughter, you need to man up. I'm ready to put the pieces in place to tank Gellar Industries' stock. Tell me that I can go ahead with it."

I pause. Cash doesn't know I've already signed the merger paperwork with Annalise. It wouldn't hurt my company to tank the stock and let Gellar Industries twist in the wind. But it will complicate things with Annalise.

I know Cash is only trying to provoke a reaction. But the mere suggestion of betraying Annalise sends a shiver down my spine. I push myself up on my elbows and glare at Cash.

"Things with Gellar Industries are in a fragile place right now. I don't want to do anything hasty." My intention is to sound detached, but a tremor in my words robs them of confidence.

"What the hell is going on right now?" James asks. "You've never been one to waver with business, Nate. What's different this time?"

I'm acutely aware of their scrutiny. Still, I can't admit that I might have a heart. Not even to my brothers, let alone everyone else. My brothers would lose all respect for me.

I swallow the lump in my throat and force a smirk onto my face. "Nothing's different," I lie, my tone dripping with disdain. "I've got everything under control."

"Give me the word, then. I'll start lining everything up for Gellar Industries to take a swan dive."

I swat his words away. "Fine! If it will make you leave me the fuck alone, you can put the pieces in place. But I'm telling you, Cash. Don't do anything more than that. I'll pull the trigger when I'm ready."

Cash's eyes gleam with excitement. He leaps up from the bench, clapping me on the shoulder. "I knew you'd come around. You won't regret this. We are going to be *rich*."

"We're already rich," James says. "Try again."

"Okay, so we'll be filthy *stinking* rich. Is that better?"

I grimace and check my watch. "Let's get going. I have meetings this afternoon that I have to get to."

Cash claps me on the back. "There's the cold, money-machine I know and love."

As we head back towards the park entrance, I force myself to keep pace with my brother's long strides. But my brain slows down, thoughts of Annalise making me struggle to keep up.

Her captivating smile, fierce determination, and how she challenges me like no one else. I picture her face when she realizes I've just sold her out for a few million.

It makes my chest feel tight.

My brothers' laughter and teasing resumes as we continue our jog. It's as if nothing has changed. But I can't help but feel the weight of the decision I've just made.

Can I follow through with it even if it means losing the one woman who's managed to break down my carefully constructed walls?

Twenty-Three

God. What am I doing here?

The answer is simple. I'm going out without Nate. It seems like lately, all I do is go to work and then have passionate sex with Nate at his place. While I'm all for the multiple orgasms Nate gives me, a thought has nagged me for the last couple of days.

It feels like I'm starting to depend on Nate Fordham to have a good time. And I can't have that. Nate and I have a very specific relationship. One that was outlined in a contract, for god's sake.

I need to exist outside of Nate and his expectations for a night. And it just so happened that my cousin Dana texted me an invite to go clubbing. She always sends them, but I've never answered.

Until tonight.

I swallow tightly. The bass pulses like a second heartbeat. It thuds against my chest as I step into the room. Neon lights streak across a throng of people on the dance floor. The bodies in motion lit from above are a strange new art form. The air is thick. I smell designer fragrances mixed with the tang of sweat.

Do I really want to go any further?

My mother's voice, a ruthless echo of etiquette in my head, screeches at full volume in my head. I swivel my gaze and take in the scantily clad dancers. At the bar, a group of men down a shot. A woman in a ruby-red dress makes out with a man twice her age.

There are so many things that Monique Gellar would hate with a passion. But the Annalise she raised to sit primly, legs crossed, and lips sealed, is not here tonight.

The strobes catch my reflection in a nearby mirror as I follow my cousin past it. Blonde curls bounce untamed around my petite shoulders. A sparkly white minidress clings to my frame. I even catch a glint of rebellion in my eyes. For once, I'm not the nice girl.

I'm someone else entirely.

My cousin Dana catches my hand. "I'm so glad you came out!"

"I'm glad you invited me," I intone. But I'm pretty sure that the pulsating music's chaotic sounds swallow my words.

Dana is undoubtedly crowing in victory at the sight of me finally stepping off the pedestal of perfection. Our whole lives, I've been the good one, while Dana has been the one my parents whisper about.

Poor girl, caught out partying at all hours. She's only thirteen!

I remember, all too well, the satisfied smirks my parents shared in secret. They were gleeful because they liked to see others struggle. Or maybe because they knew that their little girl would never dare to be caught out late?

What would Archer and Monique say now? I don't even have to wonder.

"Hey! Keep up with me, please! I don't want to lose you in this crowd," Dana says. "I know this is your first time at a club, so it's vital that you stick to me like glue."

My stomach does a flip. Dana's perfect smile, and perfect pinup blonde locks, do little to reassure me.

"Okay," I mumble. Inside, I'm wondering if this was a terrible idea.

Dana grins. "No need to look like I'm marching you to the firing squad. Cheer up! It's a party!"

Taking my hand, Dana sails back to our secluded VIP nook. In the dark, a champagne bucket and glasses sit, chilling.

Her grin is as effervescent as she pops the cork and pours champagne for us both. A waitress swishes by our table and sets down a tray clinking with shots of clear liquid.

Without a word, Dana passes the woman a hundred. My cousin turns to me, her excitement evident. She waves her hand over the tray. "I ordered some tequila for us."

I shake my head. "Uh, no thanks. I've never had tequila before."

"Come on, Annalise, live a little," she teases. She nudges a shot toward me. It's an invitation to sin, wrapped in good-natured camaraderie.

I hesitate. Isn't this exactly why I agreed to come here? To loosen up and experience something I haven't before?

"Should we toast to new experiences?" I ask.

"Damn right," Dana shouts over the music. We clink the small glasses together and take the shot. I only get half of it down my throat before the burn of the alcohol makes me gasp. I cough and try to suck in a breath, spitting the rest of the shot onto the floor.

"Whoops!" Dana laughs, pounding my back. "It's okay. That's why I got a bunch of shots."

She hands me a couple of cocktail napkins. I splutter as I dab at the tequila that I spilled on my dress. "Sorry, Dana."

"Seriously, don't give it a second thought. Just sit back and get comfy." She squeezes my arm. "I'm stoked you called me. This place?" She gestures expansively to the club full of gyrating bodies and pulsating lights. "This is where I reign."

"You come here a lot?" I ask. I flush. Do I already sound drunk?

"Yep. I've been coming here for a decade," Dana says.

My eyes bulge out. Dana is only twenty-four. Is she saying that she came here at fourteen years old?

The sound changes and she lets out a howl. "Oooh, I love this song! Come on, Annalise. We have to dance!"

She stands up and does another shot. When I hesitate, she puts the shot glass to my mouth and tips it up. I can only open and accept the flood of alcohol she pours down my throat. My mouth fills quickly and the extra tequila sluices down my chin.

I wipe my mouth as I swallow. It suddenly occurs to me how much taking tequila shots is like having a man come in your mouth. The thought makes me gasp with laughter.

"Ready?" Dana asks. It isn't so much a question as a summons. The dance floor awaits.

"Ready as I'll ever be," I declare. I can feel the alcohol now. It's igniting a rare recklessness within me.

I think I like tequila, I decide.

Hand in hand, we leave the safety of the VIP lounge. The entire dance floor is laid out before us. A pulsating mass of bodies moves in sync with the beat. Dana plunges into the fray. She's absolutely uninhibited, and as she pulls me along it's all I can do to hang on for the ride.

She finds a spot for us and throws her hands up in the air, swaying to the music. I feel like I'm nothing but sharp elbows and awkward steps. Watching the people around me shimmy and swirl euphorically only makes me more anxious.

"I'm a bad dancer!!" I shout into Dana's ear.

"Practice makes perfect! Nobody's watching," Dana shouts over the music. She moves her head in time with her arms. "You have to feel the rhythm!"

I paste a smile on my face and carry on. Slowly, I realize that most of the people around me have their eyes closed. That helps me to feel like they're not staring at me. A current of electricity starts to seep up from the soles of my feet to the tips of fingers. The beating pulse of the music envelops me.

It's freeing to discover that no one cares. Not about my clumsy steps. Not about my money or my job. Here, I am truly anonymous. I'm free from the scrutiny that accompanies my last name.

I dance with abandon. The seductive allure of being a secret hidden in plain sight lures out a side of me that I didn't know existed!

"Look at you!" Dana laughs as she twirls around me. "Who knew the ice queen could melt?"

"Watch it," I retort, playfully.

But she's right. I feel alive in a way that I never have before.

We dance for a few more songs before Dana cups her hands around my ear. "Let's take a break!"

I nod enthusiastically. We retreat to our velvet-lined haven in the VIP section. The music softens once we sit in the leather booth.

Dana wipes her forehead with the back of her hand. "We've set that floor on fire."

"That was so fun!" I crow. I fan my face, feeling flushed.

"It only gets more fun the longer you stay." Dana winks at me and offers me a glass of champagne.

I giggle and sip. This time, when Dana takes another tequila shot, I do one along with her. I'm feeling loose and hot, and I'm grinning ear to ear.

Why have I never done this before? I wonder.

As I sink into the plush couch, a familiar face causes a jolt of electricity to arc through me.

Nate —imposing and impossibly handsome—casually sits down in our booth. His gray eyes seem silver in the sporadic flicker of the strobe lights.

"Look what the cat dragged in," Dana purrs, sliding over to Nate with a confidence that borders on audacity. "Nate Fordham, as I live and breathe."

"You two know each other?" I ask. Suddenly, I'm wracking my brain to remember if Dana ever mentioned having a crush on a Nate. But I come up empty.

Nate leans forward, pinning me in place with his gaze. "We've met," he concedes. "We don't know each other that well, though."

I gulp. "That's... nice."

"It's a rare pleasure to get Nate here all to ourselves," Dana yells. "Don't have to get up early, I assume?"

"No." He doesn't even make eye contact with her.

I'm sweating over here.

She bombards him with questions, each more intrusive than the last. He parries them with the ease of a man accustomed to dodging prying inquiries. His politeness is disarming. But it's clear to me that he's not here to play twenty questions with my cousin.

At last, Dana gets bored and excuses herself to go to the restroom. I don't move to join her, and she huffs as she turns to go.

"How did you find me?" I ask once she's out of earshot.

"Maybe I wanted to relax in this loud, hot room. Ever think of that?" He tilts his head.

I narrow my eyes at him. "I think you're full of it, Nate."

He chuckles, a low, resonant sound that dances down my spine. "I have eyes everywhere, Annalise. I wasn't looking for you, but I still found you."

"Here I am. Now that you've found me, what are you going to do about it?"

An unspoken challenge hangs between us. A test of wills that's as intoxicating as the top-shelf liquor that's flowing in this club.

"Wouldn't you like to know?" His reply nonplusses me.

I stand up and do another shot. Nate's eyebrows rise. I smirk at him. "I think you're just here to torment me. And I hate it. Come dance with me."

"I enjoy watching," he drawls. He eyes me with an intensity that scorches my skin.

"Scared you can't keep up?" I tease. I'm probably going too far, but I don't care.

"I'm just here to watch the show." He sits back, draping his arms over the back of the couch.

Frustration nips at me. I down another shot and liquid courage fuels my determination. The fire left behind in my throat is nothing compared to the feeling Nate ignites in me.

"Your loss," I toss over my shoulder. I hope the words are an invitation.

But he doesn't follow me as I push out onto the dance floor.

For a minute, I shimmy and slide around the dance floor. But soon, a man starts to dance closer and closer. I welcome him, moving my hips in a way that I judge to be seductive. It works, because his hands soon find purchase against my hips. His fingertips graze my skin through the fabric of my dress.

I should feel uneasy. This is a stranger, after all. But instead, I feel a provocative thrill. I'm *desired*.

I can't see Nate. I know he's watching, though. I flirt with danger with every swaying step, daring this man to pull me closer.

Really, I'm daring Nate to react. To see what's normally his for the taking getting rubbed up against and grinded on.

The stranger's grip tightens. He is making a possessive claim that sends a jolt of alarm through me. Too much, too soon. His eagerness seems like a stark contrast to Nate's controlled detachment.

"Easy," I warn. "You're hurting me."

But the man seems deaf to my warning. He growls and tries to grab my face. I think he's trying to kiss me.

"No!" I hiss. My heart is a hummingbird in my chest.

The stranger's hands clamp down even harder on my body. My breath hitches. I try to extricate myself, but he's a determined wall of a man.

Panic crests within me like a tidal wave ready to break. "Let go," I plead. "You–"

Out of nowhere, Nate explodes onto the scene, a storm of fury and dark hair. Like a crack of thunder, his fist sends the stranger crumpling to the floor. The stranger howls and holds his jaw, but the sound is lost into the sound vortex of the club.

Nate leans down to my ear. "Nobody touches what's mine," he growls. His voice, low and primal, resonates with a possessiveness that shoots shivers down my spine. "You're mine, Annalise."

He grips my hand. The nightclub becomes a blur of lights and shadows. As we escape into the cool Manhattan night, Nate doesn't pause. His purposeful strides carry me to a sleek SUV idling at the curb and I follow him inside.

He doesn't say a word to me as the driver pulls away from the curb. His presence is an electric current charging the air between us. He studies me, his slate-colored eyes taking my measure.

Without warning, Nate surges forward. His lips crash against mine. My hands come up to press against the wall of his chest.

The kiss is a maelstrom, fierce and demanding. It scorches through my doubts, ignites my desires. It brands me as irrevocably *his*.

I melt against him and surrender to the overwhelming sensation.

Nate is all I want. Despite my feelings that I might be getting hooked on him, the fact remains. He's *my* protector. *My* tempest. *My* billionaire, with eyes only for *me*.

TWENTY-FOUR
NATE

I'm standing in Annalise's immaculate penthouse, clenching and unclenching my fists. Annalise, the beautiful blonde bombshell who turned my world upside down, was much too drunk for me to fuck last night. There was some intense kissing, and I sucked her clit while she *screamed* my name, but that was it.

She'd left scratch marks on my upper back. Kitten, indeed.

After that, I played the gentleman and put her to bed. She begged me to fuck her. And my body ached to do so. But I still found my own bed and stroked my cock alone until I came. Then I did it again four more times.

Annalise will be the death of me, I swear. Suffice to say, I did not sleep well last night.

"Ready?" Annalise's voice jars me back to the present.

She's standing in the front entryway, looking at me with this quizzical gaze. She's dressed in the Valentino couture that I picked out for her. Floor length white sequins with these jaw-dropping slits cut up the thighs. We're just going to a poker tournament but *damn*. I wanted her to dress to kill today. And might I say that I nailed it.

She looks *divine*.

The tension from last night hasn't left my body. I still feel jumpy, on edge. Something about this woman has changed me. She's awakened feelings I didn't know I possessed.

Annalise is mine. And I'm going to show her off today, albeit not in the way that she deserves. I'm just taking her to a tournament, not to Bryant Park. It's a shame with how she looks right now.

"Nate?" she prompts. "Are you okay?"

My mouth twitches. It's funny that she would ask me that. Am I okay? I really don't know anymore. "Of course," I reply. "You just look ravishing. Especially for someone who threw up this morning."

Okay, so maybe I am still irked that she got so fucking intoxicated the night before. As if reading my thoughts, she smiles sweetly and teases me. "Sorry I was such a mess last night. You must think I'm quite the party animal."

"Hardly," I scoff, my tone betraying my annoyance. "You do look good though. Really good."

I walk over to Annalise. She turns her face up to me, expecting a kiss. I grab her, pull her against my body, and growl as I kiss her neck. She giggles. "You're such a beast, Nate."

"Yeah? You'll find out what a beast I am when we get home. I'm going to fucking ruin that pussy, Kitten."

She arches an eyebrow, affecting surprise. "More than you did last night?"

"Way fucking more." I set her down and slap her ass. "Now let's go."

We make our way down to my sleek black sports car. I can't help but glance at her petite frame and her golden curls that bounce as she walks. In the Valentino dress, she looks like a damn supermodel. Maybe a little short, but she's got the charisma needed. A feeling of possessiveness claws at my chest. I've experienced that before with Annalise. But today the feeling is all I can think about.

She is *mine*.

The sensation is as unsettling as it is thrilling.

We drive up to the tournament, which is happening just on the other side of the Lincoln Tunnel at a trendy bistro on the water. When we get out, I toss the car keys to a valet. But I'm not really paying any attention. If the car were to be stolen and the cops asked me who the valet was, I'd be at a complete loss.

Today, I can hardly focus on anything but Annalise.

Her presence is both intoxicating and infuriating. She makes it impossible for me to concentrate, even on just the act of walking. We walk down the pier to where the bistro has set up an outdoor casino. But every little thing distracts me. My mind is filled with images of her nude form wrapped around mine.

"Earth to Nate," Annalise says, waving a delicate hand in my face. I blink, realizing that I've been lost in my thoughts again. "Are you okay?"

"Fine," I say. "I just didn't sleep much last night."

Annalise is mine. But I don't want to say it out loud in a public space. That makes it seem too real.

She slips her hand into mine and wrinkles her nose. "Sorry. I'll have to make it up to you later." She gives me an innocuous glance, belying her words. I can't do anything but smirk.

What is it about this woman that is making me question everything I thought I knew about myself? I'm rethinking my concept of desire. It's a dangerous game we're playing.

I'm not sure I'm ready for whatever the consequences will be.

We enter an area with several tables specifically designed for high-stakes poker games. Plush velvet chairs surround the polished mahogany tables. Poker games like this are where deals are made and empires built.

Or, in Annalise's case, they're destroyed.

We grab a drink from the outside bar as I try to scope out the competition. Better to focus on that than my feelings for Annalise.

I ask for a rum old-fashioned, but when the bartender asks her for her order, my date wrinkles her nose. "Just a sparkling water for me. After last night, I don't think I'll be interested in drinking for quite a while."

I smile. With our drinks in hand, we stroll around, checking out the set-up of tables.

"Playing poker and negotiating deals share the same core principles," I explain to her. "You need to be able to read people, bluff when necessary, and most importantly... know when to fold."

My brothers, Cash, James, and Grant enter the room as if on cue. All their eyes immediately go to Annalise. Like wolves stalking their prey, they close in on her, each vying to win her attention.

"Annalise! It's so nice to see you again." Cash immediately starts trying to separate her from me. He's using the old introduction trick, where you shake both the woman's hands and then pull her away from the man she's with.

"Stop, Cash," I intone. I put my arm around Annalise, feeling like she's some precious gemstone, then introduce the other two. "Annalise, these are my brothers. You already know Cash. This is James, and the other one is Grant," I say, trying to maintain a semblance of control over the situation.

James gives her a mock bow and Grant a lazy wave. As

they swarm around her, I can see the glint of apprehension in her eyes.

"Nice to meet you all," she says hesitantly. She's clearly overwhelmed by their sudden interest. "All the Fordham brothers at once? I've really lucked out."

"Getting us all in one place is a rare pleasure," Cash jokes. "Seriously, though. Nate has told us a *lot* about you."

"He's being sarcastic," says Grant. He clears his throat. "Er, if that wasn't clear."

"What is there to tell?" Annalise says. She looks at me, sucking in a breath. "Your brother has been teaching me in the ins-and-outs of being a CEO."

"I just bet he has. At all hours, I imagine," James says blithely. Grant hits him on the arm and James mouths, "Ow!"

Annalise tenses. Sensing her discomfort, I slip my arm down, letting it land protectively around her waist. I can create something of a barrier between her and my brothers. She rolls her eyes but doesn't protest.

"This is certainly an interesting way to introduce me to your family, Nate."

I feel the back of my neck heat. "We already planned to meet up here," I mutter. My grip tightens around Annalise's waist. "I wasn't going to bail just because you needed saving last night."

A delicate blush creeps up her cheeks, making her look even more enticing than before. Shit, I think I embarrassed her. That was not what I was going for.

"Thanks," she replies quietly. I can't tell if she's being sincere or not. Before I can say anything, my brother saves the day.

"Anyone need a drink? I'm going to head to the bar," Grant says.

"I'll go with you!" Annalise blurts. "I could use some juice or something."

He offers her his arm. She takes it and swans off with Grant, not bothering to look back.

Once they're out of earshot, James turns to me. "She's too young for you, Nate," he warns, his tone harsh. "You shouldn't even be sleeping with her."

"Relax," I scoff, rolling my eyes. "I'm not going to marry Annalise. We're both just having a little fun."

I resent his interference, but a part of me wonders if he's right. She *is* too young. She should be with someone her own age, someone also just starting out...

"Isn't that worse?" James counters, raising an eyebrow. "There's more than a ten-year age gap between you two. People will talk."

"Let them," I snap, my irritation rising. I don't need anyone else dictating my life choices, especially not when it comes to Annalise. "I'm still the richest motherfucker in this whole damn place."

James rolls his eyes. "Uh huh."

I can't help but feel chagrined by James's words. I glance over to see Grant talking animatedly with Annalise. I'm not worried about him hitting on her. Grant has always focused more on his passions, like robotics and AI, than on romantic pursuits.

But I wonder if Annalise isn't using this as an opportunity to discover what skeletons I might be hiding in my closet. And with Grant's obsession with telling the truth? He might just give them to her.

"James," I call out, motioning for my brother to join me. "Keep an eye on those two, will you? Grant can get intense when he talks about his projects."

"Sure thing, Nate," James replies with a nod. He makes his way over to them and cuts in on their conversation.

With that taken care of, I join Cash at the poker table. I'm trying everything in my power to regain control over the situation. But as the dealer shuffles the cards, my eyes drift back to Annalise. Her laughter fills the air. I swear I can smell her distinctive fragrance.

As the game heats up, I fold again and again. I just can't pay attention for the time it takes to play a whole game. Is last night's sleeplessness the cause?

Or is it something more?

"Your head's not in the game today, Nate," Cash teases me when I lose yet another hand. "I have a feeling that it has to do with a certain pretty blonde. Could it be that you're *in love?*"

"Shut up," I snap, glaring at him. My heart races in my chest, though I refuse to explore the reasons why I have such a visceral reaction. "I'm just tired."

"From your night with Annalise?" he presses with a smirk. "It's just that you've never had trouble focusing with a woman around before. Hell, we've been coming to this poker tournament for five years, and this is the first time that you've brought a *date.*"

"Enough, Cash." I grit my teeth.

My situation with Annalise is just a fling, I remind myself. It's a temporary distraction from the cold, calculated world of business that we both inhabit.

I glance across the room and watch Annalise's eyes light up with curiosity as she listens to Grant talk. Most women would be desperate to leave by now because Grant likes to monologue about whatever nerdy thing he's fixated on lately. But not Annalise. She is genuinely engaged, not merely listening to Grant's endless stories.

Annalise's patience and kindness make her all the more desirable to me. I can't help but wonder if my feelings for her run more deeply than I am willing to admit.

When Cash leans his head close to my ear and whispers, his voice almost compassionate. "Give it up, Nate. You're not fooling anyone. You've caught feelings for her."

I shoot him a stony glare. "For Archer Gellar's daughter? I'm just sleeping with her."

He folds his arms across his chest and shakes his head at my stubbornness. "I can't believe that the most business-minded of my brothers is acting like a teenaged boy with a bad crush. It's stunning to watch."

"Pay attention to your damn cards," I growl. I refuse to let him see how much his words have affected me.

I put all my focus on winning the next hand.

The room seems to close in on me as I lose anyway. I'm usually so good at reading everyone, but it seems that I've lost my touch.

As I open my mouth to excuse myself, a couple walks down the pier, arm in arm. I stand up as I stare at them.

My parents are here. Jesus fucking Christ, like I need this kind of trouble today.

Douglas and Celia Fordham scan the tables. When they locate me, my hackles instantly rise. I'm already questioning everything about my relationship with Annalise. The last thing I need to add to the mix is their scrutiny.

Cash notices my parents too. "Shit. I thought they were still on their year-long trip through Europe." He coughs into his hand. "Heads up."

My parents are bad news. They are in the US very rarely, but when they are present, they throw everything into chaos.

"I see them." I push back from the table. "Do me a favor and head them off. I'm going to get Annalise out of here before Mom and Dad rip her to shreds."

"On it." Cash stands up and makes a beeline for Mom. "You're already done traveling? How time flies!"

I reach Annalise's side, gripping her arm firmly.

"Hey, Mom and Dad are here," Grant says.

I make hard eye contact with him. "I'm going to escort Annalise out."

Annalise looks bewildered. "What?"

"Come with me," I whisper harshly.

Annalise's eyes widen slightly in surprise. But she doesn't protest as I lead her away from the tables and hurry toward the exit. "Is everything okay?" she asks.

"Fine," I lie, forcing a tight smile. "I am just hoping to help you escape—"

"Nathan!" My mom shouts.

I freeze in place, my mind going blank.

"Fuck," I mutter.

Licking my lips, I turn around. My parents are walking toward me. My mom looks Annalise up and down with a calculating glance.

I grit my teeth. The last thing I want is for them to see any cracks in my façade.

"Nathan, darling," Mom says. "It's too late to run, I'm afraid. We've arrived."

Her accent is very posh and British. She has short dark hair that's stylishly shot with gray, and she wears a loose black caftan with pink roses embroidered on it. Dad looks like exactly what he is: a wealthy man in a herringbone sport coat and khakis, who would always rather be playing golf than be wherever he is.

"Annalise," I say with a sigh. "I'd like you to meet Celia and Douglas. My mother and father."

The frosty tone of my introduction is a testament to my agitation.

Mom's cold gaze sweeps over Annalise. Her mouth curls into a tight smile that doesn't reach her eyes. "You can call me Mrs. Fordham. How do you do?"

"It's a pleasure to meet you both," Annalise replies. She inclines her head but makes no move to shake hands. She seems confident and unbothered, impressing me despite my agitation.

"Annalise is a business associate," I interject. I'm eager to establish some boundaries before my parents start prying.

"Really?" my father chimes in, his eyebrows raised. "She seems a bit too young for you, Nate. To do any kind of *business* with, that is."

My jaw clenches. I struggle to bite back a retort.

Annalise jumps into the fray and easily laughs at my father's comment. "Age is just a number, Mr. Fordham," she assures my father. "Nate has been tutoring me in all the skills I need to run my father's business."

"Is that right?" my mother asks. Her gaze narrows. "I can't imagine what form that tutelage takes. Can you, Douglas?"

The implication alone ignites a fire within me. It's a fight to keep my expression neutral. Instead, I simply nod and say, "Well, it was lovely seeing you both, but I have a meeting to attend."

"On a Saturday morning?" Dad chortles. "I'll just bet you do."

"Don't let us keep you." My mom smirks and looks at me. "Darling, while we are in town, we should have lunch. I'll have my assistant call yours and set something up."

"Uh huh," I say, not committing to anything. "I'll see you both later."

Gripping Annalise's hand, I guide her away from my parents and down the pier. The wait for the valet feels everlasting. My chest tightens each minute until we get into the car. I rub my chest and take a few deep breaths.

"That was... interesting," Annalise says. She looks at me, putting a hand on my shoulder. "Are you okay?"

I shake off her touch and start the car. "I'm fucking fantastic." I peel out with a squeal of tires. Annalise scrambles to put her seatbelt on. It's not until we're back in the tunnel that I feel the tightness in my chest ease.

"Your brother Grant seems like quite a character," Annalise says, attempting to lighten the mood with conversation.

"Yeah?" Annoyance flares within me. I snap, "You should just date Grant then."

Her eyes widen at my outburst. She levels her gaze at me and scans my face. "Is that what we are doing?" she asks softly. "Dating?"

My teeth grind together as I struggle with my response. My pride twists my words, making me lash out. "All you are to me is a hot piece of ass, Annalise."

I see hurt flash in her eyes before she quickly hides it behind a mask of indifference. "I would like to be dropped off at my building. It's on the way to yours."

Glancing at her, I furrow my brow. "I'm not done with you yet."

Silence stretches between us. The sound of her phone buzzing shatters the moment. Her hand darts into her purse. She checks the caller ID and frowns as she answers.

"Mom?" Annalise's voice is breathless. She listens for a second before she lets out a curse. "Oh, god."

Twenty-Five

Annalise

I run through the gleaming lobby of my penthouse, my heels clicking *tip-tap tip-tap* on the polished marble floor. Waiting on the elevator to reach the top floor is an anxiety-inducing activity.

My mom wouldn't say exactly what the nature of the emergency was.

But she said that word, *emergency*.

Is my father dying?

Why is my mom in my apartment again?

So many unanswered questions ring through my mind. The elevator doors open, and I burst into my apartment, almost in tears.

But when I run into the living room, I find my mother reclining on a leather couch, laughing as she talks to a pretty young woman. Mom has been at work in this room because it's completely bare. The sofa and a single matching chair are the only pieces of furniture in the vast living room. There's nothing on the walls, and no sign of where all the stripped art and furniture went.

Fuck. Mom's been in my penthouse unattended for *hours*.

My fears are confirmed when Mom spots me and calls out. "We're in here!"

I walk into the room, looking for somewhere to put down my purse. I swing left and right, and then growl in exasperation. "Mom! Where the hell did my furniture go?!"

Mom doesn't skip a beat. Her smile remains wide and unbothered. "Annalise, *language*. I stopped by a little early to tidy up for Scarlet."

I drop my purse on the empty floor and grit my teeth. "You said that you were having an emergency! You know that I thought that Dad had another stroke, don't you?"

My mother pats the chair opposite herself. "Sit down, Annalise. You're being rude to our guest."

I turn my attention to the young brunette. She's poised and polished, wearing a strapless, flamingo-pink, knee length dress.

Scarlet is absorbed in her phone. But at the word 'guest,' she looks up at me with a diplomatic smile.

"Scarlet Espinoza," she says. She extends a hand to me, showing off a fluorescent pink manicure. I shake it, uncertain of who this person is. "Matchmaker. My motto is *Making Matches, Creating Magic*."

She waves her hand in a flourish, smiling.

"I'm sorry. Why are you here, exactly?"

Scarlet's smile falters. She looks at my mom for help. "I can come back at another time if you'd prefer?"

"No, no!" Mom says, squeezing Scarlet's hand. She turns to me. "Darling, you know that Scarlet here is the best matchmaker in the country. She helps young people from good families find suitable matches. Isn't that right, Scarlet?"

"Well…" Scarlet hesitates. "I have a knack for pairing up soulmates."

"Soulmates who are wealthy enough to pay for your services." I sit down primly, folding my hands in my lap. "I can't imagine you would have great luck with people who aren't looking for that connection."

Scarlet smiles. "Women in my family have been match-making for a hundred years. It's in my blood. *Literally.*"

She says the last bit as if it's a joke and laughs at herself to boot. I stare at her, perplexed. Who is this crazy person that my mom brought into my house?

Mom cuts in. "Scarlet's going to find you the perfect man."

"Mother, I already told you, I don't need that," I try to protest.

But Scarlet interrupts me with a dismissive wave. "Annalise, listen. I know what you want in a partner." She looks dead into my eyes. "You're a strong, independent woman. You're not just a pretty face. And you're not looking for the first rich guy you see. Otherwise, you would have found Mr. Right already." She tilts her head. "Am I getting warm?"

"Well… I– I–" I stammer. My mind flashes back to what Nate just told me on the drive over here. *You're just a piece of ass.* My face contorts. "I guess…"

Scarlet reaches out to me and touches my hand with gentle fingers. "Let me walk you through my process. Maybe show you some photos of potential matches. You don't have to do anything you don't want to do. I promise."

I throw up my hands. "Fine," I say. "If it will get you both off my back, I'll look at some pictures."

"It'll be painless. I promise." Scarlet begins to talk brightly about how her service works.

I lose interest after a few moments and look at my mom,

who is gazing at Scarlet like she's got the solution to end world hunger.

Serious eye roll.

I cross my arms, my frustration mounting. I stare at the iPad that Scarlet confidently thrusts in front of me. The sleek device displays a gallery of potential suitors, each one impeccably dressed, each one posing with practiced charm. On any other day, I might have been intrigued. But today, it feels like an insult.

I grit my teeth and force myself to swipe through the profiles. Each man is more generic than the last.

My mind drifts to Nate, the infuriatingly smug businessman who has somehow worked his way under my skin. In comparison, these men seem bland and utterly forgettable. I flip through a dozen profiles before handing the iPad back to Scarlet. "I don't need a matchmaking service to find a man."

"Annalise, darling, just give it a chance," my mom pleads. "You never know who you might meet."

"Is there something wrong with them?" Scarlet asks. She seems genuinely perplexed.

"Of course not," I reply. "They're all just so... predictable. Predictably rich, predictably handsome, and predictably boring."

"Annalise, don't be ungrateful." Mom looks nonplussed. "Just pick a few."

"No! Mom, this is my life we're talking about. It's too much! Be a CEO! Find a husband! Have kids! I can't do every single thing all at one time."

Mom narrows her eyes and leans toward me. A threatening look blooms on her face. "You *will* look through these profiles. You *will* choose someone appropriate to date. And you *will* do it with a smile. Or else."

"All right." I stand up, putting my hands on my hips. "I'd like you both to leave now. Please."

"Oh!" Scarlet's eyes widen. She turns bright pink. "Of course. I didn't mean to cause you any offense."

She scoops up her iPad and shoulders her purse. I reach out and touch her arm. "There is no way you could've known. My mom is a witch. She enchanted you, I'm sure."

My mom huffs. "I did no such thing!"

"That's great." I start shooing them out of the living room. "Mom, before you leave. Where the fuck is the rest of the living room?"

"*Language*, Annalise." She scowls at me. "I removed the excess furnishings for you. You're welcome."

"I'm going to fire whoever let you in this building," I say mildly.

Mom hustles toward the front. I stand back and watch Scarlet open the door, only to be stopped by the tall man standing in her way. My eyes widen.

Nate glares at Scarlet. "What are *you* doing here?" he asks.

"We're just leaving." Scarlet grabs my mom's arm and waits until Nate steps back to let her through. Then both women vanish toward the elevator.

Nate runs his hand through his hair and turns back to me. "You had a matchmaker here?"

I turn on my heel and walk to the kitchen, calling, "Wouldn't you like to know?"

"Did you invite her here?" I hear him shut the door and his footsteps following behind me.

"Would it matter if I had?" I grab a wineglass and pour myself a glass of chilled wine. "If you care to remember, we're not even a couple."

"Wow." Nate shakes his head. "It took you like an hour to throw my words back in my face."

He's so full of shit. "You said it, not me. I'm just a piece of ass." I take a long sip of wine.

Nate purses his lips. I am ready for him to tell me why it's my fault. Or even to yell at me. But he doesn't do either of those things.

No, Nate Fordham actually *apologizes*.

"I'm sorry, Annalise. I was all stressed out about seeing my parents, and I took it out on you. It was unfair." He moves closer, his gray eyes glinting. "That's why I came here. I felt like shit after you got out of the car."

His admission knocks the wind out of me for a solid few seconds. "What world is this?" I look to my left and right, feigning distress. "You admitted that you were wrong about something? Unbelievable."

"So you accept my apology, then?"

"Saying that I'm nothing but a hot piece of ass was pretty harsh." I tap my chin. "Tell you what. I'll think about it."

His lips twitch with humor. "Fair enough. Who was the other woman that was with your mom?"

"Oh, my new bestie? She's a matchmaker. My mother texted me 911, then she showed up with Scarlet as a surprise."

"Ah." Nate seems to digest that. "So we both had unpleasant run-ins with our parents today." He grimaces. "Nice."

"Real nice."

He pulls me close. "You can think about accepting my apology while I eat you out, if you want."

"Oh yeah?" My lips twitch with humor. "Well, if you think it will help…"

He chuckles as he kisses me again.

TWENTY-SIX
NATE

Kissing Annalise feels as vital and important as breathing. I grip her hair and tug her head back, running my lips down the column of her throat. So many ideas are running through my head for things I want to do to her. Choosing one is a daunting task.

I want her in every conceivable position known to man.

As I nibble at her collarbone, Annalise digs her hands in my hair. She murmurs, "Teach me something, Nate."

"Oh? Ready for another lesson?" I ask, my cock hardening.

She looks at me with half-lidded eyes and nods solemnly. "I'm your willing student. Do whatever you want with me."

God, Annalise knows how to make a thrill run through my blood.

"First things first." I close the distance between us, my hand resting possessively on the small of her back. "Do you have any lollipops?"

She laughs. "No. Why?"

"I need one for what I'm about to teach you."

"Umm..." She turns her head, looking back toward the

kitchen, her brow furrowing. "I have a pack of popsicles. Will that work?"

The idea of Annalise licking a popsicle does wicked things to me.

"Perfect. Stay right here." I settle her on the bed.

I walk to the kitchen. Sure enough, there is a pack of high-end popsicles in her freezer. They're long and thin and will work perfectly for what I have in mind. I select the red color – it's flavor is probably cherry or strawberry.

My lips curl into a satisfied smile as I open the packaging. Carrying it into the bedroom and seeing Annalise waiting for me on her snow-white bed does something to me. I can't help but smirk as I watch Annalise's eyes widen as I sit down beside her with the popsicle in my hand.

Her cheeks flush a delicious shade of pink. She tilts her head inquisitively. I know she's wondering what I have planned for our little lesson.

"Here," I say, handing her the popsicle. "I'm going to teach you how to suck my dick. This popsicle will be your prop."

"That's a creative use of what I have lying around." Annalise hesitantly takes the popsicle from me. Her fingers brush against mine. I bite my lip as a jolt of electricity rushes through my body.

I touch her chin with a finger and stare into her eyes.

"First, you need to get on your knees," I instruct. The power dynamics at play are crucial here. I want Annalise to understand that, at this moment, she's submitting to me.

The fact that she's usually so hard-headed only makes it that much more thrilling.

She narrows her eyes at me, clearly not thrilled about being told what to do. But to my delight, she complies without complaint. She hops off the bed and sinks to her knees. She grips the popsicle in one hand, awaiting my instruction.

"That's a good girl," I praise her. I run my hand over her hair, caressing her. "Now, I want you to treat this popsicle like it's my cock. Show me how you will make me feel good, Kitten."

It's as if a switch flips inside her. Gone is the hesitant, uncertain young woman from moments ago. An eager, seductive vixen replaces her. Annalise gazes up at me with those bright hazel eyes and perfect, pouty lips. My cock twitches in response.

Ever so slowly, Annalise brings the popsicle to her lips. She parts them ever so slightly before taking the tip into her mouth. She begins to lick and suck on it, her tongue swirling around the tip before venturing further down the stick.

"Fuck," I groan. The sight of her sucking on the popsicle as if it were my cock drives me wild. The way her lips wrap around it, the way her cheeks hollow, the sucking sounds she makes. It's almost too much for me.

She must sense my arousal, for she glances up at me with a wicked grin. She never breaks eye contact.

"Keep going," I order, my voice thick with lust. "You're so fucking hot, Kitten. And I'm the only one who gets to touch you. *Fuck*, I'm lucky."

Annalise's eyes shine with pleasure as she guides her tongue down the side of the popsicle.

"Keep your eyes on mine," I instruct. I lean in closer. "Swirl your tongue around the tip like this." I demonstrate with my finger and make sure she's paying close attention. When she shifts and changes her tongue movement to match my request, I groan. "That's it, just like that. And don't forget to use your hand around the base. Keep a firm grip, but let it slide easily along the length. Yes, just like that."

After watching Annalise work the popsicle in and out of her mouth, I can't wait another second.

"Ready for the real thing?" I ask her, my gray eyes probing her blue ones. She pauses and swallows, then she nods.

"*Fuck*, Kitten. You're making me so damn hard."

With a wicked grin, I put the popsicle aside and slowly unzip my pants. I push my pants down and free my cock. Her breath catches in her throat when she looks at it.

"Eyes on me," I murmur. Annalise blinks and then trains her gaze on my face. She's fully submitting to the power dynamics. It's incredibly erotic.

"Just relax, Kitten. Remember what I taught you." My heart races as I anticipate how good her hands and mouth will feel. I bury my hands in Annalise's blonde curls. Her eyes lock onto mine. "Show me what a good student you are."

Annalise fists my cock. Her full lips part as she takes me in. I let out a low groan, feeling the heat rise between us. "Use your tongue like I showed you, swirling it around... just like that."

She does as I request, but adds a little twist. While her tongue swirls around the tip of my cock, she moans quietly. The vibrations emanating from her throat shoot arrows of pleasure into my bloodstream. My toes curl.

"God, you're so incredibly sexy," I murmur. Annalise's eyes sparkle. She likes me talking dirty to her as I watch her attentively follow my instructions. The sight of her on her knees before me is intoxicating. The urge to take over and thrust into her mouth is overwhelming. But I know that would be too must, too fast.

I have to take it slow. Annalise has to enjoy this too,

otherwise the likelihood of getting head in the future is slim. My hand tightens in her hair, urging her on.

"You have no idea how much I want you right now, Annalise."

Her cheeks flush with the praise. But she knows what she's doing now. She doesn't break eye contact with me. I can feel my control slipping away. The intensity of her magical mouth sends shivers down my spine.

"Keep going, just like that," I encourage. Looking at my girl on her knees before me, I know that my arousal is only heightened by her submissiveness. "Only I get to see this side of you, Annalise. Only I get to fuck your mouth."

I lose myself in the moment, allowing the pleasure to wash over me. Annalise's hot mouth and talented tongue crumble my cool façade. Unable to maintain my composure any longer, I come in her mouth, my fingers gripping her hair tightly. She milks my cock for all it's worth, her mouth sucking and slurping as I shoot long jets into her throat.

Fuck. *Fuck!* God, she's so perfect.

With shaking hands, I gently withdraw, my cock sensitive to touch. To my surprise, Annalise instinctively licks the tip of my cock, cleaning the come from my body. It's clear she's willing to do whatever it takes to please me.

The thought sends another wave of desire coursing through my veins. I need to show her that a performance like that gets *rewarded*.

"Annalise." I pull her to her feet, kissing her. "You have no idea how fucking good that was."

"Did I do it right?" she asks. I can see the excitement and satisfaction in her expression, mixed with a hint of vulnerability that makes her even more alluring.

"Come here," I growl, grabbing her waist and hoisting her up effortlessly.

She gasps in surprise, her legs wrapping around me

instinctively. I stride toward the glass wall of the penthouse, the city lights sparkling below us like diamonds. Pinning her against the cool surface, I can feel her shiver beneath my touch.

My hand slips under the hem of her skirt. I bunch it up around her hips. Her breath hitches in anticipation.

"You like when I touch you, don't you?" I smirk at the growing need in her eyes. I kiss her neck.

"Please, Nate," she whispers, her voice desperate and needy. It only fuels my desire for her.

"Patience, Kitten." I lower myself to my knees before her, keeping her pressed tightly against the glass. The power dynamics between us shift, yet there is no doubt who remains in control.

I start by pressing soft kisses on her inner thighs, licking and sucking at her sensitive skin. With each teasing touch, I can feel her body trembling. A moan escapes her lips, urging me on. Her fingers curl as they press into the glass behind her, desperate for something to grip.

"God, Nate," she whispers. "Don't tease me."

"Trust me, Annalise, I'm going to make you come," I reply. My hot breath ghosts over her clit. She writhes against my hands where they grip her legs.

A trickle of need sluices from her opening, taunting me. I kiss her clit and her muscles tense, her body releasing another wave of her juices.

I lavish my attention on her clit, licking and sucking it, swirling my tongue around it in tight circles. Annalise lets out a desperate cry, her hips bucking against my face. She's already so far gone. It makes me insane. The taste of her desire is so sweet and intoxicating.

A second later, Annalise's inner muscles tighten. She shatters, convulsing and crying out my name. Watching her come, knowing that I made her orgasm, is deeply fulfilling.

"Such a needy little Kitten, aren't you?" I tease as I wipe my mouth with the back of my hand, smirking at her flushed face.

She stammers, her cheeks burning red with embarrassment. She's never experienced anything like this before. *I'm* the one introducing her to these forbidden pleasures. I let her ass slide down the glass and then help her to her feet.

"God. Shut up," she mutters, avoiding my gaze. The vulnerability in her voice only serves to make me want her more.

"Or what?" I challenge. I press her back against the glass window with my body. "You'll call that matchmaker of yours?"

"Leave Scarlet out of this. She's just doing her job."

"Her job," I chuckle. "To pair you up with some pompous old-money fool who won't come close to satisfying you the way I can." My fingers trail along her thigh, a reminder of the pleasure we've shared. "You don't need a matchmaker, Annalise. Not when you're being fucked by a sex god."

"Is that what you think you are? A sex god? You're an arrogant asshole, Nate Fordham."

"An arrogant asshole who made you scream his name," I remind her, smirking. "And I'd wager that no one else has ever done that before."

"Stop it," she hisses, pushing me away. "This doesn't mean anything, Nate. It's just sex."

"Is it, though?" I ask, my voice soft but insistent. "Because for someone who claims this is 'just sex,' you certainly seem to be enjoying yourself quite a bit."

"Maybe I am. But that doesn't change the fact that we're not good for each other, Nate."

I raise an eyebrow.

"Who says we have to be? Maybe we're just what the

other needs right now. So why don't we just focus on what feels good?"

Annalise is quiet for a beat.

"I don't intend to let Scarlet set me up. Right now, I have... whatever this is between us. That's all I can handle."

"Are you admitting that you're falling in love with me?"

"It's not like that," she retorts. She straightens her skirt and steps away from me, frowning. "I'm just saying that maybe there's more to life than the perfect pedigree and the right connections. There's something to be said for passion and chemistry."

"Is that what we have, Annalise? Chemistry?"

"You know damn well what I mean. I don't have feelings for you, Nate. This is just... convenient."

I touch her cheek. "Is that all I am to you, Annalise? A convenient distraction?"

"Maybe," she says softly. "Is that not what you want?"

Her question makes my stomach flip flop. Instead of answering, I kiss her lips, kissing her so thoroughly that we're both left breathless at the end.

But her question still plays in my mind. What do I want out of this relationship? I don't know, and that disturbs me.

TWENTY-SEVEN

NATE

The door to the Manhattan bar swings open on silent, subtle hinges. Their qualities a testament to the kind of customers that frequent this place. Power brokers, hedge fund managers, and finance bros alike come to play here.

My gaze sweeps the room. High ceilings crowned with angular light fixtures cast a subdued glow on the patrons. The kind of people who possess the type of wealth that isn't spoken of aloud. It's whispered through the cut of their suits and the subtle glint of bespoke accessories. The air smells like aged whiskey. The undercurrent of deals being made swirls through the room.

At the far corner, I find my brother Cash, and our VP Drew, occupying a table that commands a strategic view of the entrance and the rest of the bar.

"There he is," I hear Cash murmur as I approach. The smirk in his voice is unmistakable even before I see it manifested on his face.

I pin Cash with a look as I take a seat. "You're looking perky. Apparently, at three a.m., you were doing shots off of a model with a bunch of your friends egging you on. I saw you tagged an Instagram post."

"Social media is designed to make it seem more fun than it was." Cash motions to his pint of beer and the glass of ice water in front of him. "Besides. I'm hydrating."

"Seems healthy." I nod curtly at Drew. He acknowledges me with a nod. Then I wave a hand. "Let's cut to the chase."

Cash leans forward, elbows on the table. The light catches the sharp angles of his face. "Gellar Industries," he starts. He taps the screen of his tablet to bring up a series of graphs and numbers and then props the tablet up so we can see it. "It's particularly vulnerable to stock manipulation right now. As you see here, the stock is slowly gaining value after word got out that Archer Gellar is ill. I propose buying as much as possible through a dummy corporation and making a short sale. We could make ten or twelve million without breaking a sweat."

He points to a graph. My kneejerk reaction is anger, but I suppress it. Quickly, I lean back, catching a waiter's eye. I point to the beer Cash is drinking, masking my irritation.

"Hmm." Drew leans forward, looking at the charts on the tablet. "How would you suggest that we approach the situation? Assuming that Nate gives us the okay to start buying up stock, stealthily."

"You two can't pick a company I am not about to merge with?" I ask. There's no heat to my voice, but my tone is heavily sarcastic.

Drew purses his lips. "You do realize that a short sale would help you, right? You will make money, and Gellar Industries will be incapacitated. Fuck a merger. They'll sell to you for next to nothing and be glad for the charity."

"We should do it. And I know how." Cash's lips spread into a grin that doesn't reach his eyes. "Once we buy all the stock, we plant a story with a friendly journalist. Maybe

Constance Lee with the Wall Street Times. A strategic leak here, a rumor there. Enough to cause a flutter of doubt among the shareholders."

"Timing is everything," I caution. My mind is alight with visions of stock prices plummeting. I can see Gellar Industries' shares tumbling like a house of cards at the slightest nudge from our invisible hand.

"Of course. We'll tread carefully. As usual, the FTC is monitoring all trades. And I, for one, wouldn't want to draw unnecessary attention to our short sale." Drew folds his hands and looks somber.

"I'm just not ready to move on Gellar Industries yet," I say. "Maybe in a few months."

"Is it the company that you're protecting?" Cash leans forward, that ever-present smirk etched onto his face. "Or a certain pretty blonde a decade younger than you?"

I can feel the heat simmer beneath my collar. "Careful, Cash." The warning drips from my tongue. "You're messing with things you don't understand."

"Are you getting pussy-whipped by Little Miss CEO?" His grin widens. "Never took you for the type to get tangled up in bedsheets when there are boardroom battles to be won."

My hand clenches into a fist, knuckles whitening. "Contrary to what you believe," I say, with lethal calm, "not everything I do revolves around the boardroom. This decision is about power, not passion."

"Sure, Nate," Cash drawls, unimpressed. "Keep telling yourself that."

I rise, towering over the table, my suit a second skin of authority. I have an idea. "I propose a trade. It's a strategic pivot to buy myself time."

Cash leans back in his chair, his smile reminding me of a

reclining jackal's. Drew's brow arches, intrigued. "A trade?" Drew asks. "Keep talking."

"I have a stock tip that's as solid as this table." I drum my fingers on the wood in front of me. "I'll share. But in exchange, you agree to delay any movement on Gellar Industries for the foreseeable future."

"Nate, are you hedging now?" Cash laughs. "Since when do you need breathing room?"

"Since I started playing chess, not checkers," I retort smoothly. "This isn't about needing room. My concern is controlling the board."

Drew and Cash look at each other, conferring silently. Then Cash shrugs. "Okay. We'll hold off for a month." He lifts a finger in warning. "Not forever, though. Gellar Industries is vulnerable. Word will get out soon enough. You'd better hope we make our move before anybody else does."

"Good enough." I write a quick tip on a cocktail napkin and slide it over to Drew. "And now, gentlemen. I have places to be."

Cash looks at Drew. "Nate has to go screw Annalise."

Fast as lightning, I reach across the table and grab Cash's tie, pulling him close. "Wanna try that again?"

"You're awfully sensitive, big brother." Fire flashes in Cash's eyes. "Do what you're going to do. I'll still talk about you and Anna–"

He doesn't get to finish his sentence. I grab the back of his head and ram his nose into the table with a sickening crack. Blood immediately spurts out of his nose, and he claps his hands to the wound. "Whadefugg?" Cash cries. "Christ, Date!"

He sounds hilarious. I make a note to tell him about how funny his voice was when he's not freaking out. Rising from the table, I lean in to tell him, "See you around, little brother."

I can feel Cash's glare right between my shoulders as I leave. A bartender rushes toward the table with a fistful of cocktail napkins. But I don't look back.

Cash deserved it. And I'll break his pretty nose again the next time he says anything about Annalise. The only person who can bully her is *me*.

TWENTY-EIGHT
ANNALISE

"Wow," I breathe. I stand at the window of the hotel room that Nate surprised me with, unable to believe it. I'm staring directly at the Notre-Dame de Paris, or the Notre-Dame Cathedral as Americans usually refer to it. The other window has a view of the river Seine, with a corner of the Louvre at the edge.

It's early in the morning in Paris, but I still feel like it's the middle of the night because of jet lag. Still, I am thrilled to be here. Nate couldn't have known this, but I've never been to Paris as a fully realized adult. I've never strolled the beautiful streets, bought a French pastry, or even visited the Eiffel Tower on my own.

And now I'm *here*. One private jet flight later, I'm spending my morning in a spectacular Parisian apartment. The place is a quarter block and decorated with large windows, chic white furnishings, and Parisian coffered ceilings. Even, thin, gold flourishes are painted around the panels of the white wood walls. And when you step outside onto the balcony, you get this view.

It's *breathtaking*. I don't know if Nate intended to

sweep me off my feet, but I am decidedly impressed by this casual Parisian vacation. Nate says that we're here to attend a conference on geothermal energy... but we're in Paris, for God's sake.

My phone buzzes in my skirt pocket. I pull it out with a sigh, not wanting to look away from this multi-million-dollar view.

The text is from Nate. *Where are you? The conference starts in a few minutes.*

Right. I'm supposed to meet him at the conference hotel. I check the time and realize with alarm that drinking in the Paris skyline has made me quite late. I text Nate that I'm just about to leave the apartment.

It's not strictly true. I have to change into a business-appropriate yet chic white linen dress. I pile my curls on my head and clip them there, then add a little blush and lipstick. After I slip on a stylish pair of Manolo Blahniks and add a set of pearl earrings, I grab my purse and rush out the door.

The Parisian sun glares off the pavement as I dash through the bustling streets. I weave around tourists and locals alike. I probably look insane. My heartbeat pounds in my ears. This is the first time that I have to meet Nate at a business function. And I'm late. How shockingly gauche, as the French would say.

"Excusez-moi!" I narrowly avoid a collision with a street vendor selling vibrant bouquets. The scent of roses and lilies mingles with freshly baked baguettes wafting from a nearby boulangerie. My stomach growls. I should have had breakfast at the apartment, but I was too busy daydreaming.

"Get it together, Annalise," I chastise myself.

At times like this, I can practically hear my mother's disapproving voice in my head. The voice berates me for not being more like her ideal version of a daughter. A young woman who'd marry rich. A woman who'd let someone else handle the responsibilities of Gellar Industries.

It's hard to tell that ever-present voice to *shut up already.*

I turn a corner and slow down as the smooth pavement ends and lapses into uneven cobblestones. Shit. In my high heels, this bit of street presents a challenge. Should I just flag down a cab?

In my haste and indecision, I misjudge the distance between two cobblestones. My foot gets caught, and my ankle twists painfully beneath me. I stumble, biting back a cry of pain as I fall to the ground. The world seems to blur around me as my ankle throbs with pain, sending waves of agony shooting up my leg. I blink back tears, gritting my teeth as I try to stand up.

There is no one around. I pull my heels off and hop toward a set of steps only a few yards away. Sitting down, I examine my ankle. Even the gentlest probing touch sends a bolt of pain up my leg.

"Fuck." I dab at my eyes, taking a calming breath. There is no way I can navigate a large conference today.

Pulling out my phone, I tearfully text Nate. I feel like a stupid little girl as I explain what happened and where I am. I'm letting Nate down. Not to mention the fact that my company probably needs the kinds of contacts that I would make at this conference. Great. What kind of stupid, flighty CEO skips the conference she's in Paris to attend?

When Nate doesn't text me back immediately, I wonder if I should try to get back to the apartment. Can I hobble? I try to stand, but the waves of shooting pain send me back to the pavement.

Should I Uber? Do they have Uber in France?

"Annalise?" A voice cuts through the haze of my distress. I look up to find Nate jogging toward me, his gray eyes filled with concern. The sight of him momentarily throws me off guard. We're rivals in the business world. And our competitive natures are constantly clashing. But his usually smarmy smirk is absent.

Instead, his look is one of genuine worry.

"Are you all right?" he asks, crouching beside me. His towering presence makes me feel even more vulnerable. I struggle to keep my composure.

"Fine," I answer weakly. "I wasn't paying attention to where I was going. Then I tripped."

"Let's get you up," he says. His strong arms pull me up and steady me. I wince at the pressure on my injured ankle. What a wounded baby deer I am.

"Thanks," I say softly. "I didn't think you would come."

He shoots me a look like I'm crazy. "Did you crack your head? You're not making any sense."

My entire face heats. "I'm fine."

He looks at me, his eyes narrowing. A calculating look comes over his face. "Can you walk?" Nate questions. "I think I should get you back to *l'appartement*."

"I probably can't make it alone," I admit reluctantly. I close my eyes. God, I hate the vulnerability and weakness in my voice.

"Let me carry you," he offers, without hesitation. My eyes open, and I start to protest, but he gently lifts me into his arms.

"You can't carry me!" I squawk. "Nate, this is ridiculous! I thought you were going to call a cab or something."

My breath catches as I feel the warmth of his body against mine. His strong arms wrap around me protectively. From here, I can smell his cologne. "It's only a few blocks. Just relax."

"Put me down, Nate," I demand half-heartedly. The truth is that I don't want him to let go of me just yet. The feeling of being cradled in his arms sends shivers down my spine. My traitorous heart demands *more*.

"You can argue with me later."

As Nate carries me through the bustling Parisian streets, I question everything I thought I knew about him. His usually arrogant demeanor has given way to a surprising tenderness. I feel stupid for thinking that he would just leave me on the side of the road.

"Thank you, Nate," I say softly.

He doesn't respond, but I hear a contented rumble from his chest. He's enjoying this.

Without complaint, Nate carries me back to the apartment building and up the ancient elevator. I expect him to put me down when he sweeps into the living room. But he carries me back to the bedroom and deposits me on the bed. He drops my forgotten high heels by the foot of the bed. Then he looks down at me.

"All right. Let's take a look at that ankle." Nate kneels beside me. His gray eyes darken with concern as he gently lifts my injured foot. "Does it hurt when I do this?"

He applies the slightest pressure. I wince, biting back a gasp of pain. "A little," I mumble, trying to sound tough. The truth is, my ankle hurts like hell.

"Sorry," he says softly. His fingers skate in light circles over my sensitive skin. "We need to get some ice on your ankle."

"Thanks, Dr. Fordham," I joke. "But I don't need you to fuss over me."

"Too bad," he retorts, smirking as he gets to his feet. "You're hurt. Now I'm here to baby you until you feel better."

"Fine," I huff. I still feel incredibly silly.

My heart pounds as I watch Nate stride from the room. He reappears a minute later, waving a bag of ice. I bite my lip as he props my ankle up on a pillow and arranges the bag across it. As much as I hate to admit it, there's something undeniably thrilling about having Nate Fordham at my beck and call.

Even if it is only for a little while.

The ice slowly does its job. Soon my ankle is chilly, verging on numbness. I flip through the pages of a Parisian style magazine for a while. The warm glow of the afternoon sun bathes the room in a golden haze, casting shadows across the room.

Nate returns, sits at the end of the bed, and checks on my ankle. The cold compress numbs the pain, but when his fingers graze my skin, I feel flames licking up my thighs that have nothing to do with my injury. I almost can't reconcile the gentle way Nate touches my ankle with how he usually behaves. It's so different from his usual brash demeanor.

"Your ankle should be fine," he announces. "Just try to stay off it for a bit."

"Thanks," I reply softly. I lick my lips, acutely aware of how close he is to me. A charged silence fills the room.

"What should we do now that attending the conference isn't on the agenda?" I ask.

Nate smiles. "The conference was just an excuse to take you to Paris for a weekend."

"I knew it!" I laugh. "I have to admit, this little getaway is romantic."

"Isn't it?" He grins and splays out on the bed next to me. "It's nice being here with you. There aren't any VPs breathing down my neck. No pressure from my brothers. No expectations at all."

Nodding, I agree with him. "Yeah. It's nice to get away. I know my mom is scheming at this very moment to marry me off to some troglodyte who wants twenty babies and zero backtalk. But the view from this room allows me to forget about that for a while."

Nate frowns. For a long moment, he's quiet. He seems lost in thought. Then he says, "My parents have always expected greatness from me. My mom told me once that I was expected to run for president, even though I have never shown the most remote interest in politics. In her view, running for president was the next linear step in my evolution. First a kid, then a young man, then CEO of my company, then president of the whole country."

I raise my eyebrows. "You'd be a terrible president. No offense."

He shakes his head and smiles. "You're right. I have too much of a temper."

I lean closer, appreciating the way that Nate is talking to me. At the moment, he's a confidante, not a rival. "It sounds like we both have controlling parents," I say softly.

He sighs. "Having parents with extremely high expectations is an odd thing. Like I'm boxed in, and told what to do and how to feel about it. Like my wants and needs don't even matter."

"Even if it means hiding who you actually are?" I question. My heart pounds in my chest as I realize the vulnerability we're both displaying. This conversation feels as dangerous as it is exhilarating.

"Sometimes," he confesses with a shrug. "I doubt either of my parents knows who I am. They can list my business accomplishments with no problem, though."

I had no idea that he felt that way. Prompted by his openness, I confess, "You know, I'm constantly trying to prove myself. Not just to the board but to my mom as well. Before my dad got sick, he was no better. My parents have such high expectations for me. I feel like I'm drowning under their weight."

"Annalise," he says softly, his hand reaching out to brush a stray curl from my face. "You don't need to prove anything to anyone. You're more than capable, and I know you'll do great things."

"Thank you," I whisper, my breath hitching as our eyes meet again.

"Maybe we're just two people who happen to be good at hiding their true selves." He tilts his head.

"Is that what you've been doing all this time? Hiding?"

He pauses, thinking. "Isn't that what we all do, to some extent?"

"Maybe," I concede. "But sometimes, it's worth removing the mask. It's a risk, but you have to let others see the real you. Maybe just one person."

"Is that what you're doing right now?"

I take a deep breath. "I'd like to show you."

We're drawn together like two magnets. The moment our lips meet, it feels like the world catches fire around us. It's a struggle to breathe, yet I can't be bothered to do so; I am consumed by hunger, a primal need. Our tongues tease and explore. His kiss is hard and demanding. Each taste of him sends shivers down my spine.

I need him. I'm desperate, starving.

Nate sees me. Really sees me. And I'm not hiding anymore.

TWENTY-NINE
NATE

As I stand outside the Louvre, its grandiose glass pyramid glistening beneath the Parisian sun, I feel a sense of awe. Not just of this city, but of Annalise as well. Paris is a creature unto itself. It teems with people from all walks of life, going in every possible direction. The city is stunning, from the first rays of sun at dawn to the dying evening glow.

And while the city's beauty is undeniable, I only halfway notice because Annalise is by my side. Laughing, firing off quips, shooting me glances that make my heart stutter in my chest. Right now, her golden curls shine like a halo around her angelic face. She has a look of intense concentration as she gazes up at the iconic museum.

"Isn't it breathtaking?" she murmurs.

"Absolutely," I agree. But I don't really mean the museum.

Annalise is just fucking *beautiful*. She has this uncanny ability to make even the most stunning sights pale compared to her presence.

She turns to me, tucking a strand of blonde hair behind

her ear, smiling a bit sadly. "I don't want to leave the Louvre. I could explore the exhibits for days. But we only have today and tomorrow in Paris. So... I guess I'm ready to move on."

Nodding, I pull out my phone and text the driver I've hired. "Where to? Notre-Dame?"

She nods, then wrinkles her nose. "I hate that we can't just walk everywhere. Stupid ankle."

Reaching out, I put my arm around her shoulders and pull her in for a kiss. "Next time."

Annalise looks surprised by my words. When I think them over, I realize that I have introduced the concept of *time* to our otherwise magical day together. We've been floating in a bubble, unbound by the limits of time and space. I didn't mean to compromise our happy ignorance like that.

I cough into my hand and pull her toward the SUV that's coasting to a stop. No need for either of us to get bogged down by reality today.

We continue our exploration of Paris, venturing from the Louvre towards Notre-Dame Cathedral. Annalise catches my hand when we enter, her awe evident on her face as she stares up. The impossibly high arched ceilings and dramatic stained-glass windows are truly something to behold.

"Can you imagine all the history that's unfolded here?" Annalise asks. Her head is on a swivel, eyes tripping over one sight before catching on the next.

"No. I can't. It is beautiful in a way that nothing in New York is, though," I reply.

Annalise looks up at me, her eyes shining. "There is something different about our time here in Paris. Don't you think?"

I can only nod. I agree with her. That much feels

obvious to me. But I don't want to screw anything up by saying it aloud. Labeling the heady mix of chemistry and intimacy I've found with Annalise seems dangerous.

It's better to stay silent.

As we stroll around the Pantheon, I find that I want to let her see the man behind the cocky exterior. Can she handle that?

There's only one way to be sure.

"You know, I am the oldest son by twenty-seven minutes," I remark. I try to pretend it like it's not a big deal. "When we were talking yesterday about feeling that our parents' expectations are high, I thought about talking about that. I feel enormous pressure from my parents to live my life by their strict standards. My brothers obviously don't feel the same kind of pressure."

Annalise nods slowly. "I doubt Cash feels that kind of pressure about anything. He seems to be entirely without conscience." She hesitates. "What was your household like when you were growing up?"

"Quiet. My father was a billionaire, always preoccupied with making more money. And my mother... well, she was cold and distant. She rarely had anything to do with her sons. A very strict group of nannies raised us."

"Is that why you're so guarded?" Annalise questions gently.

"That's a part of it. I've just – I've always felt driven. Make more money. Crush my competitors. But with that comes a certain..." I search for the right word. "Loneliness."

"Loneliness? Really? Even surrounded by your brothers?"

"My brothers and I are close, but there's always been this wall between us. We're all afraid to show vulnerability. Letting someone else in seems foreign."

"Is that what you want? To let someone in?" Annalise's touch is warm and reassuring as she takes my hand in hers.

I screw up my face. "It's not easy for me. I've spent my entire life building walls."

"Maybe it's time to do things differently." She clings to my arm, curling in. I put my arm around her and take a deep breath.

The next words I speak are past my lips before I can shove them back down my throat.

"Do you want kids, Annalise?" I blurt out.

She furrows her brow, momentarily caught off guard by my question.

"I... I've never really thought about it," she admits, her voice soft and uncertain. "I'm really young. I have plenty of time to decide on the big questions after I get the company straightened out."

"Maybe it's time to consider what you truly want," I suggest. "Life is about more than just success and power. It's about legacy. And, I guess... love."

"Are children a deal breaker for you?" she asks. Her eyes search mine intently.

"No. I think it's quite the opposite," I reply. "I have always imagined having a large family like the one I grew up in. Except, you know, I'd actually spend time with my wife and children."

"Oh!" Annalise bites her lip. "I see."

As we continue our walk, I can see the wheels turning in her mind. Working over the new information I've presented, trying to create an idea of what being with me would be like.

I'm trying to do the same thing.

After we finish the tour, we pause outside a charming café, drawn in by the mouthwatering aromas wafting from within. We sit just inside, next to large windows opened wide to capture the last of the sun's rays. I order espresso and *moules frites*. Annalise orders a *croque monsieur* and an Orangina. We eat, with her stealing half my fries. I can't complain.

We're in Paris. The temperature drops, making Annalise move closer, ducking under my arm to steal some of my body heat. She's telling me a story, her eyes shining. The world is *perfect* right now.

"Tell me something you've never told anyone else," Annalise challenges me once she's finished telling me about a prank her class played on their French teacher. A playful glint flashes in her eyes.

"Hmm." I give her request some thought. "When I was younger, I secretly wanted to be an artist."

"Really?" she exclaims, clearly surprised by my revelation. "That's so unlike the Nate I know. You're a ruthless businessman. You're always laser-focused on power and money."

"There's more to me than a high-powered suit," I say. I narrow my eyes playfully at Annalise. "What about you? What's your secret?"

"You mean besides who really put the dead mouse in Mademoiselle Duchamps' bag?" she laughs. For a moment, she hesitates. Finally, she sighs, her gaze meeting mine with a newfound vulnerability. "Sometimes... sometimes I worry that I'll never find love. I fear that my desire for success will overshadow everything else."

"Annalise," I say softly, my heart aching for her. "You deserve love, happiness, and everything life has to offer. Don't let fear hold you back."

"Thank you," she whispers. She grasps my hand when I offer it, kissing the back of it and then lacing her fingers with mine.

This feels so *right*. I just have to make sure that Annalise is on board before I make a radical move. "Do you ever think about what our lives would look like if—"

My words are cut off by the shrill ring of her phone, shattering the idyllic moment. She pulls away from me, her eyes widening as she glances at the screen. "Sorry. I have my phone set to only ring for my parents."

I shake my head. "Of course. Answer."

She picks up the phone. "Mom?" I watch as her face falls. I swear I can see the light visibly draining from her eyes. "Dad? He's awake?"

She stands right up, as if she's going to run straight home from thousands of miles away. Her strained tone sends a jolt of concern through me. I knew their relationship was far from perfect, but it's rare to see Annalise so visibly affected.

Gently, I stand and place a hand on her shoulder, trying to offer support without intruding on her private conversation. She grips my fingers and looks worried. "But I'm in Paris," she blurts out. I can't make out her mom's words, but I can hear her shouting. "Mom– mom, slow down."

She listens for a few more minutes, her eyes sliding to me. "Uh huh. Okay. I'll be there as soon as I can, Mom."

Hanging up, she turns to face me. I thought she might tear up, but she just looks shocked. "Nate, my father just woke up from his coma. I need to go home."

"Of course," I reply without hesitation. I toss a wad of cash down on the table. My mind races, making the arrangements for our swift departure. "We'll leave Paris immediately. I'm here for you, Annalise. Whatever you need."

"Thank you," she murmurs. She looks up at me, taking a huge breath. "I don't know what I would do without you."

"Of course."

As we rush back to our hotel to pack our belongings, I can't help but feel an overwhelming sense of responsibility for her. I've always been fiercely protective, but this is different. Deeper, somehow.

I am cool and collected as I arrange for the jet to be ready. I've always been good in an emergency. "Have you got everything?" I ask, scanning the room for any forgotten items.

Annalise nods. Her eyes are already on the door. "I think so. Let's just get going."

As I zip up my suitcase, my phone buzzes in my pocket. I glance at the screen, expecting a message from the flight crew or perhaps one of my brothers.

Instead, I see an unexpected name: *Maybe Archer Gellar*. It's a text and it says simply: *Wednesday. 12pm. My Hamptons estate. Don't tell my daughter. Come alone.*

That's ominous as fuck.

My fingers tighten around the phone. What could Annalise's father want with me? And why the secrecy?

"Is everything okay?" Annalise asks. "Is the plane ready?"

"Yeah," I bullshit. I'm sure to tuck the phone back into my pocket so she doesn't catch a glimpse of the message. "That's it. Just some last-minute details for our flight. Nothing you really need to worry about."

"Okay," she says. She screws up her face. "Thanks, Nate. I won't forget this."

Somehow, I doubt I will, either.

THIRTY
NATE

After a very long flight back, I said goodbye to Annalise. That was two days ago. And ever since, I've felt on edge. She seemed busy with work, while I was twisted up, snarled up on my own inner thoughts.

Why does Archer want to see me? And why did he tell me to keep the meeting a secret?

I haven't seen Annalise since I got back. A mercy, since I'm keeping my rendezvous plans under wraps.

On the drive up to the Gellar mansion, I stare out the window at the luxurious beachfront properties that dot the rolling landscape of the Hamptons. In my mind, I try to explain to Annalise exactly why I'm choosing to see her father alone.

It's a conversation that we haven't had yet. Even in my imagination, it doesn't go particularly well. I guess I can't know whether I'll have anything at all to tell Annalise until after the meeting.

The chauffeured SUV pulls up and I get out. Shading my eyes, I look up at the glass and steel frame of the mansion towering before me. It's certainly impressive, standing out from the sandy terrain around it. But I note that it could be any beach house owned by someone wealthy. No outdoor furniture. No colorful rack of kayaks. The grounds are carefully groomed. Looking down to the shore, I see that even the sand has been smoothed out in a pleasing pattern.

The place has all the charm and quirkiness of a weekly corporate apartment rental.

In other words, there is absolutely nothing personal about it. Certainly nothing that would indicate that Annalise ever lived here.

Why is that, I wonder?

The sleek lines, and lack of color envelop me as a butler waves me into Archer Gellar's upscale beach mansion. The air inside the house is strangely stale; most of the sparse white furnishings look brand new. There is nothing cozy about the ultra-modern decor.

I've stepped into the Twilight Zone. How could anyone who would choose to live like this have produced a nice, fairly normal girl like Annalise?

As the butler ushers me to the back of the house, my head is on a swivel. There are no signs of Annalise anywhere. Not a single picture of the family on the walls. No personal items that could hint at her presence.

From what I've seen so far, the relationship between Annalise and her mother is frigid at best. Annalise hasn't mentioned her relationship with her father, really. But Archer wanted to wager her in our last poker game, as if she was just some chattel to be owned.

The mere thought enrages me. So what the fuck am I walking into here?

"Mr. Fordham." The butler waves me toward the grand metal staircase, suspended from a million thin wires. Walking up it seem like the butler is asking me to perform a death-defying feat. "This way, please. Mr. Gellar doesn't like to be left waiting."

"I'll just bet," I mutter to myself.

I'm pretty sure that Annalise has already been here to see him. Knowing Archer, he will already be angry about something, though he has only been awake from the coma for less than a week.

As we reach the top of the stairs, I'm ushered into Archer Gellar's bedroom. The man himself lies in bed, swathed in silk monogrammed pajamas, propped up by a mountain of pillows. His wife stands beside him, holding a glass of water with a tight grip.

"Here, darling," she coos, offering the water to her husband.

"Get that away from me!" Archer snaps, slapping the glass away and sending water splashing onto the expensive carpet.

Monique makes a face like she's smelled something bad. Without so much as a greeting to me or a move to clean up the mess, she retreats to a white sofa on the other side of the room. She picks up a magazine and pages through it, pointedly ignoring me.

Fine by me. I could do with less Monique Gellar in all aspects of my life.

Archer makes an attempt to sit up, but fails. I walk closer to the bed, feeling like an interloper in his private time. "Archer. Good to see that you're still with us," I say.

"Nate," he says. His voice is strained, but it drips with arrogance. "You're late."

I'm not late. I'm actually a few minutes early. But that's trivial. "You called me. I came," I retort. My eyes flicker around the room, searching for even the slightest indication of Annalise's influence. Surely there will be a family photo here?

But here too, her essence seems conspicuously absent.

I'm so captivated by Annalise. How can her parents be so unmoved?

"Let's get down to business," Archer grumbles. "I have to rest soon."

"So what is it you want from me, Archer? What could possibly be so important that we had to meet in your bedroom? Surely it could've waited until you could dress yourself, at least."

"Careful with that tone, Fordham," he warns, though I can see the glint of amusement in his eyes. Archer smirks, though it seems strained. "Very well. This is about my legacy and the future of Gellar Industries."

"What about your legacy?" I lean forward slightly. "Do you mean your daughter?"

That elicits a rough, raspy laugh. After a few seconds, Archer starts coughing. The cough turns into violent hacking and a nurse appears, summoned by the sound. "Do you need–"

Archer shakes his head, dismissing her with a flick of his wrist. "Fuck off," he wheezes. "I'm..." He coughs again. "Fine."

I cast a gaze over him. Has Archer been awake for a while and is just now seeing visitors? Or might there be lingering cognitive issues from the stroke and the following coma?

Clearing my throat, I push ahead. I don't know what Archer wants from me, but I think it's wise to defend what I've been doing. "You know, Annalise has been doing damn well as CEO while you've been... under the weather. I've been helping her get her footing. But she has a real talent for the job."

I let the words hang in the air and watch Archer's reaction closely.

A gravelly sound that might be laughter bursts from his throat. Archer glares at me, his eyes filled with nothing but contempt.

"Annalise?" he scoffs. "That little girl couldn't run a lemonade stand alone. Gellar Industries won't last the quarter with her at the helm."

My temper flares. What he's saying makes no sense. I clench my fists, struggling to maintain my composure. "Then why leave her in charge?"

"Maybe I wanted to see how long it would take for her to fail," Archer replies. "Or maybe I'm testing her mettle. Maybe I just wanted someone weak to hold my position so that I can take over again once I'm ready."

"Please," I tilt my head and narrow my eyes. "I don't think you are capable of thinking about a world without you in it."

The tension in the room is palpable as Archer's cold eyes bore into me, his disdain clear. I brace myself for whatever curveball he's about to throw my way.

That's why his next words are such a shock.

"Buy Gellar Industries from me, then."

My jaw clenches. I'm thrown, trying to keep up with him. "What?"

"You were responsible for its recent stock surge, were you not?" Archer smiles, but it doesn't reach his eyes. "You obviously know how to run a company. So make me an offer."

I purse my lips. "I've had little to no control over the stock price. I have plans to cut labor and move the company's offices to a better building. But none of that has been put into place yet."

"So you're saying the stock just rose on its own by twenty dollars?" Archer scoffs. "I don't think so."

"Actually, it was your daughter's efforts that led to

Gellar Industries' sudden burst of success. She did it completely on her own."

"Annalise? Are we talking about the same person? She's far too weak to have led the company to success. That, or the stock rising is just a complete fluke."

"You're so full of shit, Archer. Why can't you give her the credit?"

"I know my daughter. And she doesn't deserve a single thing!" he barks, his face contorting with anger. "Take the deal or leave it. Just remember, Nate. This opportunity won't come around again."

I want to strangle the man. Hell, if his wife weren't here, I might actually do it. But I force a tight-lipped smile.

"I won't make a large purchase without conferring with my money manager." That's not true, but I have to have enough time to game out every possible action and consequence.

"Fine," Archer snaps. His impatience is palpable. "You have twenty-four hours. After that, the offer is off the table."

My eyes widen. "You're looking to unload your company in a day??"

He sinks back into the pillows. "I'm a sick man, Fordham. Now run along."

I take that as my cue to leave. Without waiting for the butler, I jog back downstairs to the front door. My head spins.

Buying the company outright would save me a lot of hassle. But there's no way that any board would choose Annalise as their CEO when I'm in the picture. I'm a rain maker in the business world. And the board members always, always go where they know the money is.

Annalise will be crushed if I take her position. But if I don't... Cash might ruin the company just to make a buck. Can I put a stop to that? That's currently unknown.

As soon as I'm in the backseat of my SUV, I whip out my phone and dial Cash's number. He answers after several rings and sounds groggy. "Nate? What the hell, man? It's early."

"I need you and Drew to meet me at Joe's Diner in Manhattan. It's urgent."

"Urgent?" he repeats.

"Get your ass up and get there. I'll be there in forty-five minutes."

"Shit," Cash mutters. "All right. I'll call Drew."

After a very tense helicopter ride, I race down to the meetup spot. The neon lights of the diner cast a sickly glow over the grimy tables. I slide into a booth, waiting for Cash and Drew to arrive. My fingers drum impatiently on the tabletop.

My mind is still reeling from my meeting with Archer Gellar. What the hell am I going to do?

"Nate," Cash says. I look up as he and Drew slide into the booth across from me. Their eyes are alert, curious, and a little worried. "What's got you so wound up?"

"Archer Gellar just offered to sell me Gellar Industries," I blurt out.

"Are you serious?" Drew asks, his eyes widening in shock. "That's... interesting."

"Dead serious," I confirm, my jaw clenched. "But I told him I needed to think about it."

"Damn, Nate," Cash breathes. Excitement glints in his eyes. "If ViaLife buys Gellar Industries, we could take the valuable sonar technology and make a mint. Then the rest of the company would just be stripped and sold for parts. This could be huge for us, man."

"Or it could be the biggest mistake of my life," I counter. "The money would be good, sure. But Annalise will be out on the street. There is no way that this ends happily for her."

"What the fuck do we care?" Cash says, puzzled. "I know that you're getting your dick wet, Nate. But... you can get what she's giving you anywhere. Fuck her."

"That's not true," I mutter. I hate hearing my brother talk about her like that.

Cash pins me with his silver gaze. "I asked you this once. I'll ask it again. Are you going to marry this girl? Because if you're not, it would be stupid not to buy the company."

"Yeah. Since when did you start putting a woman before business?" Drew challenges, raising an eyebrow. "Buying and junking the company is the only fiscally responsible thing to do. You can't pass up this opportunity."

My mind races. Annalise's face flashes before my eyes. How could I ruin her life like that?

At the same time, can I really turn down this offer?

"Look, I know you've got a thing for Annalise," Cash says, leaning in closer, his voice low and serious. "But you can't let feelings get in the way of business."

"Feelings?" I scoff, trying to brush off the obvious truth. "This is about more than that."

"Oh yeah? Like what?" Cash rolls his eyes. "You're a businessman, Nate. Don't throw away the reputation you've earned over some girl."

"Annalise isn't just 'some girl,' Cash," I snap back. My temper flares. "She's special."

"*She's special,*" Cash mocks. "Yeah. I know Nate, you bloodied my nose about her, that was a first. Gag. Here's what I think. You called me here to talk you into buying Gellar Industries. And I'm here to tell you yes, go ahead."

"Yeah. It sounds like you've already made up your mind, Nate," Drew observes. His eyes flash with mischief.

I slump down in my seat. *Is Cash right?*

"I need to weigh everything before making a final decision."

"Look, man," Cash says. He slams his palm on the table again for emphasis. "If you don't pull the trigger, I will. You can't pass up this opportunity."

That's all the time that Archer gave me, anyway. Glaring at my brother, I say, "I need a day to think about it."

Drew leans in. "A day is all you have, Nate. Man up and do the deal. Don't let your pathetic little *fee-fees* screw this up for us."

"Fuck off." I slide out of the booth, dropping a hundred-dollar bill on the table. "You don't tell me what to do."

I stomp out of the diner, Annalise's face in my mind.

Thirty-One

ANNALISE

Last night, a thought woke me in the dead of night.

I'm starting to have real feelings for Nate.

I'm not sure if it was a leftover feeling from a dream I had or just the realization that I can't wait until the next time I see him. Whichever it was, the thought hasn't left me since I had it.

Now the city skyline stretches out before me, a glittering canvas of lights and steel. I stand in Nate's living room, my heart fluttering with my newfound realization. Feelings for him course through me, undeniable and intense.

Feelings that are dangerously close to *love*.

I take a deep breath as I walk through the penthouse.

"Annalise," Nate says, a note of surprise in his tone. He comes out of his bedroom, shirtless. "What are you doing here?"

I look at him, all six and a half feet of cut muscle, and practically drool. I need this man, right now.

"Should I go?" I ask hesitantly.

"Never," he replies firmly. He walks over, closing the distance between us and capturing my lips in a hungry kiss.

My heart races as I respond to his touch, my hands gripping his shirt.

He pulls away. His silver eyes search mine. "You only make things better when you're around."

I laugh, my nerves easing a bit. "That's the first truly kind thing you've ever said to me."

"Is it? Well, maybe I'm just starting to see the light."

Running a finger down his jaw, I bite my lip. I'm horny and nothing can satisfy me but Nate.

"Kiss me," I murmur. "Kiss me like you need me, Nate."

Nate's lips find mine again. His hunger is evident in the way he devours me.

He mutters against my lips. "I always need you, Annalise."

I giggle, my cheeks flushing with a mix of excitement and curiosity.

"What do you mean?" I ask, breathless.

He doesn't answer at first, instead trailing kisses down my neck, igniting a fire within me that I've never felt before. His hands roam over my body as if trying to memorize every inch of me. I can feel my need growing, the wetness growing between my thighs. The anticipation of his next words drives me wild.

"Tonight, I want to take your ass," Nate whispers into my ear. His hot breath sends shivers down my spine. "I want you to feel how amazing it can be to surrender yourself completely to me."

My whole body clenches at the unexpected request. My pussy grows even wetter.

A mixture of fear, excitement, and uncertainty swirls within me. The look in his silver eyes tells me that he's serious. This step could solidify our connection.

Maybe it will bind us together in a way that nothing else can ever touch.

"Are you sure?" I ask. I feel so safe here in his arms. It's almost silly to even ask the question. Nate would never do anything to me that could hurt me.

"Yes, Kitten." His fingers brush the sensitive nape of my neck. I shudder, unable to look anywhere else but directly in his eyes. "I promise, you'll fucking love it."

"Okay," I whisper. "You're my teacher."

A sudden surge of power courses through Nate. He scoops me up and throws me over his shoulder, carrying me toward his opulent bedroom.

In one fluid motion, Nate lowers me onto the silken sheets, his strong hands working quickly to undress us both. His muscled body looms over me. I can feel his gray eyes burning with intensity, probing me. He leans down, capturing my lips in a searing kiss before trailing his mouth along my neck, his teeth nipping and teasing my sensitive flesh.

It's almost too much. I groan, digging my fingers into his shoulders, the gesture hard enough to leave marks. He growls.

"Your body drives me wild," he murmurs. His lips move against my skin, his warm breath raising goosebumps all over me. He moves lower, his skilled lips lavishing attention on my breasts, swirling around my nipples until they're taut peaks of pleasure.

"Please, Nate," I beg, my hips arching off the bed in desperation. "Touch me."

He grins and murmurs, "You'll have to be more specific, Kitten."

"Touch my pussy," I gasp, unable to hold back any longer. "*Please.*"

"Such a good girl. Asking for what you need..."

Nate's eyes darken with lust as he obeys. His large hand trails down my stomach and between my trembling thighs.

He presses a single finger inside my channel, teasing me for a brief moment before slowly sinking it inside my pussy. My moans echo through the room.

"God, Annalise. I love listening to you moan." His breathing is heavy with need. "It's the hottest thing I've ever heard. I want to savor every inch of you."

He takes his time, kissing and worshipping my inner thighs, his tongue occasionally flicking tantalizingly close to where I crave him most. The sensation is maddening. He drives me to the edge of insanity as I squirm beneath him, desperate for release.

"Please, Nate. *Please?* I need you to lick my clit."

"Your wish is my command."

Nate's warm breath fans over my aching, wet core as he lowers his head between my trembling thighs. The anticipation is electric. I feel myself clenching in anticipation of his skilled tongue. A moment later, that tongue makes contact with my throbbing clit.

For a second, my eyes roll up in my head. I swear, the world around me seems to shatter into pieces.

"God, Nate," I gasp, my fingers tangling in his dark hair, urging him closer. "Don't stop. Don't ever stop. You're too good."

"Never." He growls against me, his voice vibrating through my sensitive flesh, intensifying the pleasure. His tongue continues its expert ministrations on my clit. After a moment, he slides two thick fingers inside me, stretching my hot, wet pussy.

I can barely think straight, let alone form coherent thoughts. My body is entirely at his mercy. I'm *his*.

As Nate's fingers pump in and out of me, he begins to explore further. His free hand trails down past my soaked folds to probe my virginal ass. The sensation is foreign and slightly uncomfortable, but not wholly unwelcome.

Intrigued by this new experience, I find myself pushing back against his exploring fingers.

"Relax for me, Annalise," Nate coaches, sensing my tension. "I promise I'll be gentle."

With that reassurance, I do my best to relax, focusing on the incredible sensations coursing through my body. As soon as his finger breaches the tight ring of muscle, he sucks my clit hard. My body goes rigid but he doesn't slow down for even a second.

My orgasm hits me like a tidal wave. It crashes down and leaves me breathless and shaking in its wake.

"Fuck, Nate." I groan, still reeling from the intensity of my release.

"I'm not done with you yet. Get ready for more." I can't see him, but the way he grits the words out makes me shiver.

"More?" I echo. I'm unsure if I can handle any more pleasure than what he's already given me. Nate grabs a tube of lube from his bedside table and flips me onto my stomach. I find myself clenching in anticipation.

He's about to fuck my tight ass.

I feel the slippery-cold drip of the lube on both my asshole and pussy. I take several deep breaths, attempting to steady myself for what's to come. Nate's fingers slickly glide over my body, his touch somehow both gentle and commanding.

I look back over my shoulder. Nate strokes his cock, his eyes hungry and possessive. "I need you, Annalise. I need to claim you completely."

My heart races, but I have no hesitation in my voice. "I'm so wet for you, Nate."

"Damn right," he growls. His voice is thick with lust.

Nate thrusts his big cock deep into my pussy, going slow, allowing my body to adjust to his size. I groan, pushing back against him. He picks up my hips and I push up onto all fours as our bodies meld together like two puzzle pieces made for each other.

"God, Nate, you feel so good inside me," I pant.

"Just wait," he promises. "Just wait until I've filled you up all the way, Kitten."

He pulls out, only to position his cock at the entrance to my asshole, teasing me with shallow thrusts. The taboo sensation of being stretched in this new way overwhelms me. I can't help but release a sultry moan in response.

"Touch your clit, Kitten. Let me know how good you feel."

My fingers find the sensitive nub and work it in tight circles. A shiver of satisfaction runs through me as Nate continues to push into my ass. He is taking control of my body in a way no one ever has before.

"Oh god," I whisper. "Oh god, Nate..."

"That's it. Touch your clit. Feel how full you are right now. Let yourself go, Annalise."

His voice is a seductive spell that I can't resist. As we move together, I know that I'm falling even deeper under his spell.

My heart races as Nate works himself deep inside my ass, his rhythmic thrusts filling me completely. I rub my clit in time with his movements, pushing back into him, desperate for more. The pleasure is raw and consuming.

I've never felt so completely *taken* as I do right now.

"Come for me, Annalise," Nate urges, his voice tight with desire. His pace quickens, each thrust harder and faster than the last, driving me closer to the edge of ecstasy. "Come for me, Kitten."

My mind spins with the intensity the moment. I want this connection with Nate to go on forever. As I'm on the brink of orgasm, a realization sweeps through me.

I *love* Nate. I'm stupidly, deeply in love with him.

My orgasm makes me shudder. There are no boundaries between my body and his. In this moment, I've given myself over to him completely. I open my mouth, caught up in the maelstrom of pleasure. "I love you, Nate," I whisper.

As if my confession has unleashed something within him, Nate lets out a guttural moan. He surges forward, his cock twitching inside me, and he fills my ass with his hot seed. "God, Annalise..." he groans. He pants as he pulls out and turns me over. "Do you mean it?"

His gray eyes lock onto mine. They're full of some deep, unnamed emotion. My heart squeezes. I nod, feeling my face heat.

"I know we're just business rivals. But I think somewhere around the fourth time you called me a brat, I started to fall for you. I... I *love* you."

"Fuck, Kitten." He reaches out to caress my face and tenderly tuck a piece of my hair behind my ear. "I love you too. I've been obsessed with you for months, Annalise." He sucks in a breath. "I know what I said about not wanting to fall in love. I know what I said about how we're nothing but business rivals. But with your intelligence and beauty, what choice did I have? You've proven yourself to be more than a match for me in every way."

Hearing Nate say that is everything I've ever wanted. His approval plunges into my body, courses through my veins, sinks down to my marrow. "I think I've always loved you," I admit quietly. I trace my fingers along the sharp lines of his collarbone. "From the moment I laid eyes on you."

He kisses me then, slowly and meaningfully. We haven't given our love a timeframe yet, but I feel my soul vibrate with connection. I want this man. Not just right now, in this moment. I want him *forever*.

If I have any say in the matter, there will be lots of lounging around naked, declaring that we love each other, and talking about the future together to come. For now, I just bask in the glow of Nate's love.

Eventually he jumps up. He disappears into the bathroom and I hear water running. He returns and I watch as he uses a gentle touch to clean me off with a warm, damp cloth. The tender care he takes is in stark contrast to the raw intensity we shared moments ago.

He leans down and captures my lips in a slow, lingering kiss. His gray eyes are locked on mine. His touch sends shivers down my spine. *This man will ruin me. And I'm going to love every second of it.*

Is it possible to be drunk on a feeling? Because if it is, I'm love-drunk.

"Stay with me tonight?" He murmurs his offer against my lips. His voice is a mixture of desire and vulnerability. Strange, I think this might be the first time he has *asked* me to do anything.

"Of course," I reply. "I can't imagine wanting to be anywhere else."

When Nate lies down beside me again, I can feel the steady rhythm of his heart against my back. His strong arms wrap protectively around me, cocooning me. I close my eyes, enjoying the sensation, drifting pleasantly.

As the seductive lure of sleep tugs at my body, making my limbs heavy, I become vaguely aware of a sudden vibration. I try to focus on it for a second and then realize it is coming from Nate's phone on the bedside table. He stirs behind me, disentangling himself from our embrace. He grabs the device and the screen flashes on.

Even half asleep, I catch the low, frustrated curse that slips from his lips. I crack an eye, watching him read a message on the screen.

"Fuck," he utters. He glances at me, his features pulling into a look of worry. "Kitten, I have to go."

"Now?" I ask. "It's so late."

Nate shoves a hand through his hair. "It's an emergency."

"Is everything okay?" I mumble sleepily, fighting to keep my eyes open. I'm not entirely sure what's happening.

"Nothing you need to worry about." His tone is dismissive, but I can sense the tension in him as he hastily dresses. "I'll be back as soon as I can. Try to get some sleep."

"Promise you'll be back soon?" I force my eyes open just long enough to catch a glimpse of his conflicted gaze.

"Promise," he confirms. He leans down for a searing kiss before striding out the door.

As I lay there, drifting back to sleep, Nate's absence leaves me with a hollow feeling in the center of my being.

Thirty-Two
Nate

It's the dead of night in downtown Manhattan. The lobby of my office building is quiet. The night concierge nods at me as I cross the echoing space. If he's surprised to see me, he doesn't show it.

I take the elevator up to my office, almost vibrating with anger.

911. Your office. Now. That's all Cash texted me.

The tension in the air is palpable as I stride into my office. The windows are dark, and only a single small light-bulb glows at my desk. Drew and Cash sit on my couch, waiting for me. Their sober expressions raise my hackles.

"Which one of you two idiots was complaining the last time we had a meeting?" I ask, striding over to the sitting area imperiously.

They exchange a glance. Then Cash clears his throat. "We need to talk about Gellar Industries. We have found out some pretty serious information that complicates things with the purchase."

I wave a hand. "And this couldn't wait? You had to tell me right now?"

"You're such a prick," Cash mutters. Drew doesn't say anything, but defiance sparkles in his eyes.

What the fuck do these two cretins think is going on here? I shake my head. "I've thought it over. I'm not interested in short selling Gellar Industries. I'm bringing them into the fold. It doesn't make sense to sell them for parts."

Cash rolls his eyes. He tosses a thick stack of papers onto the coffee table between us. "Shut your face hole. Look at these financial disclosures Gellar Industries sent over, Nate."

I raise an eyebrow and pick up the papers. My eyes widen as I look at the charts and rows of figures before me. My breath catches as I flip page after page. I'm not a finance bro like Drew, but I can tell when numbers simply don't add up. The figures swim before me, revealing a discrepancy that can't be ignored.

"Drew, what the hell is going on? These numbers are off by millions. Tens of millions, maybe." I scowl at the pages as if they will change their mind with a little intimidation by me.

"Someone's siphoned millions from the company," Drew says. His tone is heavy with concern.

Aghast, I give my head a little shake. I look at the numbers again. "Who could've done this?" I mutter under my breath, trying to make sense of the situation. A horrible thought occurs to me. "Annalise?"

A vision of her blonde curls and defiant blue eyes flashes through my mind, somehow both enticing and infuriating me. She's stubborn, yes. But could she really have orchestrated such a massive theft? It seems so improbable.

"It could have been her. It also could've been any of the board members," Drew suggests cautiously. Obviously, he senses my hesitation to blame her outright.

What. The. *Fuck?* I clench the papers in my hand, crushing them. Could my sweet little Annalise be hiding something so heinous? I just told her I loved her. And now I find out that the same girl could be a thief?

No. It's not possible. Is it?

"We need to get to the bottom of this," I say, clenching my jaw. "And if it means taking over Gellar Industries to do so, then so be it."

Cash smirks at my words, clearly pleased with the shift in my convictions. "Listen, Nate," he says, leaning casually against the floor-to-ceiling window, "not only should you take Gellar Industries over, but you should get it at a fraction of the price."

"Are you out of your mind?" I snap, my fingers tightening around the damning financial documents. "This isn't some game we're playing here."

"Actually, brother, it is." Cash smirks, his eyes glinting with cunning. "And right now, you have the upper hand."

As if on cue, Drew chimes in. "If you don't agree to this, Nate, I'll move to unseat you as CEO of Fordham Enterprises. We'll install someone more... *dynamic.*"

"Dynamic?" My blood boils. With one swift, decisive motion, I close the distance between us and punch Drew square in the face. He stumbles backward, gripping his nose as blood spills through his fingers. "You're fired," I growl, my voice low and dangerous.

"What?!" he gurgles.

"You heard me, motherfucker. Get the fuck out before I do more than just punch you."

Drew spits, clutching his bloody nose as he makes a hasty exit. "You're making a mistake!"

I turn on Cash. He raises his hands, jerking his chin at the financial disclosures in my hand. "The numbers don't lie. Your girlfriend stole a massive amount of money. That, or she was complicit in the cover-up. Either way, no board will let her retain control of the company. Annalise is on her way out. It doesn't matter whether you drop the info on her in a bid to buy the company for cheap or not."

I've had enough. I can barely think. I point toward the door, scowling at Cash. He rolls his eyes, shoves his hands in his pockets, and slinks out of my office.

For almost a minute, I don't move. Staring at the open doorway, I try to think of a way that Annalise could possible not be involved.

But damn, I can't come up with anything.

How do I even go about confronting her about this?

I can't shake the image of her from my mind. She's stubborn and determined. Certainly a force to be reckoned with. But could she really have orchestrated such a massive theft?

If so, I have to fire her. The fucking FTC will be all over me as her business partner if I don't act immediately.

But can sweet little Annalise really be guilty? My mind just can't process it.

My knuckles ache from the impact on Drew's face. But thinking about the girl I left only an hour ago hurts more.

I can just see Annalise, all vulnerable and betrayed. Annalise, caught in the middle of the coming storm. I know I have to confront her. I will find the truth that lies somewhere deep below the surface.

My gut twists itself into knots at the mere idea.

To distract myself, I work out at my company gym, take a shower in the private ensuite in my office, and dress for the upcoming day. Then I sit on the couch, mulling over my options.

They are few. And the options I do have are repulsive.

At seven a.m., I text Annalise and ask her to meet at her office. Then I steel myself.

I may be in love with Annalise, but that doesn't mean she is blameless in this situation.

At eight a.m., I stride through the imposing glass doors

of Gellar Industries. The tightness in my chest is a constant companion today. Am I going to have a fucking heart attack if I find out that Annalise is a thief?

Maybe.

Upstairs, I'm met with an eerie silence from the office floor. The once-bustling office now a veritable ghost town. It seems word has somehow spread about last night's findings. The rumor mill runs rampant on Fifth Avenue and Wall Street.

Gellar Industries is a company in turmoil, its future uncertain. The vultures will soon begin to circle. And by vultures, I mean *me.* My stomach turns as I approach Annalise's office.

She's here, relaxing on the couch in a sleeveless gold minidress. She looks up when she hears me approach and smiles. She looks worried, though. "I guess the employees heard about the layoffs."

She gestures to the mostly empty office. I shake my head. There's no time for that right now. I come right out with it, not wanting to beat around the bush.

"Annalise, some serious accusations have been leveled at you."

She stills, her cheeks flushing. "What? By whom?"

"That doesn't matter," I snap. My patience is thinner than thawing ice. "There are millions missing from this company. It looks like someone embezzled from the employee pension plan."

The look on her face isn't entirely surprised. She swallows.

Fuck. Could Annalise actually be guilty?

"Just wait," she says, her voice raspy. "Let me explain."

"Christ." My stomach clenches hard. "So you did know. Did you take it?"

"*Me?*" Her eyes widen. "No! Of course not."

I sag onto the couch beside her. "You were just complicit in covering it up. That's great."

"Nate." Annalise reaches her hand out to touch my arm. I rear back like her hand is made of flames. "Look at me, please."

"How long? How long have you known?" I stare at a point in the distance. It's taking everything I have to remain calm.

All I can think about is the fact that I said I loved her last night. What was I thinking?

"A few months," Annalise admits. "Lori came to me about the missing money. We've been trying to trace where the money went, but it disappeared in a labyrinth of shell corporations and offshore bank accounts. Lori hired some forensic accountants–"

I stop her with a hand. "Lori was in on it too?"

She hesitates. "She found out about the missing cash when I did. She has been searching the company records and asking questions. I told her that I planned to pay the money back–"

"Wait." I shake my head. "Why would you do that if you didn't take the money in the first place?"

"Well, the employees were going to find out eventually."

"Bullshit. If you embezzled the funds, I need you to tell me right now. Then you can start explaining to me how you only told me that you love me to manipulate me."

Hurt flashes in Annalise's eyes. She grabs my hand and pushes it away. Heat laces her tone. "I didn't steal anything. And I do love you. I can't *believe* you would question that!"

"You're really going to sit there and lie right to my face??" I scoff. "Unbelievable."

"Nate, I wouldn't lie to you. I love you."

"I can't sit here and listen to you lie to me. I'm done." I cross my arms, my heart thudding painfully in my chest.

"Here's what is going to happen, Annalise. I'm going to make a very, very lowball offer to buy Gellar Industries. And you're going to take it."

"You would buy Gellar Industries? We're already merging! Why would you want to buy a company with so much liability?" she chokes out.

"Because I can take the lab employees and their work product. When I buy the company out, they and their work become part of ViaLife. Everything else gets scrapped."

Her eyes bug out. "You can't be serious!"

"Deadly serious," I reply, smirking at her reaction. "Your father approached me about the acquisition, Annalise. He wanted me to take over and clean up this mess. What do you have to say about that?"

Her eyes flash with betrayal. Her delicate hands bunch at her sides. "My father? You expect me to believe that he would willingly hand over his life's work to you? He despises you!"

"Believe what you want," I sneer. "But I'm telling the truth."

"Truth!" she scoffs, finally regaining her composure. "How can I trust anything that comes out of your mouth, Nate? My dad doesn't believe in doing serious business over the phone. Which means you snuck off to see him without telling me. He *just* woke up from a coma, for god's sake! You were talking business with him on his sickbed?"

My temper flares up like a hungry lion escaping its cage. "Look who's talking," I spit out. "Where did the money go, Annalise? Because it certainly looks like you embezzled it."

"Are you really accusing me of stealing from my own company?" she hisses.

"Convince me otherwise," I challenge.

Our faces are mere inches apart. The heat between us grows with each angry breath we take. Her eyes lock onto mine and she jabs a finger into my chest. "You are so arrogant. I can't believe I thought I was in love with you!"

My heart goes cold. I glare at Annalise. "You are a manipulative witch," I hiss. "And if it's not clear, we are over."

"God, Nate!" Annalise's lips quiver. She screws up her face. She seems like she is seconds away from bursting into tears. Then again, what do I know? She's obviously been working me since we met. "I don't know who stole the money. Maybe my dad, maybe our VP..."

I bleat a surprised laugh. "Of course you'd say that. Your dad makes a perfect scapegoat."

She pins me with a desperate look. "I didn't even work for the company when the money started going missing. I was a little kid then. I swear I'm innocent."

"Then how could you keep something so important a secret from me?" I bellow. It's hard to believe that someone as intelligent and resourceful as Annalise wouldn't have known about her father's indiscretions.

"Because it was my family's fuck up," she replies defensively. "I wanted to fix it myself. I wanted to prove that I can be a real CEO."

"Don't make me laugh. You're complicit in this, Annalise. The FTC is going to rake me over the coals just for being mixed up with you. You might be going to *jail*, sweetheart."

Annalise's jaw drops. "I didn't do anything wrong!"

"Tell it to somebody who cares. Preferably a very expensive lawyer."

The defiant fire in Annalise's eyes burns into me. She straightens her spine and waves an angry hand in my face.

"Enough! I've had enough of being controlled!" she yells. "First my dad. Then you. I won't let either of you dictate what I do with my life."

I arch a brow. "What are you going to do? Quit?"

"Maybe that's exactly what I need to do." Her eyes never leave mine. "Maybe it's time for me to forge my own path. I'm sick of men trying to exploit me and use me as a pawn in their sick little games."

I throw down a gauntlet so casually and icily that I barely sound like myself. "Once you leave this office, there's no coming back."

"I'm done with Gellar Industries." Her eyes promise that I'm going to feel pain. "And I'm done with you."

"Where are you going to go? Your dad is the one who sold you out."

"No." Annalise's mouth twists with aggravation. "You did that all on your own."

As the door slams shut behind her, I'm left standing alone in the office, a maelstrom of conflicting emotions churning within me.

THIRTY-THREE
ANNALISE

The sky is a darkened steel color. The clouds gather, churning. Buckets of water are pouring from the sky by the time that I get to Nantucket.

Not that it matters anyway. My whole life is *ruined*.

As I run up the steps of Lori Parker's remote coastal estate, tears blur my vision. The salty ocean breeze stings my puffy eyes. I sniffle and ring the doorbell. The door swings open.

Lori always looks so poised. Even on vacation, her demeanor is a striking contrast to my disheveled state. She looks me up and down before hustling me inside. "Annalise? What's wrong?"

I choke back a sob and lean into her open arms. "Lori... I've lost Gellar Industries."

"What do you mean?" She pauses. "Wait. Let's go into the living room to talk."

Lori leads me to a luxurious couch facing a window that overlooks the stormy sea. She whisks a blanket off the back the couch, urges me to sit, then heads to the kitchen to make us both a cup of mint tea.

As I sink into the plush cushions, my heart feels as heavy as the dark clouds looming outside. The time it takes the tea to steep gives me a minute to regain my composure. Lori is right. She knows just how to calm me down.

Hell, she's known me for my whole life.

Lori returns and presses a fine teacup into my hands. She draws very long, practiced breaths, urging me to do the same.

Breathing along with her feels silly, but it is calming. I manage to stop crying long enough to speak. "Nate found out about the missing money. He... he just fired me as the CEO of Gellar Industries."

Lori looks shocked. "What? He can't do that. Only the board can vote to remove you."

"He'll call a meeting tonight or tomorrow. And they'll be happy to vote against me. They always expected me to fail." I sniffle and sip my tea.

"God, what a mess," Lori mutters, shaking her head as she sits down beside me. "I turn my phone off for one day, and this happens. Tell me everything, from the beginning."

With a shaky sigh, I gather my thoughts. How to recount the tangled web that has become my life?

My cheeks heat as I confess, "I've been... sleeping with Nate Fordham." Saying it aloud makes it feel all too real.

"Nate? Really?" Lori asks. Her eyebrows shoot up in surprise. "I thought you two hated each other."

"You know what they say. It's a fine line between love and hate."

Lori frowns. "You love him?"

I look down at my hands wrapped around my teacup. "I thought I did." I glance up at her, hoping for reassurance.

Instead, I see worry etched across her usually calm face. My stomach churns with anxiety. I set the teacup down and clench my fists, digging my nails into my palms.

"Nate Fordham has quite the reputation," Lori begins, haltingly. "He's supposedly a love 'em and leave 'em type of guy. I would hate to see you get caught up in that. Plus, he's possessive and jealous... I can't imagine how you'd begin to deal with it."

"Trust me, I know," I reply. Bitterness rings through my words. Nate's dark gray eyes and chiseled features flash through my mind. Damn him. A blend of desire and anger runs through me and leaves me feeling even more confused than before.

"Tell me more about you getting fired. That happened today?"

Nodding, I say, "It got worse when Nate found out about the missing money. I kept it a secret from him. Now he thinks I'm part of some cover-up. He also accused me of stealing the money."

Lori's expression darkens, concern etched across her features. "That's not good, Annalise. I won't sugarcoat it. This situation looks bad for everyone involved."

"When Nate asked me who else knew, I told him the truth." I bite my lip. "I'm so sorry, Lori."

She waves away my concern. "It's okay, Annie. If you get fired, I'm probably not far behind. I'm a thousand percent loyal to you. Everybody knows that."

As if on cue, Lori's phone buzzes with an incoming text. She glances down at the screen. I can see a flicker of alarm pass across her face before she turns back to face me. "One of the VPs just informed me that you've been suspended from the company pending investigation. You're considered *persona non grata*."

A wave of nausea washes over me. My heart starts pounding in my ears.

Suspended? Persona non grata? How could this happen so quickly? The life I've fought so hard to build is crumbling around me. I feel utterly unequipped to shore up the walls.

"What am I going to do?" I whisper. My voice is barely audible above the hard rain on the windowpane. "I would normally turn to Nate for advice. Now he's the one accusing me."

"*Ach*. Kiddo." Lori pulls me into a warm embrace. "No matter what happens, you're going to be okay. You'll have me on your side every step of the way."

As her words wash over me, a feeling of gratitude and affection swells within my chest. I tighten my grip on her and whisper, "I love you, Lori."

She gently smoothes my tousled curls. Her eyes glisten with unshed tears. "You're the daughter I never had, Annalise."

I settle my head against her chest, needing reassurance at this moment. Lori strokes my hair and rubs my back until my tears dry up.

Before I can pull myself together, the doorbell rings. The fragile peace of the moment is shattered. Lori reluctantly releases me from her embrace and goes to answer the door.

Not thirty seconds later, my mother strides into the room, her face twisted with fury. She glares at Lori and snaps, "Leave us."

I'm taken aback by my mom's hostility. Why is she being shitty to Lori all the sudden? I refuse to let her drive away the one person who has truly been there for me.

"It's my living room, Monique," Lori says. "If anyone should leave, it's *you*."

I clutch Lori's hand. "Lori has been here for me. Unlike you."

"Such a spoiled little girl." Mom clucks her tongue. "Annalise. You brought this mess upon yourself."

Puzzled, I look to Lori. Lori is glaring at my mother like she'd run her through with a sword given the chance.

"What are you here for, Monique?" Lori asks.

Mom tosses her hair and fluffs her designer jacket. "I'm here to talk about some money that went missing. All little Miss-Gets-Whatever-She- Wants here had to do was keep her fucking mouth shut. But you had to tell everybody, didn't you? Well, you got what was coming to you. Nate Fordham called and warned us that he was going to fire you."

My mother's words ignite fury inside of me that I struggle to control. "You took the money, didn't you Mom?"

Lori squeezes my hand in silent support, and I'm grateful for it. I feel brave, but I might be doing something stupid.

My mom's face darkens with rage. A vicious sneer curls her pink-painted lips. Her eyes are cold as ice. "It's your fault that people found out about the missing money, Annalise! Why can't you just do what you're told for once in your life?"

"For once in my life? I did everything I could to make you and Dad happy. Look where it brought me!!" My heart skips a beat. I pause, tilting my head. "Wait. How did you find out about the missing money?"

"Perhaps if you'd bothered to turn on the television or check the news, you would know that Gellar Industries is being publicly investigated," Mom snarls, her words dripping with disdain. "It's dominating the news cycle. You're being flayed alive in the national press, darling. And now the company's stock isn't worth the money it's printed on."

The truth slams into me like a freight train, but I refuse to let her see how it affects me. "If you're so worried about the missing money, Mom, maybe you should be the one trying to find it. After all, it was under your watchful eye that this mess began."

"Excuse me?" Mom's eyes narrow dangerously.

Little does she know that I'm not done yet. Before I can speak, Lori cuts in.

"I brought in three forensic detectives to investigate this months ago. We knew that the embezzlement started twenty years ago. The forensic detectives traced the transactions back to Archer's computer. But when we checked the dates of the transactions with his old work calendar, we found that the incidents only happened when Archer was away." She presses her lips together. "It was someone who had his password. Someone comfortable with his office. Someone who knew when he wouldn't be in the office..."

My mom pales. "Just what are you accusing me of, Ms. Parker?"

"Just admit it!" I blurt out. "You stole the money. You logged in and wired the funds to dummy corporations under the guise of paying for office supplies."

Mom lifts her chin, going on the defensive. "Watch yourself, Annalise. I'm your *mother*."

I stare her down. For too long, I've let her control me. She and Dad molded me into the puppet they wanted me to be. But no more.

Now, I am a woman who refuses to be manipulated by anyone ever again.

"You are always looking to guilt and manipulate me," I tell her. It feels good standing up to her for the first time in my life. "It's not going to work this time, Mom. I don't know if you stole the money on your own or Dad was in on it. But I'm going to call the FEC and tell them the truth."

"Annalise Rebecca! You will respect me!" Monique's eyes flash. She's so worked up that flecks of spittle fly out of her mouth when she yells. "You need to accept the punishment. Surely they'll be easier on a young girl like you than a business giant like Archer."

I blink in disbelief, unable to fathom how my own mother can be so cruel and indifferent to my plight. "But I didn't take the money!" I cry out. "I have no idea where it went!"

"The money was spent on our living expenses," Monique explains with a casual wave. "I had no choice, really. It was all your dad's idea. Keeping up with the Park Ave lifestyle isn't cheap. Oh, and you had to go to expensive private schools. You had so many clothes. Fancy cars. Vacations with your girlfriends... If the FTC knew the kind of life you have lived, they would lock you up and throw away the key."

The betrayal of my parents cuts deeper than any blade ever could. "So it was you." I whisper, my voice barely audible. "You fucking stole twenty million dollars! And then you set up your own daughter to take the fall!"

Monique shrugs nonchalantly, clearly unaffected by my anguish. "I tried to tell you that you shouldn't take the CEO role. Didn't I? But you did it anyway. Always thinking you know best."

I stare at Monique, openmouthed. There are ten things that I could say to tear her flimsy argument into pieces. But I don't say any of them.

I realize that the world my mom lives in is very different than my own. It's more cutthroat, and full of reasons why she should do whatever she wants. There's no point in arguing with her.

"Monique," Lori interjects. "Why would you even tell us all this? You know I could—"

"Testify against me?" Monique scoffs dismissively, rolling her eyes. "Please, Lori, you're Gellar Industries' lawyer. I understand how lawyer-client privilege works.

Besides, do you really think I don't know where your loyalties lie?"

Lori's face twists up. I know that face. I've seen it a thousand times. Mom just told her something factually inaccurate and Lori is doing her best not to call her out on it.

Mom waves her hands. "And as for Annalise... My darling daughter wouldn't dare turn on her own mother."

In that moment, I want nothing more than to prove her wrong. Show her that I am not the weak and submissive pawn she believes me to be.

I would turn on her in a heartbeat.

"Listen to me, Annalise," Mom says. "Stay quiet. M'kay? Accept whatever punishment they decide to give you. This will all blow over. It's for the best, really." She squeezes my shoulder and gives me a stiff smile. And with that, she breezes out of the house as if she hasn't just shattered my entire world.

My heart pounds as I stare at the empty doorway.

What the hell just happened?

"Can you believe her?" I hiss, clenching my fists. "She sets me up as the fall girl and then has the audacity to act like it's my fault!"

Lori watches me carefully, her eyes radiating sympathy and concern. "Annalise," she begins, her voice gentle yet firm. "We'll figure this out, I promise you. We won't let Monique, or anyone else, destroy what you've worked so hard for."

She then strides purposefully across the room and grabs her phone. Before I can say anything, she's making a phone call. "Yeah. It's me. I need you to call the police."

"Wait, what?" I ask. "Why? You can't talk about what Mom just told you."

Lori covers the microphone with a hand. "Yes I can. Your mom doesn't understand the law. She thinks that, because I'm the company's lawyer and you're her daughter, neither of us can testify against her. But she's wrong. Having three people present broke privilege."

"You can't *prove* that she said anything, though."

"Wanna bet?" Lori points to a clock on the mantel. "I had a problem a few months ago with a maid stealing things. To catch her, I had cameras mounted in all the rooms. So I recorded the entire confession. We can report this, and we will."

I gape at her. She uncovers her phone and continues to order the person listening around?

"Yeah, Ryan? Okay. I'm going to send you the confession that I just got on tape. You're going to call the local police, the SEC, and... I don't know, call the FBI too for good measure." Lori smiles coldly. She cocks her head. "What's that? You have the name of someone at the IRS? Well, it couldn't hurt..."

She walks off toward her home office, presumably about to bring down the hammer on my mom.

Suddenly, I am shaking.

Nate, the man who dominated my most intimate moments and took my virginity with passion and desire, has betrayed me. My parents, the people who should have protected me, used me as their pawn. Now, Lori is my only remaining friend. She's my sole confidante in this twisted world.

I've lost my company, my reputation, my family... and Nate...

THIRTY-FOUR
NATE

Why am I here? I wonder.

This charity gala is as boring as the last one, and the one before that. I'm already three drinks in, my tuxedo rumpled and hair disheveled from the sleepless night that preceded this gala. I tossed and turned, thinking about the last time that I shared my bed with Annalise.

Where is she right now? Probably holed up somewhere. The news that Annalise was fired from Gellar Industries is everywhere. She's unlikely to show her face when it's being splashed across the front page of every newspaper, along with the headline *CEO Fired. Investigation Of Embezzlement Looms!*

And as for me? I'm skulking around the ballet gala, hoping against hope that she'll be here in spite of all that.

I don't know why I want to see her so badly. She made me weak. And yet, I'm here, skulking around and hoping to catch a glimpse of Annalise.

"Pull it together, Nate," I mutter under my breath.

I shouldn't be here, not with Annalise haunting every

corner of my thoughts. But I couldn't resist the chance to make sure she's doing okay after I forced her out of her company. It was just business. That's what I've been telling myself. Nothing personal.

But I know better than anyone how much Gellar Industries meant to her. It was her family's legacy. She was determined to prove herself worthy of it.

Now she's the punchline to many New Yorkers' nasty jokes.

My phone buzzes. I look at it and find yet another alert for Annalise's name. It reads, "Annalise Gellar, the latest CEO of Gellar Industries, has been fired by the board after she was found embezzling over twenty million dollars."

The information that this article is based on is blatantly wrong. I scroll up and squint at the author's name. Constance Lee.

I know that name. She's Cash's pet journalist.

Well Constance, you can go fuck yourself. And take your shitty source with you.

Was firing Annalise what I wanted? Yes, sort of. But now, articles are being written and YouTubes are being made that point to her as the obvious suspect. Somehow, I didn't anticipate that part.

Though it seems obvious now. I should have anticipated this.

As the orchestra begins another elegant waltz, I scan the room for any sign of her. Those golden curls or that fierce, stubborn gaze that had once held me captive.

But she's nowhere to be found. I didn't expect her to show up. Still, disappointment claws at my chest.

"Looking for someone, Nate?" A voice interrupts my brooding. I turn to find James, smirking in his perfectly tailored suit. My twin brother knows me too well. The bastard was always able to read my thoughts as if I were an open book.

"None of your business," I snap.

"Come on. We both know you're searching for Annalise. How's she doing since you took over Gellar Industries? Are you enjoying playing the ruthless businessman?" he taunts, but there's no heat behind his words. He may enjoy poking fun at me, but he also understands the weight I carry.

He, too, feels the loneliness that comes with being a Fordham.

"Like I said, it's none of your business," I reply, my voice sharper than intended.

James raises an eyebrow, studying me for a moment before speaking again. "Look, Nate, you're not fooling anyone. Your heart was never in this takeover. I'm surprised that you went through with it! It's clear you care for Annalise. I thought you brought her to the poker tournament to test the waters for announcing your relationship."

I push out a harsh breath. "She's the daughter of my business rival. I'm a capitalist through and through. At the end of the day, I only care about money. It was destined to end this way."

But with Annalise gone, why do I feel like I've been run over by a steamroller? Flat, dull, lifeless. Am I really this sad about a break-up?

James looks at me intently, pursing his lips. "Why don't we get out of here?" he asks. "The Porter's Club is right around the corner. We can catch up in relative privacy."

I swing my tired, slightly drunken gaze around the room. All around me, there are deals being made and jokes being cracked. I'm not in the mood for any of it.

Besides, there is no sign of Annalise. Why bother staying?

"Fine," I begrudgingly agree. "As long as they have more scotch."

My brother pushes me out of the room, shaking his head. Together, we leave the gala behind and make our way down the darkened Manhattan streets.

We soon arrive at a discreet brownstone building tucked between two modern high-rises. The contrast between the old and new façades is stark. James punches a code into a sleek keypad and hustles me in the front door.

The interior is rich and masculine, with dark wood paneling and plush leather furniture. A hushed murmur of voices drifts up from the downstairs lounge. Uniformed waiters drop drinks off to guests and collect empty glasses. On any other night, I would be tempted to join this room.

But James knows my moods too well for that. He pushes me toward the back of the foyer. We ascend the elegant staircase to a private library. I look at the walls, lined with leather-bound volumes and exquisite pieces of art.

An impeccably dressed employee appears almost instantly, a testament to the level of service in this exclusive sanctuary. "Bottled water for both of us," James orders without hesitation.

"Make that a Scotch for me," I counter.

"We're fine with water," James says firmly. He levels me with a serious gaze. I shrug and the employee disappears to fetch our drinks.

As I sink into one of the overstuffed leather chairs, I feel a sense of foreboding. Whatever James has to say, it's bound to be something I don't want to hear.

But a part of me hopes that he has an answer to the gnawing emptiness inside me. An emptiness that seems to grow every moment since I pushed Annalise away.

The chilled glass bottle of water lands on the mahogany table between us with a soft thud, accompanied by two crystal-clear glasses. The employee vanishes as silently as he appeared, leaving James and me in the dimly lit library.

"Let me guess," James says, pouring his water. "You listened to Cash's advice about Gellar Industries?"

"Unfortunately," I mutter. I slouch down in my chair.

James throws his head back and laughs. He quickly catches himself. "Sorry, Nate. But you've got to admit, Cash isn't exactly the best person to give relationship advice. He's in it for the money, not for the... emotional *whatever*."

"Tell me about it. Sometimes I think that guy is destined to be one of those billionaire seventy-year-olds who marries a girl young enough to be his granddaughter."

"Or he'll never settle down at all, knowing him." James fills my glass and nudges it toward me. "Drink this. It's not a good look to wander around drunk in public. For fuck's sake."

I gulp the water down, then go right back to lamenting my decision. "The point is, I screwed up with Annalise. I tried to do what I would normally have done. But... I'm starting to think that was a mistake."

James snorts. "Ya think?"

"I thought you were here to console me." I rub a hand over my face, blearily.

"Sorry. Old habits die hard." He crosses his legs and gives me a serious look. "You screwed up. Go on."

I shrug. "And now she's dumped me. Or we broke up? The details are kind of fuzzy."

"Let me ask you a question. Did you and Annalise ever use that four-letter word? You know the one."

"Love?" I feel like my stomach is lined with icy rocks. "Just once. The night before I fired her, actually."

James blinks. "You fucking fool," he mutters.

"Thanks for the vote of confidence, brother." But deep down, I know he's right. I've been an idiot.

"So. You've driven her away. How are you going to fix this mess you've made?"

I run my tongue over my teeth. "Do you think I can?"

"Depends. Can you continue on this path you're on?" His voice is heavy with concern. "You seem lonely and miserable."

"I am." I sigh, admitting defeat. "But even if I apologize to Annalise, it won't undo any of the damage I've caused."

"Then you must *grovel*."

"Grovel?" I scoff, the word sticking in my throat like bitter poison. The thought of begging for anything goes against every fiber of my being. But for Annalise...

I need to have her in my life. In my bed. As my wife, if she'll agree to it. What if groveling is the only way to get her back?

"Fine," I concede, clenching my fists in determination. "I'll grovel if that's what it takes."

"The things worth having sometimes require us to," James replies. Then his phone buzzes. He checks it, making a face of disgust. "Shit. I have to go, Nate. Derek needs me."

"You can't leave! Derek's just a friend. I'm your *twin*."

James shakes his head. "He's in the hospital, asshole. I'm going to pick up his daughter and take her over there."

"Oh." I wince. "I guess that's more important."

"Nate, good luck. I know you'll figure out the best way to beg for forgiveness." He gets up abruptly, dialing his phone as he strides across the room.

As the door shuts behind him, I sink deeper into the leather chair. The weight of the situation presses down on me. My fingers drum impatiently against the armrest as I pull out my phone, lost in thought.

How can I convince Annalise that I'm not the villain she believes me to be? Okay, I am the villain. Or rather, my brother is the villain. But I'm sure that Annalise won't see it in such black and white terms.

But how can I tell her that I know I did the wrong thing? A grand gesture, perhaps? No, Annalise is far too intelligent to be swayed by empty theatrics. It needs to be personal, meaningful, and most importantly, sincere.

A sudden thought strikes me like a bolt of lightning, illuminating the darkness clouding my mind.

THIRTY-FIVE
ANNALISE

I'm curled up on the couch in my Manhattan apartment, watching bad reality TV. After discovering that I'm all over every fucking news channel, I have retreated into the familiar world of fake reality.

Two impeccably dressed women are currently arguing onscreen. "You betrayed me!" one woman howls. She jabs a manicured fingernail at the other woman. "You're a betrayer, Deborah!"

"I was doing what was best for my family!" the other woman sobs.

The first woman crosses her arms. "You are dead to me."

There is a long shot of Deborah reacting. I cheer on the absolutely terrible acting. "Oh, Angie. I know that feeling all too well."

The program goes to commercial. I mute the TV and fast forward the program, eager to see the fallout.

A knock at the door makes me jump. I turn and look suspiciously at my front door.

Maybe the Thai food that I ordered is already here? It's

only been a few minutes, but... I climb to my feet and pad to the door.

Of all the people that I thought would be on the other side, Nate Fordham is the very fucking last.

Seeing him on my doorstep makes my heart stutter. He looks good. Way too good for how much I hate him. My mind might have made up its mind, but my body tenses at the sight of Nate.

He did a good job making my body fall in love with his.

"What are you doing here?!" I ask.

"Annalise." His gray eyes search mine for any sign of forgiveness.

They find none. "Go away, Nate." I start to shut the door on him. "I've had enough betrayal and manipulation to last a lifetime."

"Wait!" He sticks his foot in the door and stops it from closing. "Can I apologize?"

I laugh, then I realize that Nate is one hundred percent serious. "What? No! After what you accused me of, why would you think that I want anything to do with you?"

He reaches and gently grabs my wrist. A shudder runs through me at the feeling of his fingers on my skin. "Please, Annalise. Just hear me out,"

I hesitate, studying his face. It looks like he's been through the wringer. The pain etched across his features tugs at my heartstrings.

I can't let myself fall into his trap again.

Nate looks at me with those gray eyes of his, pleading, and I'm lost. I find myself agreeing to let him talk, even though we both know what I'm going to say at the end of his little speech.

Get out and never return.

"Two minutes," I warn. I open the door wider to let him in. The scent of his cologne fills my nostrils as he moves closer. I'm reminded of the last time we fucked. When we were naked in his bed, the whole damn room smelled just like that.

"Thank you, Kitten," Nate murmurs. He steps inside and shuts the door behind him. His presence in my home feels like an invasion. But I'm tougher than he knows. I won't let him see how much he affects me.

My voice is sharp as a razor's edge when I speak. "Start talking."

Nate has the audacity to look both contrite and determined. His eyes lock onto mine. "Annalise," he begins. "I have been walking around all week, completely miserable. Not understanding why I felt this... this sense of doom. I wrecked your life and then tried to walk away from you. Like you aren't the only woman who ever made me feel anything at all."

I suck my teeth. "I'm so sorry your life has been so hard, Nate."

Glancing at the clock on my phone, I'm almost ready to call an end to his two minute time limit. Nate grabs my hand, pleading.

"Not just hard. It's been impossible. My life stopped in its tracks the second I pushed you away. I was a fool, Annalise."

"I don't see how any of this is my problem." I cross my arms, trying to ignore my galloping heartbeat.

"I love you." Nate stops me cold with those words. "Annalise, I hurt you. I pushed you away. But I only did it because I got scared. It got too real for me. Saying I love you was not in my plans."

I stare at him, perplexed. "Scared. Scared of what?"

He waves his free hand. "Of you, baby. I was really scared of the way you made me feel. Until now, I've only cared about money. But then you came along and messed with my *priorities*."

"I need to sit." I walk back toward my couch and turn off the TV. I beckon him to sit. "So you dumped me, and publicly humiliated me in this spectacular fashion because... you're emotionally a little boy?"

For the first time ever, Nate's face flushes bright red. "It was a convenient escape. My associates were planning to take over Gellar Industries anyway. It was going down either way."

I curl my fingers into fists at my sides, nails biting into my palms. My anger simmers dangerously close to the surface.

"I'm beyond sorry for what I've done, Annalise," Nate confesses. His voice is laced with genuine remorse. "But I think I know how I can make it up to you."

I scoff, the sound harsh and bitter. "You think you can fix this? You destroyed my life, Nate. My company? My reputation? In ruins. Everything I've worked so hard for is gone."

"Give me a chance to prove myself," he pleads. "Please, Annalise."

"Prove yourself?" I repeat. "You expect me to give you another chance after everything you've done?"

He swallows hard and looks down. In that moment, I see a glimpse of vulnerability beneath his arrogant facade. It doesn't sway me, but it does give me pause.

Maybe he isn't a two-faced rat demon after all.

"I made a mistake," he admits. His voice cracks on the last word, sending a chill through me. "I'm sorry. You have no idea what a piece of shit I feel like. But I want to set things right. I promise you, I can make amends."

"You publicly humiliated me, Nate," I hiss. "I am the

laughingstock of the business world because of you. And now you waltz back in here, asking for my forgiveness?"

"Annalise."

I stop him short with a gesture. "Tell me how I can possibly forgive you after what you've done? What kind of grand plan do you have for that?"

"Give me two days," he says. He grabs my wrist, imploring. "Please. Two days to make things right."

"Two days? What could you possibly do in two days that would erase all the damage you've caused?"

"I will put you back in the CEO position. I'll give you enough money to cover the rest of the embezzled funds. Then if you're not satisfied, I'll never bother you again. Let me set the record straight about you with everyone that matters."

My heart races in my chest. As much as I despise him for what he's done, I can't deny that I want my job back. It's what I've been fighting for, after all. But can I trust him?

THIRTY-SIX
ANNALISE

The stench of betrayal hangs in the air as we stalk into the Gellar Industries boardroom, a dank space with a long wood conference table in the middle of the room. There are large windows that should show off the Manhattan skyline. But the windows are dirty and the view is dull.

The room is full of rich men and women who are all, to a man, bored and ready to get out of here. When the board members see Nate, then clock me right behind him, it's clear that they don't know what's about to happen.

It's funny, because I don't either.

I can feel my heart pounding in my chest as I sit down at the polished oak conference table. My mother and father are here, at the far end. Familiar faces fill out the rest of the table. I've known many of these people since I was a child.

"Annalise, dear," my mother begins. Her voice sounds painfully saccharine and extremely condescending. "Are you sure about this?"

"If you need to talk, sweetheart—" my father adds.

Nate cuts them off with a sharp gesture. "Enough."

As Nate addresses the room, I sit demurely. Trying to pretend that I'm not so anxious that I'm worried about my heart.

"So. When we met last week, I told you that over twenty million was missing from the company. And Mr. Gellar was happy enough to jump up and tell us that the only answer was to remove his daughter as CEO. Everyone remembers that, right?"

The room is silent. The board members look at each other, trying to communicate with their eyes.

"I'll take that as a yes. Let me tell you what's about to happen in this room." Nate paces the floor. "The unethical business practices of this board have gone unchecked for far too long. I think we should all talk about it."

He opens a laptop and projects damning documents onto the wall behind him. As I watch, emails, financial records, and transcripts all pop up on the screen. It looks like the FTC's wet dream, from what I can see. I can feel the tension in the room mounting. A palpable energy crackles like static electricity.

"Mr. Thompson!" Nate yells, singling out one man in particular. "Did you honestly think your insider trading would go unnoticed?" He presses a button and several graphs pop up. "You got a tip here... and one here... should I continue?"

"No..." The man squirms in his seat, his face turning an alarming shade of red.

"Very well. Let's move on to Ms. Patel." Nate smiles widely. "Embezzling funds from the ballet company's charity foundation? Despicable."

"I... I did not!" Amrita Patel stutters. "It's not what it looks like. I swear!"

Nate opens his briefcase, flips through the file folders, and tosses one to her. "There you go. There is all the evidence. You did a shitty job of covering it up, by the way."

Amrita's mouth drops open. She looks at the file folder for a second. Then she reaches out a shaky hand and draws it toward herself. She opens it, muttering, "Shit."

Nate goes around the table, pulling file folders from his briefcase and putting them in front of each of the board members. Most of them look at what's inside for a moment before closing the folder silently. A couple of people don't even check what's inside.

I think that means that they already know their darkest secrets have been exposed.

"Well, that's everybody. Everybody except Archer and Monique." Nate smiles, showing all his teeth like a fucking shark. "I don't want you two to feel left out."

My mom stands up. "I don't need to listen to this."

"Sit the fuck down." Nate makes a down gesture. My mom glares at him and then turns to walk out of the room.

"Monique embezzled the missing twenty million dollars from this company!" Nate cries.

My mom's gait slows, then stops. She turns around slowly.

"You can't prove that!" she hisses.

"We can, actually. We have the confession you made to Lori yesterday on video," I cut in. "It's pretty cut and dry."

"You little bitch!" Mom's eyes widen for a second before her expression turns angry again. "My lawyers will have you for breakfast."

"Now, Monique." Nate clucks his tongue loudly. "We also have you on the security tape on the days of the embezzlement, breaking into Archer's office. The time stamps line up quite nicely."

Nate presses another button and several still shots from crystal clear security cameras pop up onscreen. They are taken from inside in my father's office, time stamped as clear as day. And right in the middle of each shot is my mother, sneaking into the room.

My mom's jaw drops. "You—you can't use that! It's... confidential!"

"Nice try. It's a funny story. Apparently, Archer installed a nanny cam in his office. News flash: your husband doesn't trust you, Monique. I assume that you started embezzling as a solo project. When your husband caught on, you were forced to cut him in. Isn't that right, Archer?"

The tension in the room is a thick, suffocating fog as Nate focuses his piercing silver eyes on my parents. I watch, heart pounding, as he coolly delivers the final blow.

"How do I know?" Nate asks, as if someone has voiced the question. "You hid the money in bank accounts across the globe. I have you both on tape, walking into banks in the Grand Caymans, the Czech Republic, and Kenya. That was insanely stupid of you."

My mother's face turns ashen. Her muted pink lipstick is suddenly garish against her pale skin. My father clenches his jaw, his eyes narrowing dangerously.

I feel nothing but a cool numbness as I stare at my parents. They perpetrated a large financial crime and had the fucking balls to try to pin it on me. I'm just lucky that they're both dumb enough to think they wouldn't be caught.

But my trust in them is now shattered like a priceless vase carelessly dropped onto an unforgiving marble floor. It can never be put back together.

"I did no such thing!" my mom yells, her face turning red. "Archer, say something, for god's sake. Defend my honor!"

"Monique, dear..." My father, who is dressed in a black suit that makes his pallor stand out all the more, clears his throat. He shifts in his seat, still clutching his cane. "I think it's best if neither of us says anything. We don't want to make any statements, period."

Mr. duBeck, the head of the board, climbs to his feet. "Excuse me, Archer. If Nate didn't call this meeting for any reason other than to harass you—"

"You?" Nate points at him. "Sit down. Shut up. Or else I will start telling the other board members all about your overseas sex tourism. Laos? Gambia? Ukraine?"

Mr. duBeck staggers and collapses in his seat as if someone had fired a shot at his center mass. His eyes protrude like they are about to pop out of his head.

"Good man." Nate sweeps his gaze over the assembled board members. "If I go to the press with what I've uncovered, you'll all be fucked. You were on a board for years while financial improprieties went on under your nose? Who would hire you if word got out? You would be tainted by scandal."

"Mr. Fordham, I don't think—" Mrs. Smythe starts in, her gray coiffure quivering. She looks like a large, graying lump of Jell-O.

"Mrs. Smythe, let me stop you right there. I know that two of your three husbands died under mysterious circumstances. You paid the same coroner hundreds of thousands of dollars to declare the deaths heart attacks. Isn't that right?"

Mrs. Smythe gapes. "Well, I—I—"

"Right." Nate looks at me, smiling blandly. "We have the same type of information on each one of the board members. Mrs. Smythe here should be less afraid of her secret getting out than the rest of you. Corrupt sons of bitches, every last one of you. Seriously, the next one that says a fucking word gets his or her secret spilled to a tabloid."

I'm pretty sure I hear an audible gulp. Eyes around the table widen, everyone looking around at the gathered group.

"Right. That's settled. And before anyone gets any ideas, I've got a fucking dead man's switch. Fucking with me is the only way to be certain that your secrets *will* go viral."

Nate lets the threat hang in the air for a moment, allowing the gravity of the situation to settle. I can feel the balance of power shifting. Damn. Nate was right.

I could be dressed in a damn clown suit right now and no one would notice. No one else is bothering to look beyond themselves.

My dad clears his throat. "What do you want, you prick?"

Nate rubs his hands together as his eyes slide around the room.

"I have a proposition for you. Vote Annalise back in as CEO. In exchange, I'll keep your terrible secrets to myself."

The room explodes into a cacophony of protests. Nate holds up a hand to silence them.

"This is non-negotiable. You put Annalise back in charge or you prepare to face the consequences of your actions."

The board members exchange wary glances. Their expressions are a mixture of fear and resignation. One by one, they cast their votes, until it's official.

I'm back in as CEO of Gellar Industries. A wave of relief crashes over me. I push myself to my feet.

"Now get the fuck out of here," I growl.

The entire board looks at me as if I've grown another head. I slap the table, standing up. Mrs. Smythe stumbles out of her seat, running for the door. Everyone else follows her, even my scummy parents.

The parting look my mom gives me is one of immense

revulsion. I blow her a kiss and she scowls. Then she turns the corner and vanishes.

The girl I used to be three months ago would have withered under that glare. What has happened to me?

"Annalise." Nate calls me back from my thoughts. I look at him, feeling off-center. "You're back. I know you didn't want it to happen this way. But it's done. You're the CEO again."

"Blackmail, Nate? There had to be another way to get me back in charge."

He shrugs a shoulder. "I know what rich people fear most: losing their money and status. Sometimes, you have to play dirty to win. Besides. It worked, didn't it?"

My lips press into a thin line. "Only because they were more afraid of being exposed than they were of me. They don't respect me, Nate. They'll never take me seriously now."

"You've got your company back, Annalise. That's step one."

"Nate..." I look at him. "You've managed to undo one thing. But you did a lot of damage. You're talking like you want me to just fall at your feet and be thankful you even looked my way. And I'm here to tell you that isn't going to happen. You fucked up. And I'm not sure that there is a way back from that!"

I end my speech before I burst into tears. It takes all that I've got to rein my emotions in.

"You've got to give me more time." Nate touches my face. "I'm trying to make things right."

"Trying? You think that's going to cut it?" I laugh bitterly and back away from his caress. "You may be a big name on Wall Street, Nate Fordham. But when it comes to credibility with me, you have none. Zero. Zilch."

Nate reaches for me again. Desperation is etched in

every line on his handsome face. "Please, Annalise. Just give me one more day. One day to prove to you that I can change. I can be the man you deserve. If I can't make it right after that..." He swallows hard. "I swear I'll leave you alone forever."

I study him. The raw vulnerability in his gaze, the tension in his broad shoulders. Part of me that still throbs for him, despite everything. I *want* to believe him.

But the scars run deep. I can't let myself forget what Nate has done.

"I'll wait one more day. But things are far from fixed."

Meet me at the Met at 7. Wear this dress.

It's a simple text message, but it makes my heart beat a little faster. I do love the Metropolitan Museum of Art an embarrassing amount. He knows that. What could Nate have planned that involves the museum after hours?

It reminds me of our first date. But it's not, as I keep reminding myself. So why am I so damned nervous?

Now, standing outside the grand entrance of the Met, I'm nervous. Dressed elegantly in a curve-hugging black gown that Nate sent for me to wear, I draw in a deep breath. There's only one way to find out what Nate has planned.

And that is to follow his cryptic instructions.

Pushing past the columns, I brace myself. The doors open from the inside; there is an usher standing there who welcomes me. As I step into the museum, I'm engulfed in an opulent ballet-themed wonderland.

The Met's grand hall has been transformed into a dazzling venue fit for royalty. Crystal chandeliers cast shimmering light across the white and gold accents that are draped on the walls. Delicate floral arrangements topped with tiny glass ballet dancers are placed every twenty feet. Elegant ballet-inspired statues and paintings dot the length of the hall.

The atmosphere is absolutely electric. The place is packed, more full than I've ever seen the spacious lobby be. A palpable current of anticipation buzzes through the air. Tiny white note cards hang at intervals from the ceiling on long white strings. I reach up to touch one of the cards, but I'm interrupted by an inquiring voice.

"Miss? Would you like a Grand Jeté Gin Fizz?" A passing waiter extends a tray toward me, offering a frothy white cocktail garnished with a delicate pirouetting ballerina made of sugar.

I take the glass, my eyes widening. "Thank you."

I have a sip, savoring the silky, citrusy-sweet flavor. The drink is surprisingly effervescent. I take another sip as I touch the white card hanging near me. It reads simply, "I'm sorry, Kitten."

I almost spit my mouthful of cocktail on the floor. Looking around, I wonder what everyone else thinks. Will they understand that Kitten is my nickname? I have no idea.

What is Nate up to?

My gaze sweeps over the room in search of that infuriating man. Admittedly, he has both captivated and challenged me. Where is he? And what does he want from me tonight?

"Have you seen Nate?" I ask another guest, a woman bedecked in diamonds and silk.

"Who are you looking for, dear?" she inquires. She lifts an eyebrow.

"Nate Fordham." I can feel the heat rising in my cheeks at the mention of his name.

"Ah, Mr. Fordham," the woman crows. "Quite the

enigma, isn't he? I saw him make a grand entrance earlier. You might want to look for him near the stage."

I thank her and thread my way through the crowd toward where she pointed. The Met's grand hall doesn't usually have a stage. But I can see that the huge marble staircase in the center of the hall is roped off. That must be what the woman meant.

I take another sip of the cocktail, savoring its sweet and tangy flavor, and continue my search. I pass by another note hanging from the ceiling. When I check this one, it says, "I would choose you in every lifetime."

The note gives me pause. Is this what Nate actually feels? The note is scrawled on the card and the handwriting feels familiar, but I can't be certain.

And so what if it is how he feels? Is that enough of an apology for publicly humiliating me?

"Annalise!" Someone calls my name.

I turn sharply, only to see one of Nate's brothers waving at me from across the room. It's Cash. Not my favorite person, if I'm being honest. My heart sinks a little, knowing that whatever he has planned, his family is here, too.

"Hello, Cash." I force a smile as I approach him. "Have you seen Nate?"

"Don't worry. He'll find you when he's ready." Cash smiles pleasantly.

I notice that there is no attempt to hit on me. Cash seems to be a completely different person. I don't trust it.

"What, no comment on my body or how I look in this dress?" I say dryly.

Cash gives me a sober glance. "Nate told me to behave myself tonight. He also threatened me with bodily harm if I said anything to upset you."

"Did he now?" I eye Cash. "And you're respecting that?"

"Of course. Nate said the magic words. 'I'm going to marry her'." He puts his hands up as if he's surrendering. "You're off limits now."

"What?" I say, sucking in a breath. "He said that?"

"Close enough. I told Nate if he gave you a diamond, you would probably tell him where to stick it." Cash wiggles his eyebrows. "Be nice to Nate, Annalise. The poor guy is kicking himself for doing you wrong."

"No offense, Cash. But you aren't the person I want to take life advice from."

"Enjoy the evening, Annalise," Cash says with a wink. "I'll see you soon."

"What does that mean? See me when?" I call. But he's moving away.

My fingers tighten around the delicate stem of my glass. That's a huge assumption on Cash's part. Shaking my head, I move deeper into the opulent venue. If Nate's plan was to make me feel agitated, it's all playing out perfectly.

I wander around, sipping my cocktail and looking at the ballet-themed art. Nate got one part of this correct. I am pretty ballet-crazy for a girl who never wore pointe shoes.

"Annalise?" I turn to find a tall man with graying hair and sharp blue eyes extending his hand to me. "I'm Richard Palmer, CEO of Palmer Technologies. I've heard a lot about you."

"Nice to meet you, Mr. Palmer," I reply, shaking his hand firmly. "I hope the rumors haven't been too unkind."

"They haven't. It's just unfortunate that the national press was fed the wrong story about you. I've talked to Nate Fordham at length. From what I hear, you're a force to be reckoned with."

"Thank you. I try my best." I bob my head, not knowing how I should behave.

"Perhaps we could discuss potential collaborations

between our companies sometime," Richard suggests. "Your ground-penetrating sonar technology is of particular interest to me."

"That sounds..." I gulp. "Like an interesting opportunity?"

"Excellent," he replies. "I'll have my assistant get in touch."

I watch him go, trying not to gape. My mind reels from the encounter.

What is Nate planning to do here? Is this whole hall full of people he has talked to about me? I glance to my left and right. Tom Anderson, the VP of SoftPoint Software. Lisa Cheng, the CEO of Bradley Inc Investments. Djimon Hsu, an ultrawealthy patron of every charity I admire.

These people are obviously wealthy. And they could be here for the ballet? But maybe they're more than ballet patrons.

It seems like they may be the movers and shakers of Fifth Avenue.

"Hello." Nate's amplified voice booms throughout the hall. "I'd like to bring your attention to the front here. In a few moments, the NYC Ballet is going to perform the *denouement* of Swan Lake."

Nate is standing on the grand staircase. His tuxedo is impeccably tailored, hugging his muscular frame to perfection. He exudes power and sensuality as he waits for the crowd to quiet down. As he does, his eyes search the crowd.

My heart's curiosity is decidedly piqued by this exasperating man.

"Annalise," someone whispers in my ear. Lori Parker catches my elbow. She raises an eyebrow at Nate's entry, clearly intrigued. "Any idea what he's up to?"

"What are you doing here?" I ask, alarmed.

She rolls her eyes. "I don't know. I was just told to

attend this ballet fundraiser. I didn't know that you would be here. And I definitely didn't expect Nate Fordham to be behind it."

I whisper back, "I promised Nate I would listen. Other than that, I'm as in the dark as everyone else."

"Give me a signal and we'll hightail it out of here." Lori squeezes my arm. "You have an escape plan?"

Giving her a quick side hug, I exhale a long breath. "I'm going to give him a few more minutes to make his point."

The lights dim, signaling the start of the ballet program. Ballerinas glide gracefully onto the makeshift stage. They are amazing; their movements so fluid yet tightly controlled. The audience watches, mesmerized.

My eyes drift to Nate. He remains visibly attentive, clapping politely after each act. But his gaze occasionally drifts to where I sit. I meet his gaze several times but break eye contact after a moment.

I'm not swayed by anything I've seen yet. Nate hasn't made a personal, vulnerable plea to me yet. I keep expecting him to come over.

But he doesn't. I grit my teeth, frustrated.

As the final act concludes to thunderous applause, I steal one last glance at Nate. He's deep in conversation with a technician, scanning the room as if assessing its readiness for something grand. My heart hammers in anticipation.

The applause for the final ballet act dies down. Nate strides onto the steps again, commanding attention with his mere presence. He clears his throat, and a hush falls over the room. I watch him intently, trying to guess what he has planned.

"I'd like to thank Calum Fordham for lending us his ballet company," he begins, his voice smooth and rich. "I hope you've enjoyed the enchanting performance we've seen tonight. But now, I have something personal to share with you all."

His gray eyes lock onto mine, sending a shiver down my spine. I feel both exposed and intrigued.

I'm utterly unable to look away.

"Please direct your attention to the screen beside me." A large TV screen descends from the ceiling. As the lights dim, the screen casts a harsh glow on the expectant faces of the crowd.

"Roll the video," Nate commands.

As the professionally edited video begins, I see Nate. He's dressed in casual clothes, sitting in what appears to be his luxurious penthouse. He looks directly at the camera.

But his piercing gray gaze seems to be directed at me alone. I suck in a breath.

"Annalise Gellar, I owe you an apology. I was wrong to push you out of your own company. All I can say is that I was blinded by arrogance and ambition. I'm so sorry that your face was splashed all over the media. Someone leaked lies about you embezzling company funds. I'm not responsible for the leak. But the fact that I didn't correct the record when I had the chance... that's my fault."

My breath catches in my throat. My mind races with disbelief at his admission.

"The thing is, Annalise. I started to fall for you." He pauses for a long moment, then continues. "For the first time in a long time, I felt vulnerable. And I reacted the only way I knew how. I pushed– no, I *shoved* you away. And for that, I'm sorry. It was the worst decision of my life."

My mouth opens. I cover it with my hand, heart thudding. Nate is apologizing and admitting to this whole room of Wall Street sharks that I make him feel *vulnerable*?

No *way*.

"I've spent my entire life thinking that power and

success were the only things that mattered. I was wrong. When you smile at me, those things seem like faraway concepts. I don't care about Gellar Industries or the merger anymore. If it means losing you, I'll walk away from all of it."

Nate looks at the camera with such a look of intense desperation. I can't breathe. A tear slips down my cheek, unbidden. I brush it away without tearing my gaze from the screen.

The spotlight slices through the darkness, illuminating Nate. He moves toward me through the crowd. My heart thuds wildly in my chest.

"Annalise," he begins, his voice rich with emotion as he reaches me and drops down to one knee, "I know I don't deserve your forgiveness, not after everything I've done." He glances around at the captivated audience before looking back into my eyes. "But I promise you, from this moment on, I will spend every day proving myself to you."

My pulse races faster with each word he utters.

"I can't imagine my life without you in it. I love you, Annalise."

The sincerity in his voice is impossible to deny.

"Are you saying—" I start, then stop. My voice is barely above a whisper. "Are you offering to put aside our rivalry?"

"Annalise." He takes my hand, kissing my knuckles. "You are worth more to me than any empire. More than any fortune. I know that now."

I take a deep breath. Though I doubted him, Nate has done the unthinkable. He's proven that he'll do anything to be with me, including professing his love in front of his peers. To pretend that I'm not swayed by his admissions would be a lie.

"All right," I whisper. I lock eyes with him.

"Is that a yes?" he clarifies, his expression tense and hopeful.

"Yes, Nate. Yes, I'll give you another chance."

Nate's face breaks into a smile. He picks me up and I slide my hands around his neck. Our lips meet in a passionate, searing kiss. People are lightly applauding, but my brain doesn't even register it.

All there is in the entire world at this moment is Nate and me.

This, I think. *This feeling right here. I've missed this so desperately.*

When we finally break apart, Nate whispers in my ear.

"I'm ready to start making it up to you right now." His words are laced with heat and anticipation. I shiver and kiss him again.

"Maybe you can make it up to me in the bedroom instead of the board room," I whisper in his ear. "And my first act as CEO is to be on top..."

THIRTY-EIGHT

NATE

"I'm so excited to see this performance!" Annalise's eyes are bright as she talks about her passion. "I've never seen the Tokyo Ballet before. I can't wait."

My lips twitch with dark humor. "I'm glad that at least one of us is excited."

Annalise pauses, looking around at the people pushing past us to get to their boxes. She pulls me to the velvet-lined wall and puts a gentle hand on my chest.

"If you don't want to do this..." Her eyes are large and luminous.

"No." I heave an exaggerated sigh. "Taking my parents to the ballet was my idea. A bad one, almost certainly. But mine nonetheless. Come on."

I place my hand on the small of Annalise's back, guiding her into the opulent ballet theater. One of the things I love about Annalise is her perpetual enthusiasm about being in this building, with its gilded ceilings and plush red velvet seats. I can feel the hitch in her breath as we step into the box; the stage is laid out before us, curtains closed, orchestra tuning their instruments.

My parents are already seated in our private box, sipping champagne and whispering to each other. When they realize we are here, though, they turn to look at us with sharply disapproving gazes. My mom's severe look rakes over Annalise from head-to-toe, her lips already pursed in disapproval.

"I do admire your boldness, my dear. It takes a certain... confidence to dress so, *uniquely* in such a refined setting."

"*Mom.*" I slide my arm around Annalise. "Play nice. Even if you don't mean it, pretend that you can be pleasant."

"I'm just protecting the Fordham family's endowment." My mom looks at Annalise again. "You understand, don't you? Of course it's lovely that you've found a way to fit into my son's world. *Temporarily*, at least."

"Now, darling." Dad represses a chuckle. "Don't be so hard on the poor girl. *Everyone* deserves a taste of luxury, even if they're not accustomed to it."

I feel Annalise tense under my palm but she keeps her head high, a polite smile glued in place. My blood boils at their blatant rudeness.

Annalise is brilliant, beautiful, and passionate. Not only that, but she loves *me*. How dare my parents insult her?

"That's enough from the peanut gallery," I say coolly, giving them a hard stare. "Annalise is an accomplished CEO in her own right. I won't tolerate you belittling her."

Mom waves a dismissive hand. "Oh please, Nathaniel. We all know she's only playing at business until she can land herself a proper husband."

"I'll tell you this once more." I move to take Annalise's hand in mine. "I love Annalise. And I'm lucky she puts up with me. If you still feel the need to demean her, you shouldn't expect to see me at family gatherings."

My mom's jaw sets. She harrumphs and turns back

toward the stage. I arch a questioning brow at my father. He shrugs, casts his gaze over Annalise and me once more, and then turns as well.

Annalise looks up at me as she exhales a shaky breath. I squeeze her hand and whisper, "Sorry." She hugs my arm tightly. I urge her down into the box, where we take seats in the second row.

As I'm still holding Annalise's hand reassuringly, a familiar face pokes her head in. "Is this where I'm supposed to be?" Lori Parker asks.

Annalise gasps in delight, her eyes widening. "Lori! What are you doing here?"

I wave Annalise's so-called 'bonus mom' in. "Sure is. There's a seat for you right by Annalise."

Lori takes the proffered seat with grace. "Nate invited me," she tells Annalise. "He thought it would be nice for our 'families' to meet and mingle."

Annalise turns to me. "You did this? For me?"

"I know how much Lori means to you. She's like family."

"She is my family," Annalise says emphatically. She hugs Lori again. "My found family. I don't know what I'd do without her."

Lori pats her back soothingly. "Oh honey, I'll always be here for you. We're in this together."

The lights begin to dim as the ballet starts. I slide my arm around Annalise's shoulders. She leans against me in a tender way that makes me forget the dancers onstage.

I put my nose in her hair and inhale her scent. For a few moments, I am blissed out, unaware of anyone who isn't Annalise. I watch the dancers float across the stage for forty minutes, then applaud when everyone else does.

The lights roll up again, a sign that intermission is starting.

"Perfect timing. Let's head to the bar and I'll introduce you to a few more people," I say to Annalise, then call out, "Do you want anything, Lori?"

The older woman is already halfway out of the box. She flaps a hand at me. "I spotted a friend across the way. Don't get anything for me."

Annalise and I make my way downstairs. Just as we enter the crowded lounge area, I spot my cousin Calum, the owner of the ballet company, with his glamorous wife Kaia.

"Nate!" Calum claps me heartily on the shoulder. "Good to see you. And..." He looks at Annalise. "Annabeth?"

"Calum, Kaia, I'd like you to meet Annalise Gellar. She's my girlfriend." I keep an arm wrapped around her waist.

"Charmed," Kaia trills. She bounces over and air-kisses Annalise on both cheeks. "I so rarely meet any of Calum's friends' girlfriends. They are all commitment-phobes."

"Is that so?" Annalise replies, looking a bit taken aback. I can tell she's flustered by Kaia's effortless, slightly intimidating poise. "I hope it's not rude to ask, but are you a ballet dancer?"

"I am!" Kaia laughs, sharing a glance with Calum. "I danced here until I got pregnant with our daughter Charlotte. Now I lead a foundation."

"Is that how you two met?" Annalise asks.

"Yes. I was a dancer. He took over the company. We fell in love." Kaia gestures. "Tale as old as time. I'll tell you all about over a cup of coffee sometime, if you're interested."

I hide an amused smile at that, knowing how my old money family tends to look down on the newly wealthy, like the Gellars. But Kaia has always been refreshingly free of snobbery, despite her own blue-blooded heritage.

"Well..." I cough into my hand. "There's not much to tell other than it nearly ended both of their careers."

Calum rolls his eyes and puts his hands onto Kaia's

hips. "Yes, yes. Forbidden love, etc." He nudges Kaia toward the theater. "My suggestion is that we head into the Jewelry Box for a drink. Nate, your brothers are in there already."

A note of anticipation and nervousness thralls through my blood. I know exactly what Calum has planned; I arranged all of this.

"They are?" Annalise glances up at me with a questioning look. "Did you know that they were coming?"

I shrug a shoulder and smile enigmatically. "Maybe."

She gives me a funny look. I snake my arm around her waist, pulling her closer. I feel that faint pull of desire starting to thrum through my veins at her nearness. We follow Calum and Kaia away from the crowd and into the Jewelry Box, a private, stage-level box with a small bar and plenty of standing room. The entire room is decorated in pink velvet, pink satin, and black and white photos from NYC Ballet productions.

"I didn't even know this place was here!" Annalise says as I sweep her along into the room. "Oh, Lori's in here. And... your parents..."

Cash and Grant turn around, each lifting their drink in acknowledgment. James stands with my parents, whispering. My pulse picks up.

They are all here. It's time.

I take Annalise's hand. Her eyes meet mine. It has always felt like she could see straight through me. I search her face, trying to gauge her reaction to what I'm about to say. "Annalise. There's something I want to ask you."

Everyone in the room stills and looks at us. She leans closer to me, as if drawn in by some invisible force. "What is it?"

Without hesitation, I reach into my pocket and retrieve a small velvet box. I kneel before her and everything else fades away as I open the box to reveal the dazzling diamond ring inside.

Annalise puts a hand to her mouth, gasping softly. "Nate, is this–?"

"Annalise Gellar, you're an amazing woman. You are the entire package: intelligent, beautiful, and kind. You make my life complete. Will you marry me?"

Tears glisten in her eyes as she looks back and forth between me and the ring. This isn't just a proposal, it's a promise to spend our lives together.

"Oh my god. Oh my god, yes!" she breathes out. "Yes, I will marry you, Nate Fordham."

As everyone applauds, I get to my feet and Annalise flings herself into my arms. I hold her tight as her lips seek mine. She kisses me hard, her hands bracing my head.

"I love you," she whispers to me.

I grab her waist and lift her. "And I love you."

Calum is the first to congratulate me. I shake his hand, thanking him for helping me to set this up.

Grant pulls Annalise into a warm embrace, lifting her off the ground briefly before setting her back down with a laugh. His easy grin mirrors mine "Congratulations, you two!" he exclaims.

Cash joins in, his charm radiating as he offers Annalise a playful wink. "Welcome to the family! We knew Nate was too good for one-night stands, but we didn't think he'd go this far!"

"Shut up, Cash," I reply. I roll my eyes, but I'm unable to suppress the smile tugging at my lips. "I hope that you are the next brother to be tortured by love."

"Hey!" Annalise says, eyeing me. "I'm right here."

"Nate didn't mean anything by it," Cash says. "And anyway, his wishes are never going to happen. I'm not dumb enough to fall for a woman. Er, no offense."

"Um, offense taken," she shoots back. "You're just lucky I'm still walking on air from Nate's proposal."

"See, Cash? I stopped you from putting your foot in your mouth." I squeeze Annalise. "You're welcome."

Lori pushes her way into the circle, making my brothers step back.

"Congratulations, Annalise." She hugs her. "And Nate, thanks for letting me be here for your special moment."

"Of course. We're all becoming one family now," I answer mildly.

My parents eventually make their way over to us. My mom leans out and touches Annalise's arm. That's as good as a hug, in my mom's book.

"Congratulations," Mom says. "Though you could've done without the public proposal, don't you think?"

"We talked about getting married and public proposals before I popped the question in public." I tighten my arm around Annalise. "We're both very happy to be engaged. So thanks."

"Nate, Annalise." My dad claps me on the back a little bit awkwardly. "Well done. A celebration is in order, wouldn't you say?"

"Come on, let's grab some champagne!" Grant suggests, elbowing his way into the conversation. "Annalise, there is a new conductor I wanted to tell you about..."

"Not tonight," I tell Grant, eyeing him. "Some other time. Tonight, she's all mine. We'll all go together."

Laughter bounces off the plush walls as we get our champagne flutes. I can barely keep up with the excitement swirling around us.

All I know is that Annalise is wearing my ring on her finger. Finally, this woman is really all mine.

THIRTY-NINE

NATE

"Careful with those!" I hear Annalise reprimand two movers when one bumps a chair leg into the doorframe of my penthouse. I smile at the men as they hustle past me, each bearing a chair that Annalise simply refused to part with.

I watch as my fiancée steps through the penthouse door. Her golden curls frame her face, which is flushed with equal parts exhaustion and excitement. She's dressed in yoga pants and a plain t-shirt. She looks sexy, but then again, she always does. Even while muscling a much too heavy box through the door.

I step in, grabbing it from her. "Will you just let the movers handle this?"

I set the box down in a stack of other boxes. Annalise smiles at me.

"That's it!" She runs her hand over her ponytail as she surveys what used to be my penthouse. Now it looks like a U-Haul storage facility. "That's the last box."

"Oh, that's it? You couldn't find any more boxes of random stuff to have the guys bring over?" I grin at her and she shakes her head.

"You should have seen how much stuff went to the curb for people to take. I caused a minor stampede this morning."

I tilt my head, looking at her body. "In those leggings? It's no wonder."

"It was not my leggings, thank you very much." Annalise flushes. "People in New York City will take anything that's not nailed down."

I study her face for any signs of regret or hesitation. "You're happy, though?"

She comes over to hug me. "More than happy. I'm just overwhelmed. My parents being in the news hasn't been the easiest thing for me. The media might have exonerated me, but they are still hounding me to give an interview. Then I was just packing up my apartment..."

"I told you to let the moving company do all of that," I chide.

"I know. It's just... It was hard to get rid of some things, knowing that my mom would've had a fit. She has very... very strong feelings... about decor..." Her voice wobbles and she sniffles. "I just can't believe my parents fled to Montenegro just to avoid prison time. What will happen to their properties? What about the house I grew up in?"

"The one that has no sign of you ever having lived there?" I ask.

Annalise winces. "That isn't my point, Nate."

I wrap my arm around her waist, pulling her close. "I'm sorry that you're going through this. My offer to buy your dad's house when the estate is settled is still on the table." I kiss her head. "Besides. You're building your own life now. A better life. In this life, you can decorate your own house and pick out your own clothes."

"Thank you," she whispers, leaning into my embrace. "Seriously, thank you for making this feel like home."

"Annalise, this isn't just my home anymore. It's ours. And soon, hopefully, it will return to looking like a chic penthouse and not a habitat for wild raccoons."

"*Nate*." She laughs. "I'm trying to be vulnerable with you."

"Sorry." I suck in a deep breath and then exhale, looking into her eyes. "You know I love you. I always will."

"Do you promise?"

"Absolutely," I say. I brush a stray curl from her forehead. "I've got you. As long as you have me too, we'll crush any obstacles in our way."

"Sounds good to me. As long as you still cuddle me tonight."

I feign shock, my eyes widening in mock horror. "May I remind you that I am a ruthless mogul?"

"As long as you're *my* ruthless mogul, that sounds right to me.".

I give her a possessive kiss that leaves us both breathless. Just then, a lean figure in a tailored suit appears before us, his impatience radiating off him like an overpowering cologne. Javier, our stylish wedding planner, taps his polished leather shoe on the marble floor as if he's been waiting for hours.

"Don't we have a wedding to plan?" He eyes Annalise and me with a mixture of irritation and relief. "We have so much to discuss. Wedding invitations, floral arrangements, cake designs... If you follow me through this post-apocalyptic scene in your foyer, I have set up a cake tasting in the vortex of boxes that used to be your kitchen."

I raise my eyebrows at Annalise as I let her pull me into the kitchen. Javier was right; there are piles of boxes on every surface except the marble island. There, thirty slices of cake on individual plates with little toothpick signs await us.

"Behold." Javier waves his hands, clearly proud of his handiwork. "A cascade of flavors for you to taste!"

"Wow, Javier," Annalise breathes. Her eyes widen in disbelief at the sheer number of options. "Where do we even start?"

Javier is all smiles. "The bakery sent your classic vanilla and chocolate, as you can see. There are also more adventurous flavors like lavender and passionfruit."

"An impressive selection," I acknowledge. "I'll admit, looking at these cakes makes me feel a little excited about the day."

Javier's eyes narrow. "The hundreds of thousands you have already spent on your fantasy venue, top-of-the-line caterers, and ten thousand white lilies... none of that excited you. But this does?"

"It sems more real when I'm about to eat cake." Looking at Annalise, I shrug. "It's your world, Kitten. I'm just living in it."

"Well said." She brandishes a fork at me. "Let's start tasting, Mr. Fordham."

I taste ten pieces of cake before I put my fork down on a plate and push it away. "What was this one? Cappuccino? Yeah, definitely not cappuccino. *Blech.*"

Annalise tries a final cake, makes a face, and then spits it out in a napkin. "Oh god. Don't try the lavender. It's like soap. Ugh, I can still taste it." She picks another cake and samples it to get the flavor out of her mouth.

"I don't suppose you want to try any?" I ask Javier.

"No, thank you." He runs his hand over his midsection and shakes his head. "I have a gluten allergy. Thank god, because all these cakes look amazing. I would eat until I burst."

"Well, I already have a preference for my groom's cake." I pause for dramatic effect. "Chocolate cake with hazelnut filling."

"Ah, a man who knows what he wants." Javier nods approvingly. "Very well, chocolate it is for the groom's cake. How about the rest?"

"He's talking to you, almost-Mrs.-Fordham." I raise my eyebrows at Annalise.

Annalise laughs, a musical sound that warms my heart. She surveys the cakes, putting her hands on her hips. She's almost tiny enough to be mistaken for one of the confections. As a matter of fact... I'll have to make note of that for later. After Javier leaves, I'll have the bride-to-be all to myself.

"Vanilla cake. Swiss buttercream. And for the filling, I want to alternate layers of blackberry. I want it to have a sharpness like..." She makes a popping sound with her mouth.

"So it shall be," Javier says. He jots some notes down and then excuses himself, saying he has to get going.

Once he is gone, we take a moment to relax. The process of getting married invited a whirlwind of activity into our lives. I pour myself a glass of scotch and lean against the kitchen counter. Annalise curls up on one of the barstools, her designer sneakers discarded on the floor. She flips through a wedding magazine, though I can't imagine what she's hoping to find.

As Javier pointed out, at this point, this wedding is almost planned. It's been four months since I proposed to Annalise. Four months in which I repeatedly offered to elope.

But she's my girl. If she wants a wedding with all the fanfare, she's going to get it. I watch her as I sip my drink, a smile playing about my lips. She gets a glass of wine and nurses it, distracted.

Our tranquility is soon interrupted by my house manager entering the room, holding out a newspaper for us. "Mr. Fordham, I think you might want to see this."

I unfold the paper, then my gaze hardens. Annalise comes over and reads over shoulder.

The article details the sentencing of Annalise's parents for embezzlement, fraud, and ten other minor charges. The story is dramatic, highlighting their flight from justice and the impact of their crimes on New York society.

It's funny, because I escorted Annalise for several days of the trial, which was held in absentia. No one even bothered to show up for the verdict. And why should they have?

Archer and Monique Gellar certainly weren't there for a perp walk.

"Can you believe this?" Annalise murmurs, scanning the page. I try to read her face, but her eyes have little in them but acceptance.

"I know." I rub my hand in little circles over her back. "Are you okay?"

"Yeah. It's just– You know, New York society won't be the same without them. My parents were a monolith."

I can hear a hint of the anger simmering beneath her sadness. That kind of righteous indignation that would have anyone else shaking in their boots. But I know better than to fear her anger.

Like the sun and moon, we are opposite, yet extraordinary complementary. It's one of the things that I love about her.

"Your parents made their choices."

"They did." She hesitates, then blows out a breath. "Thanks, Nate.

"We're going to be partners in every sense of the word, remember? Unbreakable. If you hurt, I sense it. I will always feel protective of you."

Her lips quirk. "So you've said."

"Well, I mean it." I wrap a shielding arm around her. "You're not alone anymore. If you face it, then we have to agree to face it together. That's the only way this whole thing works."

Annalise wrinkles her nose. "You're so eloquent when you talk about our future."

"I look to the future, and all I hear are poems."

"Okay." She kisses me on the lips, long and slow. "That's like... aggressively romantic."

"That's me. Mr. Romance." I raise my glass to hers, toasting. "This is going to be our year, Kitten. Just you wait and see."

"Yeah?" She laughs. "If you're selling that, I'm buying it. Even if I don't believe a word. You know why? 'Cause I love you so much."

"I love you too, babe. Forever and ever."

My Kitten is all grown up and now she's a lioness.

———

Thank you so much for being a part of Nate and Annalise's romance! I'm so grateful to have a romance reader like you! As a special token of my gratitude, I've written a bonus epilogue with your favorite characters – Nate & Annalise. Read it here.

I must admit, I have really enjoyed writing this series. Billionaire romance is my number one love, but forbidden is a close second. I'm over the moon to write some tropes and stories that I've been longing to write for years. Get ready for me to weave a web about office romances, one night stands, guardians and wards, total Casanovas, and more!

The Fordham siblings each deserve a happily ever after!Cash and Scarlet will be the next to get a spicy, swoony love story. You can turn the page to get a taste of what is in store for them in Fifth Avenue Romeo!

FORTY
CASH

The sun glints off the Hudson River. The sleek hull of my yacht slices through the choppy water. I stand at the helm, navigating smoothly. Seven other boats are racing against me, but I don't look back to see where they are.

The key to winning anything in life is confidence. My pulse pounds in my ears. A sharp wind rips at my jacket and tousles my dark hair. With the finish line in sight, I have every assurance that I will finish this race first.

I lean forward as I jet across the finish line. Slowing my boat so as not to make any wake, I look left and right. At my yacht club, only twenty yards away, the crowd applauds. I finished ahead of the rest of the yachts, which are just now clearing the finish line in one contentious clump.

My heart pounds with exhilaration. A grin splits my face. I've clinched the solo captain's pennant for the third year running. Even after a decade as a billionaire CEO, the thrill of victory never gets old.

I do a celebratory lap, spinning the wheel and turning the boat in a wide circle. Showboating is kind of my *thing*.

As I guide my boat to the pier, I spot my friends Jack and Tom tying up their vessels.

"Well, if it isn't the man himself," Jack calls out with a smirk. "Congrats on the win, you jerk."

I flash him a cocky grin as I secure my mooring lines. "What can I say? I aim to please. And I please *regularly*."

Tom laughs, shaking his head. "Classic Cash. You'll be playing the field and breaking hearts 'til you're old and gray."

"I would resent that remark... if it weren't a prophecy." I shrug a shoulder.

"It's not a bad thing." Jack shakes his head. "You're just a shark by nature."

I force a chuckle. I know my friends are right. It's not *really* a joke. It's just the cold, hard truth about who I am. *Commitment* has never been my strong suit.

"Speaking of being a man-slut." I offer them both a tight smile. "Let's finish with our boats to get to the party. People are celebrating us. We need to be there."

The reception is in full swing when we make our way to the yacht club's opulent ballroom. Servers weave through the crowd of dark suits and cocktail dresses, loaded down with trays of champagne.

I look around, assessing the situation. At any fancy dress party, there are a few types of people. Older men, drinking scotch and socializing. Some boring married guys who are glued to their spouses. My brother Nate has recently entered that category. There are handsy, drunk cougars looking for secret relationships.

Then, there is the category that I look for: available young women who are looking for the ride of their lives.

That's where I shine. Dance a lot, drink a little, target one woman, and make her feel extra special. *Boom*. I'm hooking up in a coat closet by the night's end. It's the perfect formula.

There are only three rules I follow. No kissing, like I'm fucking *Pretty Woman*. No bringing them back to my penthouse. And absolutely no sleeping with the same woman twice.

No exceptions, even for girls that suck my cock so well that I can see God. I don't want any of these girls to get the wrong idea. I'm not a nice guy.

That's okay. Girls don't hook up with me because I'm *nice*.

Looking around to assess the situation, I'm slightly put off by the crowd tonight. Tons of cougars. Lots of married guys. But there are almost no single girls. Maybe they're all on the patio for some reason? God knows.

I spot my friend Derek sulking by the bar. His usually cheerful face is pulled into a pout. Poor guy. I didn't see him finish, so he had to have come in toward the back of the pack. I snag two flutes of bubbly and make my way over to him.

"Drink up. You look like you could use it." I press a glass into his hand.

"Nah. I shouldn't. I just got out of the hospital. If Dr. Stein knew I was here, he'd have a fit." Derek gives me the ghost of a smile.

"You are a champion." I clap him on the shoulder. "It was anyone's race out there. I only won by a hair."

"I saw the replay footage," he mumbles. "You won by forty-five seconds."

"Look," I say. I point him towards a waiter laden with hors d'oeuvres. "Have some crab cakes. Relax. We're here to celebrate."

I survey the glittering crowd as Derek reluctantly nibbles on a crab cake. A group of beautiful women in slinky dresses catches my eye. They must have been hiding behind a large group of older men. Here, I see the real reason I love these events.

The thrill of the chase. The promise of a night of passion with no strings attached. It's what I'm good at.

What I'm *notorious* for.

Derek comes to stand beside me. He notices the group of young women, and a smile splits his face. "Right, Cash. You owe me for that race. Time to pay up."

"Is that right?" I take a sip of my champagne and arch an eyebrow. "And how exactly am I supposed to do that?"

"You're going to be my wingman tonight. I need to get laid. You're going to do what you usually do. Instead of helping yourself, you're gonna help me, too."

Even as I nod in agreement, I can't help but roll my eyes. Derek does fine for himself, supposing he's not high out of his mind or rushing home to take care of his teenage daughter. He's probably the worst parent I have ever met.

And I know Celia and Doug Fordham, *my* parents. I sigh deeply.

"Fine, fine. I'll be your wingman. But you'd better play it cool."

As I scan the room for potential conquests, I can't help but feel a twinge of concern for my friend. Ever since his wife passed away, Derek's been spiraling. Drinking too much, sleeping around, neglecting his responsibilities.

I clear my throat. "Hey, uh, where's Charlie tonight?"

"With the nanny, probably." Derek shrugs, not meeting my eyes. "Don't worry about her."

The dismissive tone in his voice makes me wince. I want to press further. Someone should remind him that his daughter needs him. But I know better. Derek gets touchy when anyone brings up his parenting... or lack thereof.

Before I can change the subject, I spot a familiar face in

the crowd. Thank god. I nod my chin toward the door. "Look who just walked in."

It's Amir Ahmadi, voted 'Mr. Gotta Have Him' by the Wall Street Times. Which is their awkward way of saying that Amir is one of Manhattan's most eligible bachelors. I have to admit, he does look dope as fuck in his bespoke charcoal suit and crisp white dress shirt. Right now, Amir is strolling through the party with a stunning woman in his arm. I wave him over, curiosity piqued.

"Cash. What's up?" Amir greets me with a fist bump. "Congrats on the win today."

I nod my thanks, but my eyes fix on his companion. She's a knockout. Lithe body, long blonde hair, and sparkling green eyes. "Who's your friend?"

Amir grins. "This is Holly. Holly Barnes, meet Cash Fordham. Holly's my girlfriend."

Girlfriend? My interest begins to wane immediately. Still, I turn on the charm, flashing her a warm smile.

"It's truly a pleasure, Holly. How did you two meet? I'd love to know where I can find a woman like you."

Amir laughs. There is a knowing glint in his eye. "Sorry, Cash. That's never going to happen. Holly and I met through a matchmaking service."

"A matchmaker? Really?" I blink, taken aback. That seems pretty old-fashioned.

"Really," Amir confirms. "It's not for you anyway, Cash. We all know you're not interested in meeting 'the one'. You're only interested in hookups. My matchmaker wouldn't touch you with a ten-foot pole."

His words sting more than I'd like to admit. Is that really how everyone sees me? Just a perpetual playboy? It's not *wrong*. But I don't like being so easily quantified.

"What's that supposed to mean?" I ask, trying to appear unbothered.

Amir raises an eyebrow. "Come on, Cash. You know exactly what I mean. The parties, the revolving door of women..."

"I'm only 32. Since when did that become too old to have fun?"

But even as the words leave my mouth, I know they ring hollow. The truth is, I've been feeling the pressure lately. The sidelong glances from board members, the not-so-subtle hints from my PR team about "settling down" and "presenting a more mature image".

I purse my lips and force myself to relax. "Look, maybe you're right. Maybe it wouldn't hurt to... explore my options." I turn to Holly and flash her my most disarming smile. "Any chance you could put me in touch with that matchmaker of yours?"

Holly's eyes light up. "Oh! You're in luck. She's here tonight! The yacht race is a big event for her." She gestures towards a cluster of women near the bar. "That's Scarlet over there, in the red dress."

My gaze follows her pointing finger. I'll admit that a plan is already forming in my mind. I could use a "nice girl" to appease the stockholders. Date someone for a while, break it off, play up my heartbreak. It's a perfect ruse.

"Thanks, honey. If you'll excuse me, I think I have a date with destiny." Leaving Amir and Holly in my wake, I saunter towards the group of women. Red dress. Red dress... My eyes lock on an elegant older lady with silver hair in a red crepe dress.

That must be Scarlet, I think to myself.

"Excuse me," I say to her. "Are you Scarlet?"

The woman frowns at me. "No..."

Someone touches my arm. I turn, unprepared for what I see. A woman, a vision in red, steps forward. She looks a little puzzled. My breath catches in my throat.

"Mr. Fordham?" Her voice is like warm honey. "I'm Scarlet Espinoza. I believe you were looking for me?"

I blink, momentarily stunned. Scarlet is, without a doubt, the most beautiful woman I've ever seen. She's all curves, and dark eyes, and full red lips. She's the matchmaker? No *way*.

I recover quickly, hiding my surprise. "You know my name?"

Scarlet smiles. "I make it my business to know everybody who's anybody in New York City."

"Call me Cash. I must say, Scarlet. If the women who use your service are half as stunning as you, I need to sign up *yesterday*."

Scarlet's eyebrow arches, a hint of amusement in her eyes. "Flattery will get you everywhere, Mr. Fordham."

"Really?" I arch a brow. "How about into your bed?"

She pauses, wetting her lips with her tongue. Her gaze grows guarded. "I'm not on the market. But I know thirty women who are just your type."

"Not on the market, huh?" I chuckle and lean in closer. The hint of her perfume wafting over to my nose is intoxicating. "Is that a challenge, Scarlet? Because I do love a good challenge."

Scarlet takes a small step back, maintaining her composure and her personal space. "It's just a statement of fact. Now, should I give you one of my business cards? Or is this just an elaborate ploy to hit on me?"

I can't help but admire her directness. Most women fall for my charm instantly. This back-and-forth, this is refreshing.

Why won't Scarlet Espinoza simply fall at my feet? It's refreshing, but still fucking annoying.

"Why can't it be both? I'm always open to exploring all my options."

She studies my face for a few moments before she sighs. Reaching into her purse, she pulls a business card out and hands it to me. "Call me if you decide it's time to meet the woman of your dreams." Then Scarlet turns away, moving amidst the crowd of young women. Though I stare at her for some time, she doesn't glance my way again.

Damn. I look down at the card Scarlet handed me, running my thumb over the fine linen stock. I just met a new breed of woman. One that doesn't want me the second I walk into a room. Curious. *Very* curious.

I stroll back to where Derek is sitting. My ego is slightly bruised, but the cutthroat competitor in me is alert. Does Scarlet Espinoza know that she just roused the beast? *Doubtful.*

Derek is hunched over a mountain of seafood, shoveling crab cakes into his mouth with reckless abandon. "Easy there, champ," I quip, sliding into my seat. "Tasting like day-old seafood will not get you on the Wall Street Times' most eligible bachelor list."

Derek barely looks up, waving a dismissive hand. "I need sustenance to recover from defeat," he mumbles through a mouthful. Swallowing, he adds, "So, how'd it go with the hot matchmaker? Is she in your little black book of dates yet?"

I lean back with a cocky grin plastered on my face, masking my frustration. "Oh, Scarlet's going in the black book. Have you seen her up close? She's a wild mustang just waiting to be tamed."

Derek snorts. "Then why are you back here with me?"

"Patience, my friend." My jaw tightens imperceptibly. "The best games of chess require timing and strategy."

"*Strategy?* Since when do you need a strategy? Usually, you just mention that family name and flash that smirk."

"Let's just say Ms. Espinoza presents a..." I pause, smiling. "*Unique* challenge. Trust me, I'll have her wrapped around my finger soon enough."

"Really? Because she sounds like someone who resisted the infamous Cash Fordham charm. I'd pay good money to see you two duke it out."

"Please," I scoff. "Listen, I already have a plan. I'll engage Scarlet's services as a matchmaker. It's the perfect way in. Then I'll just meet with Scarlet and be my very handsome self. She'll beg to sleep with me once she sees what she's missing."

"Wait." Derek's eyebrows shoot up. "You mean you're going to use her matchmaking service? Now that's desperate."

I spread my hand wide, grinning mischievously, and lean close to Derek. "Care to make this interesting?"

"What did you have in mind, Casanova?" Derek's eyes sparkle with intrigue.

"I'll bed Scarlet within a week. If I succeed, I get that custom Lamborghini of yours."

"That's a pretty high price." Derek chuckles, shaking his head. "Luckily, I'm not going to have to give you shit. Look, I'll give you a month to bed her. And when you fail – because you will – *I* get your yacht."

My heart races at the idea. I love a high-stakes gamble... especially when I'm sure I'll win.

"You're on," I grin, extending my hand.

We shake, sealing the bet. I can already feel the leather of Derek's Lamborghini beneath my fingers.

"Hope you've got good insurance on that Lambo." I smirk and lean back in my chair. My mind is already churning with possibilities. "Because in a month, it'll be mine."

Derek rolls his eyes. "Don't count your chickens, Cash. Scarlet might just knock you down a peg."

I scoff, but there's a flicker of doubt in my eyes. I push it aside, focusing instead on the thrill of the chase.

"Trust me, Derek. I've got this in the bag. No woman can resist the Fordham charm for long."

As I sip my champagne, my mind races with plans. I'll need to be clever. Seducing Scarlet will require a different approach than my usual conquests. But the thought only excites me more.

After all... what's life without a little challenge?

———

Intrigued? Snag Fifth Avenue Romeo right now!

About Vivian Wood

Vivian likes to write about troubled, deeply flawed alpha males and the fiery, kick-ass women who bring them to their knees.

Vivian's lasting motto in romance is a quote from a favorite song: "Soulmates never die."

Be sure to join her email list to keep up with all the awesome giveaways, author videos, ARC opportunities, and more!

Vivian's Works

Fifth Avenue Villains
Fifth Avenue Devil
Fifth Avenue Romeo

Cape Simon Billionaires
Small Town Billionaire Romance

The Grumpy Boss Agreement
The Fake Fiancée Proposition
The Playboy Rival Arrangement

Hush Hush Club
Forbidden Billionaire Romantic Suspense
Such A Good Girl
Such A Spoiled Brat

Married At Midnight
Forbidden Billionaire Romance
Deal With The Devil
Wed to the Devil
Vow to the Devil

Ruined Castle Trilogy
Forbidden Billionaire Romance
The Single Dad
The Nanny
The Caress

Broken Slipper Trilogy
Forbidden Billionaire Romance
The Patron
The Dancer
The Embrace
Possessive

Dirty Royals
Forbidden Royal Romance
Cruel Heir
Sinful Princess
Pretend Princess

King's Capture Duet
Dark Billionaire Romance
King's Capture
Queen's Sacrifice

Sinfully Rich
Steamy Billionaire Romance
Sinful Fling
Sinful Enemy
Sinful Boss
Sinful Chance

Billionaires Ever After
Steamy Bad Boy Romance
His Best Friend's Little Sister
Claiming Her Innocence
His Fiancé To Keep
His Lovely Virgin

Addiction Duet
Angsty Dark Romance
Addiction
Obsession

Other books
Wild Hearts

For more information....
vivian-wood.com
info@vivian-wood.com

www.ingramcontent.com/pod-product-compliance
Lightning Source LLC
Chambersburg PA
CBHW070411310726
48977CB00003B/641